Nat Gould

Seeing Him Through

A Racing Story

Nat Gould

Seeing Him Through
A Racing Story

ISBN/EAN: 9783337211721

Printed in Europe, USA, Canada, Australia, Japan

Cover: Foto ©Andreas Hilbeck / pixelio.de

More available books at **www.hansebooks.com**

SEEING HIM THROUGH

A RACING STORY

BY

NAT GOULD

AUTHOR OF 'THE DOUBLE EVENT,' ETC.

LONDON

GEORGE ROUTLEDGE AND SONS, Limited

BROADWAY, LUDGATE HILL

1897

CONTENTS.

SEEING HIM THROUGH

CHAPTER I.

BLACK MONDAY

IT was settling-day, and the spring meeting of the Australian Jockey Club had been unfortunate for backers. Several well-known punters were hard hit, and there was every prospect of some of them being unable to come up to time. The scene at Tattersall's Club, in Pitt Street, Sydney, was bustling and animated. The spacious and richly-appointed club-room was filled with men well known on the turf. A babel of sound penetrated through the open windows into the street below, where a crowd of miscellaneous hangers-on congregated.

Across the road numerous men were standing on the pavement, discussing the events of the recent meeting, and adjourning at intervals to Adams's marble bar, which was almost as thronged as the club itself.

A smart-looking sulky pulled up at the entrance to Tattersall's, and its appearance caused quite a buzz of excitement in the crowded street. Men looked at the new arrival, and then spoke hurriedly to their companions :

'He's had a hard knock, they tell me,' said a seedy-looking individual to a diminutive lad standing at his side.

'Thousands out. Shouldn't care to settle his account,' responded the man child, who was a jockey.

'Some people reckoned he wouldn't be able to come up to time.'

'Then they knew very little of their man,' said the jockey. 'If there were more men like Ross Gordon, I guess the bookmakers would not have to grumble about bad settlements.'

The man alluded to as Ross Gordon stepped out of his sulky, and went up the stairs to the club-room. It was after twelve o'clock, and his appearance had been anxiously awaited. When he entered the room there was a lull in the conversation. Then some of the bookmakers present could not repress a cheer, and the effect being contagious, others joined in, until there was a hearty round of applause.

Ross Gordon nodded and smiled.

'I thought cheers were reserved for the victors,' he said. 'It's some consolation to be a loser under these refreshing circumstances.'

'There's not many losers like you, Mr. Gordon,' said Fred Otway, a well-known member of the ring. ' It seems to me it makes very little difference to you whether you win or lose—you always come up smiling.'

'Generally take things as they come,' said Ross Gordon. 'I am a bit late, but my settling will soon be over.'

He walked up the room, nodding to several acquaintances. He was a handsome looking young man, about thirty years of age, tall and well built, his athletic frame contrasting favourably with the fat, sleek persons surrounding him. His clear, piercing eyes looked fearlessly into the faces of these men, and it was evident that he was held in considerable respect.

He walked up to a man at the farther end of the room, and said :

'You can settle for me, Walsden. I have the needful for you. How much is it ? Have you figured it out ?'

'Yes, Mr. Gordon. It's a stiff sum—close upon ten thousand pounds.'

' Quite correct. It is ten thousand, all but a few pounds. There's my cheque for the amount,' said Ross Gordon. 'I will see you when you have settled.'

Horace Walsden looked after him admiringly, as he walked away, and thought to himself :

'I wonder where he raised the money. I'm dashed sorry for him. He's a man, he is, and no mistake about it.'

Horace Walsden was quickly surrounded when he announced he would settle for Mr. Gordon. He checked off the amounts as they were claimed, and gave his own cheques for them.

The last man to come up to him was a dark-complexioned, foreign-looking individual. He might have been an Italian, or a Greek, or a mixture of both, which, as a matter of fact, he was.

Horace Walsden looked at him with no friendly glance as he handed him a cheque for fifteen hundred pounds.

'That is correct, Mr. Vecchi?' he said in a tone of interrogation.

The man looked at it, and said with the faintest possible accent :

'Perfectly correct. Your cheque, I see : I am glad of that.'

The tone was insulting. It implied that he would have declined to accept Ross Gordon's cheque.

'I give my cheques merely as a matter of convenience,' said Horace Walsden warmly. 'There is Mr. Gordon's cheque. I don't think you would decline to accept it.'

When Paolo Vecchi saw the amount of the cheque, he looked surprised.

'You must have great confidence in Mr. Gordon,' he said.

'I have,' replied Walsden. 'A good deal more than I have in some people.'

Vecchi could hardly mistake the significance of Walsden's tone and look, and a dangerous gleam came into his dark eyes.

'Ross Gordon is a ruined man,' he hissed. 'That cheque represents every penny he has in the world, and where he got it from is best known to himself.'

'You appear to be well acquainted with Mr. Gordon's affairs. It may be what you say is correct, and in that case I admire him more than ever,' said Walsden. He turned away and spoke to another man, and Paolo Vecchi went to the bar.

Ross Gordon was standing there with two or three friends, and he saw Vecchi. Their eyes met, and they looked at each other as only sworn enemies can.

Vecchi raised his glass and nodded to Ross Gordon, who took no notice of him.

'I detest the sight of that fellow,' said Ross. 'Come and have a game at billiards, Danby.'

'Did you lose any money to him over the meeting?' said Danby Widdrington.

'Yes; fifteen hundred, worse luck! That is the only wager I regret having to pay. I should not have bet with him but I thought Killara was a certainty for the Derby, and I knew how he would hate losing to me,' said Ross.

' I say, old fellow, they tell me you are hard hit this time. You know how fond we all are of you—I mean our set. If there's any need of assistance, count upon us, and I shall be proud if you come to me first,' said Danby.

Ross Gordon grasped his friend's hand, and there was a suspicion of a falter in his usually cheery voice as he said :

' You're a genuine friend. I have known that for some years. You are quite correct; I have been hard hit, but it is entirely my own fault, and therefore I must take the consequences. I wanted to have a chat with you, old friend. I'm about to ask a favour of you.'

Danby Widdrington's face brightened up considerably.

' It's granted, my boy, straight away, before I know what it is. If it's money, you're welcome to what you want. Thanks to a thrifty parent, Heaven rest his soul! I have more than I care about handling. I have often wished you would use some of my spare cash for me, but you're such a touchy beggar in money matters that I dared not make you an offer.'

The billiard-room was well-nigh deserted, and the friends sat down in a quiet corner.

' I will not accept money from you or anyone else, Danby. You know that well enough. My favour does not concern money matters. I shall have to sell my horses,' said Ross, with a sigh.

'I'll buy the lot. How much do you want? I'll give you a cheque now;' and Danby seemed quite excited at the prospect.

Ross Gordon smiled at his friend's enthusiasm.

'I knew you would say that,' he said. 'You're a generous, big-hearted lump of humanity. Now, don't deny it, because you are. I cannot sell you my horses, because they are not my property. That sounds Irish, but it is true.'

'Then, if your horses are not your horses, whose horses are they, and how can I help you?'

'I only arranged with the bank at eleven o'clock this morning to get the money to settle with. I had five thousand in the bank, and they advanced me another five on my horses. I tried hard to keep Killara out of the deal, but it was no go. Now, I want you to buy Killara when the horses are sold. He's the best I ever owned, and it was not his fault he lost the Derby. You buy him, and he'll win the V R. C. Derby for you sure enough,' said Ross.

'Is that all?' said Danby ruefully. 'Allow me to inform you, Ross, that you have greatly insulted your best friends. How dare you give the bank the preference over me, for instance? If you had come to me, I would have lent you the money with pleasure.'

'I know that,' said Ross; 'it is the very reason I

did not ask you. It would not have been fair. The bank advanced the money, and they take over the horses. They'll not lose by it.'

'You bet they won't! Why, all your horses are worth a heap more than five thousand, and they know it. Bank managers know the value of racehorses. We've had experience of that.'

'Will you buy Killara?' asked Ross.

'Of course I will, and I'll buy two or three of the others. Name the best, and I'll put 'em down. I'm a beggar to forget names. Forgot my own once when I was hauled up in a dog case.'

Ross Gordon laughed as he said:

'I'd have given a trifle to have seen you before the bench on a charge of evading the lawful payment of a dog license.'

'No chaff. Give me the names of the best horses.'

'Buy Killara, and let the others go. What do you want with racehorses?'

'I have been thinking of owning a few horses for some time,' said Danby. 'This is an admirable opportunity for me to make a start.'

'I have never heard of your intention before,' said Ross. 'You generally class men who own horses as fools, myself amongst the number.'

'I have changed my mind. A man with the money I have lying idle must invest it somehow. Why not in horses?' said Danby.

'I believe you came to this unexpected determination about a quarter of an hour ago,' said Ross.

'Been thinking over it for months,' said Danby.

'Strange I have heard nothing of it,' said Ross with an amused smile.

'I didn't care to tell you,' said Danby; 'I thought you would think me changeable. Will you give me the names of the best horses to buy? If you don't, hang me if I won't buy the lot.'

'Under the circumstances, I will tell you the horses to buy,' said Ross. 'Killara comes first, of course. Next to him there's Kempsey; then Ivanhoe, Marengo and Bushboy are all worth buying.'

'Is that all?' asked Danby, who had put down their names.

'Yes; that will be a very good start for you as an owner. Killara will not fetch more than five hundred after his defeat in the Derby, and old Bushboy will go for a trifle, but he'll win you a steeplechase,' said Ross.

'Now you must do me a favour,' said Danby.

'Depends what it is,' said Ross. 'You know how the land lies when you touch upon money matters, so beware.'

'That's all right,' said Danby cheerfully; 'but I know you're not such a fool as to throw away a chance of earning money. You're not too proud to work for a living?'

'No, I am not,' said Ross. 'If you can put me

into the way of earning money, I shall be only too glad to avail myself of the opportunity, providing I am competent.'

'When I am an owner of horses, I shall want someone to manage them,' said Danby. 'I prefer a man I can treat as a friend and an equal. You are an old friend, and if I buy these horses I want you to manage them for me.'

Ross Gordon knew what this meant. His friend was determined to see him through, and this was his way of doing it. Danby Widdrington had been more like a brother to him than anything else.

'It is very good of you to put it in that way,' said Ross ; 'what your proposal means is that I am to retain the best of my horses, enjoy the management and racing of them as I have always done, and you are to find the money.'

'But think of the advantages I shall have in securing you for a manager. You know the horses better than anyone, bar your trainer, and we can keep him on. I think it is a brilliant idea on my part. As to your salary, I suppose you'll not refuse to take one ; we shall not fall out about that. I'm a bachelor, and I've got a much larger house than I require. You can live with me. You don't know what a blessing it will be for me to have you in the house,' said Danby.

'You're the best friend a man ever had,' said Ross. 'Give me time to think it over. If I come to the conclusion I can fairly earn a decent salary from you, I'll accept your offer, but you must allow me to put a value on my services.'

'Put your own value on your services with pleasure, but if I don't consider you have done justice to yourself, I shall deal with you accordingly,' said Danby.

'I'll let you know to-morrow,' said Ross. 'The horses will be sold next week. If I decide to accept your offer, I shall probably want you to buy a couple more.'

'The lot, if you like,' said Danby.

'By no means,' said Ross. 'Some of them are not worth their keep. We'll let someone else have a try at them.'

They parted at the club door, and Danby Widdrington, as he saw Ross Gordon drive away in his sulky, thought:

'What a genuine fellow he is! A real good pal, that's what I call him, and I'll stick to him through thick and thin.'

CHAPTER II.

DANBY'S OFFER ACCEPTED.

DANBY WIDDRINGTON had heaps of money; at least, men said so, when alluding to his wealth. His father had worked hard and saved money, and as he saved,

2

he bought land at a time when it could be had at a reasonable figure. When the price of land went up by leaps and bounds, Jacob Widdrington did not buy more, but sold what he had at a huge profit. Few men could lay hands on more ready money than old Jacob. He always had a big balance in several banks, and rumour credited him with hoarding up savings in divers secure places. When he died, his only son, Danby Widdrington, inherited his wealth, and was at a loss to know what to do with it. Ross Gordon came out to the colonies with a moderate fortune, and a letter of introduction from his father to Jacob Widdrington. As Jacob was dead, Ross Gordon delivered the letter to his son. The two men at once struck up a friendship, which proved lasting. They thoroughly trusted each other, and Ross Gordon soon learnt to admire the sterling worth of Danby Widdrington.

There was a vast difference in the two men. Danby Widdrington was of the slow and sure order, Ross Gordon somewhat rash and uncertain. Danby's movements were in keeping with his temperament, while Ross Gordon was full of activity and delighted in his strength. Both men were tall, and they were alike as to their ideas of what was manly and honourable.

After his conversation with his friend, Danby Widdrington went home in an amiable frame of mind. He was a generous, big-hearted lump of humanity, as Ross Gordon had called him, and he delighted in doing good to others. A big, silly fellow, some men called him—an overgrown child. They were mistaken. He was very sensible, but in some things had the simplicity of a child, and he was the more a man for it. Danby once accepted a challenge to fight a well-known pugilist who had been egged on to make sport of him. The pugilist never forgot the encounter. Danby gave him a thrashing, and this made the man his friend. It is strange how a professional fighter takes to a 'swell' who has beaten him. Beaten by one of his own calling, he would hate the victor cordially, and burn to avenge his defeat. Danby Widdrington thought very little of his feat. He thought it would have been a difficult matter to vanquish Tom Anser, but he found it comparatively easy. This did not make Danby desirous of exhibiting his prowess, but it gave him satisfaction, because he felt, if he had occasion to get mixed up in a row, he could fight his way out of it.

Danby Widdrington's house was at Rose Bay, and commanded a glorious view of the harbour. It was a comfortable, old-fashioned place, built in the early days, and the trees had grown and flourished, and consequently the extensive grounds were nicely wooded. Danby's household was somewhat extensive for a bachelor. He had a worthy housekeeper, who was devoted to him, and she had three maids to do the work for her. He had a head-gardener, with two under-gardeners to do his work, and he had a coach-man and groom, who had three helpers to assist them in their arduous labours.

Branxton, as the house was called, was a noted place, and had been specially marked as a desirable house to live in by all classes of servants. Strange to say, the Branxton servants generally remained there when they were fortunate enough to secure a place. It was some distance from Sydney, but the servants did not seem to mind this, and small wonder, when they had rooms of their own in which they assembled at night and made merry. Danby Widdrington was a generous master, and paid his servants liberally.

After dinner he sat smoking in his own den—it can be called by no other name—and gloating with intense satisfaction over the prospect of having Ross Gordon as a constant companion. Danby's den was suggestive of the man. Things in the room stood there as though they were too comfortable to be moved. Guns, fishing-rods, boxing-gloves, riding-whips, boomerangs, spears, models of native canoes, pictures of dogs, horses and pigeons, were hanging on the walls or else stuck up in corners. It was a room of many corners, and all these corners seemed to be of use. Danby's den was not often cleared out. He objected to it on principle. He had an affectionate regard even for the dust of his den, and therefore did not wish it to be disturbed. He said

he wanted one room in the house to remain in a
state of dire confusion, because it showed off the
other rooms to greater advantage, and reflected
more credit upon his housekeeper. Dogs, Branxton
dogs, loved Danby's den. They made it their
dwelling-place. It was the one spot in the house
from which they were never hunted by energetic
servants. Any dog entering Danby's den at once
felt at home. There was a doggy look about the
place that gave the visitors an impression that this
room was sacred to dogs. The assortment of dogs
at Branxton was large. There were big dogs, and
little dogs, and dogs of medium size. A huge St.
Bernard and a toy terrier were the best of friends.
Fox terriers were numerous, and a pug and a poodle
claimed their share of Danby's den. Spaniels and
retrievers were to be found at Branxton, also a
couple of setters and pointers. These dogs were the
bane of the housekeeper's existence. Half a dozen
of them would follow Danby in solemn procession to
his den, and when admitted select suitable corners,
and mats upon which to rest. Sometimes Danby, as
he sat in his chair, would call them round him, and,
as they sat contemplating him, would converse with
them in a language evidently understood by all parties.
Danby discussed various topics with them. On this
particular night, when he was thinking of Ross
Gordon, he had the St. Bernard, the toy terrier, two
spaniels, and a fox terrier seated round him.

He addressed the St. Bernard, as being the most imposing.

'We're going to have a pal here, Nero,' he said.

Nero blinked, rolled his big eyes, looked at his companions, and expressed as plainly as it was possible for a dog to do that there was no objection to a pal, provided he was one of the right sort.

'He's not quite made up his mind yet.'

A disdainful look on Nero's face, as much as to say:

'More fool he, then, when such a comfortable home is offered him!'

'But he'll accept my offer, I feel sure,' went on Danby. 'He's a real good sort, and he's fond of dogs and horses.'

A general wagging of tails by way of acclamation. Dogs wag their tails when they wish to give a vote in favour of anything.

'The sooner he comes here, the better. He'll be safe here. He'll not have so much temptation, and he'll be out of Paolo Vecchi's way.'

The mention of Paolo Vecchi caused a slight frown to pass over Danby's face.

'He's a regular bad lot. Wonder who he really is! Looks like a brigand. Not that I'm much up in brigands, but he resembles pictures I have seen. What a strange thing he should have such a daughter, and she's not a bit like him! I'm not much struck with actresses as a rule, but Vera Vecchi—well, she's a charming girl, and an exception must be made in her favour.'

Nero rubbed his master's knee with his head, as much as to say:

'Speak up; this is a bit slow. We don't appear to be in it.'

Danby patted his head, and this aroused a feeling of jealousy in the other dogs. They insisted upon being patted all round. Order having been restored, Danby resumed his meditations.

'Vera Vecchi'—he lingered over the name, and a soft look came into his eyes. 'I'm a fool. Nero, your master's an unadulterated ass. Here I'm sighing over Vera Vecchi, and all the time she's in love with my best friend, and he's equally in love with her, or I am very much mistaken. It won't do, Nero. I must not be a traitor to my friend, even in my thoughts.'

He got up and paced round the den, and the dogs followed him in solemn procession.

He looked at them, and burst into a hearty laugh.

'We look uncommonly like a lot of nigger minstrels doing a walk round. Gentlemen, be seated.'

He sat down, and the dogs did likewise.

'Gentleman to see you, sir,' said a servant at the door.

'Who is it?'

'Mr. Walsden.'

'Send him in here.'

'In here, sir ?'—in a tone of disgust.

Danby laughed as he said :

'Yes ; in here, Susan.   Mr. Walsden is a bit of a dog-fancier.'

Horace Walsden came in, and shook hands heartily with Danby.

'Pat the dogs, or we shall have no peace,' said Danby.

'They are beauties,' said Walsden.   'I always admire your dogs.'

'What's brought you here to-night ?' said Danby.

Horace Walsden looked uneasy.   He wanted to do a good action, and he didn't know how to set about it.

'The fact of it is, I want to speak to you about Mr. Gordon.'

'About Ross ?   What's the matter ?' said Danby in alarm.

'Oh, he's all right in health,' said Walsden, smiling, 'but not in pocket, I'm afraid.'

Danby looked at him, as much as to say :

'That's no business of yours.'

'I hope you will not think me impertinent, Mr. Widdrington, but I know you're Mr. Gordon's best friend : that's why I came to you.   I paid his wagers this morning for him.   I've heard it was all the money he had that he gave me.   He handed me a cheque for ten thousand.   I've got it here.   I've not

presented it. I'm not short of money, and I like
Mr. Gordon. He's a manly, straightforward young
fellow. That fellow Vecchi means him no good. He
hates him, and all the more because his daughter is
partial to Mr. Gordon. Vecchi knows Mr. Gordon is
short of money. Ruined, he said to me. How he
knows is more than I can tell. I'd like to help Mr.
Gordon, but I know he would refuse. Here's his
cheque, Mr. Widdrington. Will you ask him to
accept it from me as a loan? He can pay me back
when he makes a rise. I'd do a heap for Mr. Gordon.
He reminds me of my poor lad who's gone.'

There was a big lump in Danby Widdrington's
throat, and his eyes were blurred.

'Horace Walsden,' he said, 'give me your hand.
There, I'm better now. You're a good fellow. I
would make Ross Gordon accept your generous
offer if I could, and it were necessary.'

'Then, he's not ruined,' said Walsden. 'I'm right
glad that Vecchi was wrong.'

'Ross Gordon is my friend, and to-morrow will
be the manager of my racing establishment, when I
get it,' said Danby.

'That's good news,' said Walsden. 'Don't tell
him about the cheque; I'll bank it to-morrow.'

'Look here, Walsden, leave that to me. I may
think it proper to tell him how kindly you have
behaved in this matter,' said Danby.

'Keep it to yourself if possible,' said Walsden.

'Very well,' said Danby, 'but leave it at my option. By the way, have you heard much about Paolo Vecchi lately?'

'One does not hear much about his doings outside the club. I have heard that since Mr. Gordon has been seen so much with Vera Vecchi he's treated her cruelly at home. He's a brute.'

'If Ross hears of it, he'll do something rash. That Vecchi's a dangerous man. He has a murderous look in his face at times.'

'When Mr. Gordon left the club to-day, Vecchi said he'd soon let him know he'd have no one hanging around his girl. He commenced to abuse Mr. Gordon until I had him stopped. He was told the club was not the place for one member to make insinuations about another member in. Vecchi said, if they were too particular to hear the truth in the club, he'd tell his tale elsewhere.'

'I wish Ross Gordon had never seen the girl,' said Danby. Then his conscience smote him. He had a very tender conscience for his friend, and he added : 'I hardly mean that. I wish the girl had a different father. She's all right, but he's a bad lot.'

They sat talking for some time, and then Horace Walsden left.

Next morning Danby received a note from Ross Gordon. He recognised the handwriting, and went into his room to open it. He was half in doubt as to whether Ross would accept his offer. It was a short letter, and in it Ross Gordon in manly terms accepted Danby's offer, and agreed to live at Branxton with him.

'If you find me a bore, or get tired of me, fire me out at once,' wrote Ross.

'I'm right-down glad,' said Danby. 'It's a good thing for him, and me, too. I shall perhaps sober him down, and he'll liven me up. We shall get on splendidly.'

CHAPTER III.

UNDER THE HAMMER.

'BLESS my soul, Ross! what's the meaning of this?' said Danby Widdrington, as he contemplated his friend with an amused smile.

Ross Gordon arrived at Branxton in his sulky, followed by a buggy containing half a dozen portmanteaus and Gladstone bags of various sizes, the horse being driven by a diminutive imp, half man, half boy, with a face childlike and bland, but suggestive of humour and shrewdness.

'I thought I'd bring a few of my belongings with me,' said Ross. 'I didn't like to come to you quite empty-handed. These are all my own, including Dicky. You have not met Dicky before. He's a character; I think he'll amuse you. Thought you might be able to stow him away somewhere; he doesn't take up much room.'

'We can put him up here,' said Danby, 'and also your belongings, as you call them. I'm right glad to see you. Come into my den. Here, Bill, just see to these horses, and find a camping-ground for Dicky— he's Mr. Gordon's servant.'

They walked into Danby's den, followed by the usual canine procession.

'You can't think how glad I am you have accepted my offer,' said Danby.

'I feel like a loafer,' said Ross. 'I ought to be ashamed of myself for trading upon your generosity, but I'm afraid I am not.'

'It is very good of you to take compassion on my loneliness,' said Danby, 'and you will be able to help me a lot. I want looking after. Things get in a hopeless muddle when left to my management. You know all these, I think; they do not seem to need an introduction;' and he pointed to the dogs crowding round Ross and giving him a hearty welcome.

'They are old friends,' said Ross. 'I always feel at home at Branxton.'

'That's right,' said Danby. 'It's your home for as long as you care to remain.'

Ross Gordon quickly settled down in his new quarters, and he was much touched by his friend's thoughtfulness in selecting his rooms for him.

'I want you to feel these rooms are entirely your

own,' said Danby. 'I like a den of my own, and probably you do.'

'You are too good,' said Ross. 'Some day I may be able to repay your kindness.'

The day Ross Gordon's horses were to be sold, he and Danby drove to Sydney, and put up at Fenelly's Bazaar, where the horses were to come under the hammer.

They met Fred Otway in the yard, and after the usual greetings he said :

'I mean to buy one of your horses, Mr. Gordon. Flycatcher I like ; is he a decent horse ?'

'Not at all bad,' said Ross. 'Mr. Widdrington is going to buy half a dozen if they go at a reasonable figure ;' and he named the horses.

'You'll have to pay a stiff price for Killara, I fancy,' said Otway. 'Paolo Vecchi says he means to have him, and he'll not stick at a trifle.'

'Why does he want him ?' asked Ross in some surprise.

'I think he knows more about Killara's running in the Derby than anyone, bar the jockey,' said Otway. 'I don't want to say much against him, but he's a friend of Fally's. I was a bit afraid when I saw you had Fally up in the Derby.'

'Do you think he squared Fally ?' asked Ross.

'He'd not be above doing it,' said Otway. 'He's an unscrupulous man, and has his own ideas of what's right and wrong.'

'If he means to give a big price for Killara, he must know something,' said Ross.

'Vecchi will not get Killara,' said Danby. ' He's as good as mine now. I mean to have him, no matter what price he brings.'

' I am certain he is a good horse,' said Otway, 'and I hope you will get him.'

The yard was crowded when the sale commenced. It was seldom such a lot of well-known horses were on offer, and buyers knew what most of Ross Gordon's racers were worth.

Several lots were knocked down at a moderate price, and then Danby Widdrington bought Kempsey, Ivanhoe, and Bushboy.

Killara was the next horse put up, and there was a buzz of excitement as the colt was led round. Killara was a dark bay with black points, standing 16.2 and powerfully built. He looked a model racehorse as he threw up his head and glanced proudly round the ring.

The auctioneer expatiated upon Killara's merits, and Ross Gordon smiled as he heard him say :

' Although he just lost our Derby, gentlemen, he ran well enough to give him a chance at Flemington. I expect Mr. Gordon is sorry to part with him, but it's the fortune of war, and the colt must be sold. There is no reserve on him. What shall I say for him ? Three hundred for a start. Thank you. Four hundred. Five. At five hundred, gentlemen ; there is no occasion to pause. The colt is worth double that amount.'

Danby Widdrington had not made a bid yet, nor had Paolo Vecchi. After a few minutes Vecchi bid another fifty, and the colt gradually went up to eight hundred pounds.

'I'll bid a thousand,' said Danby to his friend; 'that will stop the opposition.'

'As you like,' said Ross. 'He's worth it, but I never expected him to fetch that price.'

'A thousand guineas,' said Danby.

This bid came as a surprise, and was followed by a cheer that startled Killara and made Paolo Vecchi scowl.

'That's put a spoke in his wheel,' said Danby, who had been watching Vecchi.

'It ought to stop him,' said Ross, 'but he's a vindictive beggar. He knows why you are buying these horses, and he'll bid out of mere spite against me. We ought to have put someone else up to bid.'

'I would rather do it myself,' said Danby. 'I don't mind the money. I want to have the satisfaction of bowling out Vecchi.'

A thousand pounds was a long price for Killara, and Paolo Vecchi knew it; but he meant to have the colt, if possible, for more reasons than one.

He bid another fifty, which was quickly capped by Danby.

At last Killara was run up to fourteen hundred and fifty guineas, that amount being Vecchi's bid.

'I'll go another fifty,' said Danby.

'Fifteen hundred guineas,' said the auctioneer. 'Now, Mr. Vecchi, don't miss him.'

'Let them have him and be d——!' said Vecchi as he turned away savagely and walked out of the yard.

'Beaten,' said Danby, rubbing his hands.

'The colt is yours, Mr. Widdrington,' said the auctioneer, as the hammer fell, 'and I hope he'll win the V R. C. Derby for you. You deserve it for your plucky bid. I am sure we are all glad the colt has got into such good hands.'

A hearty cheer followed these remarks, and Danby Widdrington was pleased.

'You have paid a stiff price for him,' said Horace Walsden; 'but, if I'm not very much mistaken, you will get it back with interest. Mr. Gordon will not be sorry to have the handling of Killara again.'

'I am delighted Mr. Widdrington bought him,' said Ross; 'but it was, as you say, a stiff price. I fancy Vecchi must have had a strong reason for bidding as he did.'

'The best of reasons,' said Walsden. 'He knows exactly what the colt is worth.'

Danby Widdrington made a couple more purchases, Marengo being one of them; and then the sale came to an end.

The friends adjourned to Tattersall's Club, Horace Walsden accompanying them.

The club-room was not very full, and Paolo Vecchi stood near the bar, talking excitedly to three or four people.

'That fellow will be expelled the club, if he does not mind what he is doing,' said Walsden. 'He has been warned two or three times about his conduct here.'

'Foreigners are always excitable,' said Ross.

'They are,' said Walsden; 'but they ought to mind what they say in their excitement.'

'You beat me, Mr. Widdrington. I wish you joy of your bargain,' said Vecchi. 'You have paid pretty dear for a beaten horse.'

'Only fifty more than you were ready to pay for him,' said Danby. 'Why did you value him so highly?'

'I fancied the colt, and when I make up my mind to have anything, I generally succeed in getting it. I won fifteen hundred from Mr. Gordon over the Derby, and I thought it would be a fair thing to buy Killara with it,' said Vecchi.

'You have a good opinion of the colt's merits, notwithstanding his defeat,' said Walsden.

'I have. He was badly ridden,' said Vecchi.

'Falby did not ride to orders,' said Ross, 'or the result would have been different.'

'Some people don't know how to give orders,' said Vecchi.

'Other people do,' said Ross, 'more especially when they are interested in a horse and want it to lose.'

'As I do not own horses, I cannot give jockeys instructions,' said Vecchi. 'If I had to give them orders, I would take care they understood them.'

'Falby's a friend of yours, I believe,' said Ross.

'He is. What of it?' said Vecchi menacingly.

'I thought perhaps he might have given you a hint that Killara was worth buying,' said Ross coolly.

'What do you mean?' said Vecchi excitedly.

'Precisely what I say,' said Ross. 'You speak English well—you ought to understand me.'

Danby Widdrington tried to take Ross away, but he seemed bent upon aggravating Vecchi.

'If you mean to insinuate that Falby had an understanding with me about your colt, you lie,' said Vecchi angrily.

'I did not insinuate anything,' said Ross. 'You appear to be fitting the cap on to your head very well. Allow me to tell you it will be better for you not to talk about lies. I am not in the habit of having my word doubted.'

'You are savage because I won your money,' said Vecchi. 'You are a bad loser. I like a man who can lose as well as win. You ought to give up racing. Actresses are more in your line. You seem to understand them.'

Ross Gordon made a step forward as though he would have struck the speaker. He restrained himself, however, and said :

'On second thoughts, I will not soil my hands with you. Remember, your daughter is an actress. Your daughter!' he added, as he looked straight at Vecchi. 'Can it be possible she is the daughter of such a man !'

Paolo Vecchi turned white, and said, in a low tone of intense passion and hate :

'She is my daughter, and I do not forget she is an actress. I know how to protect my daughter from the insults of such men as you. I forbid you to speak to her. Do you hear me ? It will be the worse for you if you disobey me, and her too ; yes, and her too. She shall know what it is to thwart *me*.'

Ross Gordon looked at the excited, furious man with undisguised contempt. Then he turned on his heels and walked away without a word.

'I dare not trust myself to speak to him,' he said to Danby. 'What a despicable wretch the fellow is ! I believe he is quite capable of using violence to Vera By heaven ! if he touches her I'll be even with him. I'll break every bone in his miserable body if he dares to lay a finger on Vera.'

Danby Widdrington tried to calm Ross and soothe his feelings. He wished the encounter with Paolo Vecchi had not taken place. He knew no good would come of it.

'I wish you would avoid Vecchi,' said Danby when they reached Branxton. 'You put yourself in his way this morning.'

'I will be careful,' said Ross; 'but I could not help giving him a turn about Falby, and he took it. I have no doubt whatever that he paid Falby to pull my horse. He showed it in his face.'

'Falby will not have the chance to pull him again,' said Danby.

'That's one blessing,' said Ross. 'I must win the Derby for you with Killara, old fellow.'

'Stick to the horses, and leave Vecchi and his set alone,' said Danby.

'I'll try,' said Ross. 'I am not my own master now. I have your interests to consider. But I cannot give up Vera. She is an angel! Hang it all, Danby, I cannot bring myself to believe that man is her father. He looks like a bandit. I should not be at all surprised if she turned out to be the child of one of his victims. She has no love for him, but she fears him. That is not natural in a man's own child. You smile, and think I am romancing. There is a halo of romance about Vera Vecchi. I always feel I am in another world when I am with her. Were you ever in love, Danby?'

The question startled Danby. He turned red and became confused.

'No!' he stammered. 'I have never been in love. I'm not the sort of fellow girls take to. I am too slow and old-fashioned. Love is not much in my line. I can love my friends, but I have never loved a woman.'

'That's not true,' said conscience. 'You are more than half in love with Vera Vecchi.'

Ross Gordon laughed.

'My question has upset you,' he said. 'I do believe your big heart is full of love for some charming girl. I expect you will bring a bride home to Branxton some day. She ought to be a happy woman. I know no man more calculated to make a woman happy than you are.'

'A bachelor I am, and a bachelor I mean to remain,' said Danby.

'Time will show,' replied Ross.

CHAPTER IV

VERA VECCHI.

VERA VECCIII was a popular actress. She loved her work and was never happier than when playing her best to a large audience. She had been brought up to the profession from an early age, and the glare of the footlights was familiar to her from childhood. She had a natural talent for the stage, and devoted herself entirely to it. To study a new character was

to her a labour of love. She endeavoured, and successfully, to imagine she was the woman whose life
and actions she portrayed upon the stage. To Vera
Vecchi the heroines of Shakespeare were living,
moving beings with whom she thoroughly identified
herself. Rosalind, Beatrice, Portia, Ophelia, she had
at various times impersonated with great success.
She shared their joys and sorrows, and delighted in
their sayings and doings. Perhaps of all the Shake-
spearean heroines she had played she loved Portia
most. The many beautiful words Portia utters were
in consonance with her own ideas and feelings. She
felt she could act as Portia acted if her lover were in
danger, and defend him with skill and vigour in a
real trial scene. She preferred Portia to Juliet or
Ophelia because she would rather live than die for
love. Rosalind, Beatrice, and Portia were more to her
than Ophelia, Juliet, or Desdemona. She studied the
part of Lady Macbeth, but declined to play it.

'I should be a failure as Lady Macbeth,' she said
to the manager. 'I am sorry to disappoint you, but
I cannot undertake the part. I hate her; she makes
me shudder. She is an impossible woman to me.
She had no love in her. She murdered Duncan
to gratify her own ambition through her husband.
She was a woman capable of any crime. There is
no excuse for her. She gloried in crime.'

And Macbeth was not played, for the manager
declined to risk another Lady Macbeth. He knew

Vera Vecchi could play the part, but he understood why she declined it. He admired her immensely, and he judged her rightly. He was too proud of her to risk offending her, and Vera was quick to take offence and as ready to forgive. She had enemies, as every clever woman who stands above the more commonplace members of her sex has, but she had troops of friends.

An actress on the Australian stage has to play a wide range of parts. Vera Vecchi was an actress fully equal to the demands made upon her. She was equally good in comedy and drama. She was young and handsome, and her fine stage presence could not fail to win admiration. Her movements were easy and graceful; she knew how to walk the stage. Her voice was clear and melodious, and she spoke without effort. She had a wondrous head of nut-brown hair, and a complexion of exceptional purity that needed very little making up. Her eyes were clear and penetrating, of a peculiar bluish colour seldom seen, and her long lashes added to their beauty. There was no resemblance between her and Paolo Vecchi. Her nature was lovable and steadfast, and her manners winning, and she was full of life and vivacity. The one dark spot in her otherwise joyous existence was the fact that Paolo Vecchi was her father. Her dislike to him was painful, and verged upon hatred. The warm Southern blood boiled in her veins as she listened to his often coarse language

and heard of his mean actions. Her small hands
clenched, her mouth set firm, and her eyes flashed in
indignation, when he spoke to her as though she were
a mere chattel, part of his household, and valued as
he would value a picture or a rare bit of china.

She knew he did not love her as a father should,
but her talent was useful to him. It was mainly
through her skill as an actress that Paolo Vecchi had
made his way in the world. Being his daughter, she
endeavoured to do her duty by him, but she would
have given much to know he was not her father.
Her mother she had never known. She had a faint
recollection of a wild life spent amidst huge
mountains and forests, of caves and huts, and of
constant hurryings from place to place, and the
presence of strange, sad-looking men. It was all so
long ago that she was tempted to imagine it a bad
fairy-tale of her childhood.

Sometimes a glimpse of this life came vividly across
her mind. She fancied she heard savage shouts and
wild yells of exultation, then shrieks and groans and
cries for mercy. She saw daggers flash and guns
fired, and then the hurrying to and fro of picturesque
figures amidst the smoke. She did not know what
it all meant, but it was there, and such scenes had
become fixed in her mind.

Her father had never told her of his early life. He
was angry and morose when she questioned him
about it. She remembered a long voyage on a big

ship, and then the new life in a new land. Australia had been her home, and her first vivid recollections of how her life was spent were connected with it.

Paolo Vecchi told her she was born in Australia, but she knew differently. He did not think she would remember the voyage to Australia, much less incidents that occurred before it, but he was mistaken. She had once told him she was not born in Australia, but he laughed at her, and said he ought to know, as he was her father.

When she first began to earn a large salary on the stage, Paolo Vecchi secured most of the money. He handled it to his advantage, for he was unscrupulous, a gambler, and a cheat. When the girl learned how he made his money, her whole soul rose in revolt. There were terrible scenes between father and child, and he generally frightened her into acquiescence.

But there came a time when he could no longer control her. Vera Vecchi was no more a child, but a woman, and with a will of her own. Then Paolo Vecchi had to adopt a different plan with her. He treated her with more respect, and he took what money she chose to give him because he dared not demand the whole.

But when Vera became acquainted with Ross Gordon a change took place in Paolo Vecchi. He hated Gordon, who had on more than one occasion exposed his crooked doings, and threatened him with expulsion from the club. He came of a race of men bred in an atmosphere of strife, hatred, and murder, who held life cheap and lived for self, and were scarce loyal to each other. Paolo Vecchi would have killed Ross Gordon, and gloated over the deed, had it not been for fear of the vengeance that would surely overtake him.

He determined at all hazards to stop the intimacy between Ross Gordon and Vera. So far he had been unsuccessful. The recent scene at the club made him furious; nay, more, it made him rash and oblivious to consequences. For the first time since she became a woman he had raised his hand to Vera. She was too astonished and indignant to speak, but she hated him for his cowardly action. He did not strike her a severe blow, but it rankled deep, and she knew it would never be forgiven.

After the sale Paolo Vecchi went home in a desperate mood. He saw Ross Gordon suspected there had been something wrong in the running of Killara, and that others were of the same opinion. He was angry at losing Killara, and cursed Danby Widdrington because he had taken Ross Gordon by the hand and raised him out of the ruin he had made of his fortunes. Everything had gone wrong with Paolo Vecchi that day. Even Falby the jockey had angered him by demanding more money than had been agreed upon for acting dishonestly to Ross Gordon.

He found Vera at home studying a new part.

She did not even look up as he entered, and this added fuel to the flame. The quiet contempt with which she had lately treated him exasperated the man. He knew she was not afraid of him, but he thought she might be afraid of something happening to her lover. He might be able to strike her through him.

'That cursed swell who admires you has insulted me again,' he said.

Vera did not look up from her manuscript.

'Do you hear me?' he said angrily.

'I can hardly fail to hear you,' she replied. 'You speak loud enough for the neighbours to hear you.'

'I say Ross Gordon has insulted me,' he said. 'He has accused me in the club of getting at his jockey who rode Killara in the Derby.'

'Which, from all I hear, is perfectly true,' said Vera quietly.

He stared at her in amazement and fury.

'Where do you hear such things?' he asked.

'I hear many things at the theatre,' she replied, 'that I would prefer not to hear if possible; that is one of them.'

'Do the fellows at the theatre say I bribed Falby?' he asked.

'The fellows, as you call them, say that Paolo Vecchi "stiffened" Killara. I think that is the way they put it,' she said.

'D—— them !' he said. 'They are a meddling pack of fools. There is no truth in it.'

She made no answer.

'Don't you believe me?' he said.

'No,' she replied.

He swore an oath in some language she did not understand. He often used strange expressions when excited and alone with her. She noticed he restrained himself when others were present, and seldom used foreign words.

'I have told you once and for all,' he said, 'I forbid you to continue your acquaintance with this fellow Gordon.'

'That is a matter upon which I shall entirely please myself,' she replied.

'I am your father, and this man insults me whenever he has a chance.'

'That you are my father I am truly sorry,' she said; 'that Mr. Gordon insults you I very much doubt.'

He took several hasty strides across the room, and, standing over her in a menacing attitude, said :

'Will you give up this man ?'

'No,' she replied, looking at him without flinching.

Paolo Vecchi's face was terrible to look upon. All the evil passions in the man were reflected in his face. It reminded Vera of the mysterious fierce men she sometimes remembered, and she shuddered.

'Then, by God, I will kill him!' he said in such a
fierce tone that Vera rose from her chair. 'Ah, that's
touched you, has it?' he said. 'I mean it. If you
do not give up this man, I will kill him, and no one
will know who has done it.'

'I shall know,' she said.

'What good will that be to you when your lover is
dead?' he said.

'You dare not injure him,' she said haughtily.

'I dare, and I will, if you do not give him up,' he
said. 'You shall never marry him.'

She looked at him in surprise, but he saw she was
fearful for Ross Gordon's safety.

'I can easily put him out of the way,' he said.
'I have not lived my life for nothing. We Vecchis
know how to war upon men and avenge our wrongs.
Think over what I have said. It rests with you
whether Ross Gordon comes to a sudden end.'

It sounded melodramatic to her, but she knew
there was danger to the man she loved in Paolo
Vecchi's threats.

'I will leave you,' he said. 'Consider well how
you act. This man is my deadly enemy. He shall
not be my daughter's lover. I have sworn it.'

When Vera Vecchi was alone, she stood for some
time in deep thought. She loved Ross Gordon with
all the intensity of her passionate nature. Was there
any real danger to him? Would her father carry
out his threat? It was possible. She knew he was

a desperate man. She must warn Ross, and put him on his guard. He would laugh at her fears. He was brave and noble, and would scorn the threats of such a man as Paolo Vecchi. He did not know of what her father was capable. Should she tell him of those visions of her early days when she was a mere infant? If she pictured to him the scenes, she sometimes imagined it might convince him of her father's desperate nature.

'Is he my father?' she said passionately. 'Sometimes I can hardly believe it. We have not one feeling in common. What he likes I loathe. He is all for evil. I try to avoid evil and learn to do good. I have no love for him, nor he for me. It is most unnatural. I hate him. How terrible he looked a few moments ago! There was murder in his eyes. There is some secret in my life I cannot fathom.'

She sat down, and remained for some time quite still, with her hands clasped together. When she had made up her mind, she said to herself:

'I will see Ross. I will tell him of the danger that threatens him. He loves me, and, oh, how I love him! Danger or no danger, we must face it together. I cannot give him up.'

CHAPTER V.

A STORY WELL TOLD.

' I AM going to the theatre to-night,' said Ross
Gordon. ' Will you come ?'

' What's on ?' said Danby. ' Shakespeare ? He's
a cut above me. I'm very commonplace. Give me
a good drama with plenty of go in it, and language
a fellow can understand.'

Ross laughed as he replied :

' You do yourself an injustice. You like Shakespeare well enough, but you won't own to it. There's
lots more like you. It is drama, however, to-night
—a revival of " In the Ranks." That ought to suit
you. There is plenty of fun in it, soldiers, girls,
extraordinary men and women, rogues and honest
fellows, injured women and——'

' Hold, enough! as William S. says,' laughed
Danby ; ' I will go. The temptation is irresistible,
and I have never seen " In the Ranks." I suppose
Vera is the injured heroine.'

' Yes, she is,' said Ross. ' Gets married in the first
act, I believe. Husband arrested as they come out
of church. Takes the Queen's shilling and his hook.'

' His what ?' said Danby.

' Hook ! Forgotten your school-days, I suppose.
Did you never take your hook when there was a
prospect of a row ?'

'I comprehend,' said Danby. 'Go on.'

'Hero enlists. Fearful troubles in the ranks. Officer a deadly enemy. Wants hero's wife. Can't get her. Hero half strangles him. Fearful scenes. All ends happily, and the audience retire satisfied.'

'Very good for you,' said Danby. 'You are improving. I suppose Vera Vecchi puts you up to all these things. You'd make a good critic.'

'Might earn a few shillings that way,' said Ross. 'I've known fellows turned on to criticise a play who are generally to be found in the bar during the performance. One man on a leading journal was candid enough to tell me he had written his notice before he left the office, in order that it might be strictly impartial.'

'Why do you want to go to-night?' asked Danby.

'A note from Vera. She wishes to see me after the play. There is something in the wind. That disreputable father, probably. I wish he'd go to sea and get foundered in a gale,' said Ross.

'Paolo Vecchi will founder sure enough one day,' said Danby; 'but it will not be in a gale. He's more likely to swing.'

'I hope he will retire more gracefully,' said Ross. 'Even when one loves a girl to distraction, a father who has been hanged is not pleasant.'

'Seriously,' said Danby, 'are you going to marry Vera?'

'Of course I am,' said Ross.

'When ?' asked Danby.

'That I will leave to her. She has no desire to leave the stage at present, and I am not in a position to keep a wife. As her affianced husband, I have the right to protect her from such men as Paolo Vecchi,' said Ross.

'He is her father,' said Danby.

'Worse luck,' said Ross.

'This being the case, I fail to see how you can interfere between them.'

'I shall forget he is her father,' said Ross. 'It will not be a hard matter.'

'I hope it will all end well,' said Danby with a sigh.

'Of course it will,' said Ross. 'Don't look so glum. There is no immediate prospect of a desperate encounter with Paolo Vecchi.'

They went to the Lyceum Theatre and found the house well filled.

Danby was interested in the drama, and he watched Vera Vecchi with an interest he had never experienced before. How lovely she was ! He did not wonder at his friend falling in love with her.

When the curtain fell on the last act, Ross Gordon said :

'Wait for me at the club. I will be as quick as I can.'

'All right,' said Danby, 'take your time. I'm in no hurry.'

4

Ross Gordon went round to the back of the stage. He was well known, and no surprise was expressed at his going to Vera Vecchi's dressing-room. She was dressed in her ordinary clothes when he entered, and received him with a glad smile.

She was very loving, more so than usual, and she kissed him so passionately that Ross felt his blood heated, and he clasped her in his arms and held her there.

'I sent for you, Ross,' she said, when he released her from his embrace, 'because I wanted to tell you a short story. It is connected with my childhood. It seems strange to me; I want to see how it affects you. My father has told me what occurred at the club. He said you insulted him. We had some angry words. He forbade me to see you or speak to you. I defied him. Then he threatened you. Oh, my love!' she went on in tones of intense passion, 'I am afraid for you. He said if I did not give you up he would kill you. There was murder in his face. He meant it. But I cannot give you up, Ross; it would break my heart. And yet I ought to do so, because I feel you are in danger.'

Ross Gordon laughed and tried to calm her fears, but he felt matters were becoming serious. He did not believe in Paolo Vecchi's threat—that was uttered to terrify Vera; but the man was dangerous, and might do something rash.

Vera could not be calmed. She was excited and

alarmed. As she looked at the man she loved, she thought how terrible it would be if he came to harm through her.

'Ross, you do love me,' she said. 'Tell it me again. I never tire of hearing it. You cannot understand how I love you. I live for you and in you. You are my life. If you died I should be dead. I might live for a year or two, but I should be dead in life. "Thou shalt have no other God but Me." But I have, Ross. You are my God. I worship you.'

'My darling,' he said, 'you know how I love you. Vera, you are more beautiful than ever to-night. You hardly know your own power. I do not deserve such love as yours, for I have nothing to offer you in return except my love.'

'Except your love,' she said. 'What more could you offer me? Your love is all in all to me. It is life, hope, fame, glory, for me. You are in my thoughts every hour. I feed on your love; it is my sustaining power. The thought of it makes me act as I have never acted before. It inspires me, and it wins me fame. Safe in your love, I can do anything, dare anything. Without it—ah, well, I will not think of that: it would be too awful.' And she hid her face in her hands.

'You need never doubt my love,' he said. 'It is yours now and for ever.'

'I believe you,' she said simply, 'and I trust you.

Thank God there are men of honour in the world still.'

'And your story, Vera? You have forgotten that,' he said with a smile.

She became serious, and said :

'I hardly know how to tell you exactly what I want you to understand. It all seems so strange and obscure. It may be true, or merely the effects of a vivid imagination. That is why I wish to tell it you. I want your opinion. I have never told all of it before. I have hinted to my father what I think of my childhood's days, but he only laughs and denies it. He says I was born in Australia, and I know that is not true.'

'Then, he must have some strong reason for concealing something from you,' said Ross.

'I have begun to think so lately,' she said. 'The way in which we regard each other seems to me unnatural. But it is late, and I will tell you my story as well as I am able.

'Strange to say, it was not until I met you, Ross, that I began to have vivid recollections of my early days. Your love, I think, must have reminded me of beings I loved then, and who loved me.

'Sometimes I dream curious dreams about my childhood. At other times I see visions when I am awake. At first I thought the romance in my nature, perhaps my profession, had much to do with this, but I do not think so now. These visions are

too real, and I feel they represent truths. I will try
to describe what I have experienced. Do not think
I am acting or romancing now, for I am sure it is all
true.

'I recollect the time when I lived in a fine old
country-house, and had everything to make a child
happy. I remember a fine, big man with a noble
face and a rich, picturesque dress. Who he was I do
not know. Then, I feel, I was a child of importance,
for people were so kind and courteous to me.
Suddenly there came a change. After being born
as it were to riches, and surrounded with luxuries, I
lost all.

'I recollect going a long journey, and the country
was wild and desolate in its grandeur. Mountains
upon mountains, deep ravines, caves, huge rocks,
forests, rushing streams, all seem to be jumbled
together in my memory of that time. I must have
been very young, a mere child, and therefore there
must have been something extraordinary to impress
all this on the mind so that it cannot fade away.

'It must have been a wild life, and the men were
rough and savage. I remember no women after
leaving the big house, nor do I recollect how I came
to leave it. I awake sometimes, even now, and hear
the clash of weapons, the firing of shots, cries and
groans, calls for help, savage yells of vengeance,
men rushing to and fro brandishing glittering daggers,
their fierce swarthy faces and bright eyes gleaming

with the lust of blood. I see curious wild pictures of mock courts of justice, with a few helpless men in the hands of a lawless mob. I am telling you how these things come to me, now. They have gradually grown upon me, until what I saw as a child appears to me now as a woman. A few years ago what I describe now I could not have pictured then. Words would have failed me, but they come freely to my aid now.

'I do not think I was treated unkindly, but I missed the kind, loving women who had before attended to my wants. The men were uncouth and savage. One scene is more vivid than any other. It was when these men, in whose power I was, quarrelled amongst themselves. It is at this time I have a full recollection of Paolo Vecchi, my father. He seemed to be the leader of these men, who had revolted from his authority. We were in a cave in the mountains. From mere word quarrelling the men came to blows. Some sided with my father, only a few, and the others soon overpowered them. I recollect my father seizing me in his arms and running for his life. We wandered about for days until we came to the seashore, where great ships were moving about and there were many people speaking in a babel of curious tongues. My father took me on board one of these ships. There was a long voyage, and then my life in Australia began. Paolo Vecchi soon saw I had talent. I was always fond of

acting. As a mere child I amused the wild men my
father lived amongst by dancing and singing baby
songs. I have told you how I became an actress,
Ross. My father took all my earnings, which were
large for a mere girl, and he used the money to
gamble and rob and cheat with. How ashamed I
am of it all! When I think of it I am crushed down.
It is horrible. Can such a man be my father? I say
to myself sometimes, and then the noble face and
form of another man comes before me, and I see him
bowed with sorrow, weeping and lamenting over
something either lost or dead. Ross, I would give
up everything. in this world, but you, in order to
prove Paolo Vecchi was not my father. Why should
he deny it when I say I was not born in Australia?
He will never tell me why we came here. I do not
know to what nation or country he belongs. I do
not even know my mother's name, and I have never
known a mother's love. The past is all shrouded in
mystery. I know Paolo Vecchi is a bad desperate
man who must once have been the leader of a band
of desperadoes. This is why I am so fearful for you,
my love, and why I tell you this incoherent story.
I am fearful for you because I know my father, who
threatens you, must have shed the blood of human
beings in other lands. He does not value life, except
his own, and he would kill you without scruple if he
found a safe way to do so. Oh, beware of him, my
love! It is wrong of me not to give you up. I place

you in danger, but I cannot let you go. You are the only being in this wide world I love.'

'My darling,' he said as he kissed her, 'yours has been a strange life, and there is a mystery about it that must be fathomed. I do not believe Paolo Vecchi is your father. I have often thought he was at one time a bandit, a member of a gang of fierce robbers. He looks it. You must remember, Vera, we do not live in the wilds of Turkey or Greece, or Italy or Spain, but in Australia, and Paolo Vecchi dare not harm me here. I do not fear him. You exaggerate the danger. Be brave, my Vera, and we will face this man together. I will never give you up, and I will protect you from him. I may be able to learn something about Paolo Vecchi's past life. You must watch him, and try to discover what he has been, and where he came from. To do this, you must still let him think you believe he is your father. That he is not I am certain. Paolo Vecchi could not be the father of such a woman as you, Vera.'

'I am glad you think he is not my father,' she said. 'It gives me hope and courage. I shall be able to act differently towards him if I can believe he is not my father.'

'I want to close up, Miss Vecchi,' said a man at the door of her room. 'I am sorry to disturb you.'

'I am ready,' she replied; and Ross opened the door.

Behind the man stood Paolo Vecchi with his hands clenched and a dangerous light in his eyes.

CHAPTER VI.

THREATS AND DEFIANCE.

FOR a few brief moments Paolo Vecchi and Ross Gordon stood looking at one another without speaking, and Vera was too startled to say anything.

'I have come to take you home,' said Vecchi to her, ignoring Ross Gordon. 'I thought you were late. I see why you were detained. It is not a pleasant discovery for a father to make—his daughter shut up in her dressing-room with such a man as this.' He pointed at Ross.

'Be careful what you say,' said Ross. 'You are insulting your daughter. I cannot permit that, even from you.'

'You cannot permit it!' said Vecchi. 'That's good—very good. I should like to know what right you have to come between us.'

The theatre attendant stood looking on. He knew Paolo Vecchi, and disliked him.

'We cannot have any disturbance here, Mr. Vecchi,' he said. 'I am going to turn off the light; you had better retire.'

Paolo Vecchi turned on him fiercely, and said :

'What business is it of yours to interfere ? Mind your own affairs. She is my daughter, and I must keep her straight if I can. I suppose you are in the pay of Mr. Gordon. He makes it worth your while to admit him here, and you keep the coast clear when he is in there ;' and he pointed to Vera's dressing-room.

' I do nothing of the kind,' said the man angrily ; ' we all respect Miss Vecchi and Mr. Gordon.'

' I think I had better go home,' said Vera to Ross.

' I'm glad of that,' said Vecchi. ' If you do not come home, it will be the worse for you.'

' That is a threat,' said Ross.

' I'll do more than threaten if you interfere,' said Vecchi.

' Vera is my affianced wife,' said Ross ; ' I have a right to protect her from such men as you.'

Paolo Vecchi turned white with rage as he said to Vera :

' I have forbidden you to speak to this man, and you have dared to disobey me. You know what I threatened to do, and I will do it. I am the guardian of your honour. There will be a scandal when it is known that Ross Gordon visits you here, and remains alone with you in your dressing-room until a late hour. I will not have it. If you have no shame, I will teach you to keep my name from being dragged in the dirt. Come home with me at once.'

' You insult me,' she said. ' How dare you say such things to me ! How dare you make such base insinuations ! Were you ten times my father, I would tell you I loathe and despise you. Honour indeed !

What do you know about honour ? Such a word has no meaning to men like you.'

She was losing control over her feelings, and forgetting her resolution to still consider him as her father.

'Mr. Gordon is my lover. I have promised to be his wife, and I will keep that promise. He is a man of honour. I would leave this place with him tonight, and trust myself to his honour. My good name would be safer in his keeping than in yours. Stand aside, and let me pass. I will go home, but not with you.'

Paolo Vecchi did not move. He glared at her vindictively. The savage nature of the man was mastering him, and with it came the cunning of a wild beast seeking to entrap its prey.

'You are dramatic, my dear Vera,' he said ; 'you were always an admirable actress.'

'Stand aside, and let Miss Vecchi pass,' said the attendant.

'Keep out of my way, or I will teach you not to thwart me,' said Vecchi.

'Let me take you home, Vera,' said Ross Gordon. 'We have had enough of this.'

'She does not leave this place with you,' said Vecchi ; 'she may go alone, but not with you.'

'Perhaps it will be better for me to go alone,' she said to Ross.

'Then, I will see you into a cab,' he replied.

'She does not go out of this place with you,' said Paolo Vecchi. 'I will not have her name coupled with yours.'

Ross Gordon was fast losing his temper. It was only the thought that harm might come to Vera that restrained him.

'Good-night, Ross,' said Vera; 'I will go home alone. Be careful,' she added in a low tone, 'for my sake.'

Paolo Vecchi would have accompanied her, but she declined to go with him, and he had no option but to remain behind. Vera shook hands with Ross, and as their eyes met he read her thoughts.

'There is no cause to fear, Vera,' he said; 'I am not afraid of any man.'

The attendant followed her out, and said:

'I tried to persuade him you were gone, but he insisted upon coming round to the back.'

'Now, you infernal blackguard, what do you mean by insulting your daughter in this manner?' said Ross, when they were alone.

'Listen to me!' said Paolo Vecchi. 'I do not care for your foul names. They come well from such a man as you. I have forbidden my daughter to meet you. She shall obey me; I have sworn it. You may smile, but when a Vecchi swears he keeps his word. If you persist in paying your attentions to her, I will find a way of stopping you. I have dealt with obstinate men before to-day, and have generally

brought them to reason. Take my advice, and draw
back before it is too late.'

'Not at your bidding,' said Ross. 'I am not at
all alarmed at your threats. Men of your stamp are
all cowards.'

'I am no coward,' said Vecchi. 'I have fought
better men than you, and I am still alive ; they are
—well, it is no matter. They are not here to
trouble me. When a snake crosses my path I
kill it.'

'That you are capable of murder I fully believe,'
said Ross. 'But we are not living in Turkey or
Greece; we are in Australia, and I defy your
threats.'

When Ross Gordon mentioned Turkey and Greece,
Paolo Vecchi seemed startled, and Ross noticed it.

'I see you know those places,' said Ross; 'I
thought as much. Perhaps you have led an honest
life there. One reads occasionally of strange things
happening in those countries. Men have captured
and held for ransom, and in some cases murdered,
men, women, and children who have been stolen
from their parents. You look like a half-bred Greek
or Turk ; I shouldn't be at all surprised to hear you
had been laid by the heels for outrages committed
before you came to this country.'

'Have a care what you say!' hissed Paolo Vecchi.
'If you think what you say is true, I have no reason
to tell you I am a dangerous man. What I have

been or where I came from is known to no one but myself. If you love Vera, as you say, think well over what I have said. If you wish to injure her, persist in your attentions to her. I have other plans for her. I do not mean her to be thrown away upon a man like you.'

'I defy you,' said Ross; 'do your worst. Threats hurt no man. Let me give you a word of warning: If you harm a hair of Vera's head, if she comes to me and seeks my help, I will give it her, and I will hunt you down until I have you at her feet begging for mercy. I will find out who and what you are. I will learn the secret of Vera's early days, and where she was born.'

'She was born in Australia,' said Paolo Vecchi.

'That is a lie,' said Ross coolly, 'and you know it. She was not born in Australia. What your reasons are for trying to persuade her such is the case I do not know, but I will find out.'

'You have had your warning,' said Paolo Vecchi. 'It is dangerous for men to meddle with me and mine. If you refuse to accept my warning, the danger will be of your own seeking.'

The attendant returned, and said: 'Come, gentle-men; I want to close the theatre. Miss Vecchi has gone home.'

Ross Gordon gave the man half a sovereign, and walked out by the stage entrance. Paolo Vecchi followed him. Both men went to Tattersall's Club.

Danby Widdrington wondered what had detained his friend so long, and was glad to see him come in.

'It must have been a long story Miss Vecchi had to tell you,' he said.

'It was,' said Ross, 'and a curious story.'

He then told Danby about the appearance of Paolo Vecchi on the scene, and of his threats.

'I don't half like it,' said Danby. 'The fellow is a desperate man, I feel sure.'

Ross laughed as he said :

'I can hold my own with such a man as Paolo Vecchi.'

'In fair fight, yes,' said Danby ; 'but such men as Paolo Vecchi do not fight fair.'

'There is no danger, I assure you, Danby,' said Ross. 'The man is a coward at heart.'

'Cowards are dangerous when they can be so with impunity,' said Danby.

'Excuse me a few moments,' said Ross ; 'there's Walsden. I want to speak to him.'

No sooner had Ross left Danby, and entered into conversation with Horace Walsden, than Paolo Vecchi came up to Widdrington.

'Mr. Gordon is your friend ?' he asked.

'Yes,' said Danby, ' my best friend.'

He hated the sight óf Paolo Vecchi, but he could not resist hearing what he had to say. He might be of some use to Ross, he thought.

'Then, I should advise you to look after him well.

You should teach him to keep a civil tongue in his head, and to mind his own business,' said Vecchi.

'Mr. Gordon is quite capable of looking after himself,' said Danby.

'I will give you a word of warning,' said Vecchi. 'If Mr. Gordon does not cease to pay attentions to my daughter, I shall find means to make him. If he is your friend, keep him out of harm's way. I am not a man to be easily thwarted.'

He walked away, and Danby Widdrington felt uneasy. The man was evidently in earnest, and was therefore dangerous.

'I'll have a good talk with Ross as soon as we get home. It is late, but I may as well have it out at once.'

The friends drove home, and Danby Widdrington tried hard to induce Ross not to see Vera Vecchi for some little time, until her father had cooled down.

'It is all very well for you to make light of Vecchi's threat,' he said, 'but I cannot do so. As a friend, take my advice, and do not visit Miss Vecchi at the theatre. No good will come of it either to you or to her.'

'How can I?' said Ross. 'She will think I am deserting her. It would be cowardly. If there is any danger, I must face it, and shield her from it if possible. It is very good of you to take so much interest in me. I know you do it because you are my friend. But you surely cannot mean me to give up

Vera because I may incur personal danger by not doing so.'

'I do not ask you to give her up,' said Danby ; 'but I think it will be better for you both not to meet for a time.'

'I cannot promise not to see her,' said Ross. 'Let things take their course. I mean to find out something about Paolo Vecchi's early days. It would give me a hold over him. I will tell you the story Vera told me to-night. It is strange and unaccountable, but that she experienced in her early childhood what she related to me I have no doubt.'

He told Danby the story, and when he had concluded said :

'I am convinced he is not her father. He must have stolen her when she was very young, in the hope of securing a ransom for her. All her recollections seem to me to point to this supposition. There must be some way of finding out who Paolo Vecchi really is.'

'I am of your opinion,' said Danby. 'It is a strange story, but, then, strange things happen in those wild countries. I will help you all I can. It will take a good deal of money to prosecute inquiries, but I have plenty, and you are welcome to it. I have a presentiment there is danger ahead, but I will face it with you. We are friends, and I will stick to you through thick and thin.'

'There is a friend that sticketh closer than a

5

brother,' said Ross, 'and such a friend you have ever been to me. I do not deserve such friendship. I am a useless member of society. I can do nothing.'

'Don't say that,' said Danby; 'you can do almost anything you set your mind on. What you have got to do at present is to count upon me to help you all I can, and you must repay me by accepting my assistance freely.'

'That I will,' said Ross, 'for I know the spirit in which it is offered. Some day I may be able to repay you for all your kindness, and when that day arrives I shall have a big account to settle with you.'

CHAPTER VII.

GOING AWAY.

VERA VECCHI had signed an agreement to go on tour with the dramatic company she was playing with in Sydney. It was to be a lengthy tour extending to Melbourne, Adelaide, and New Zealand, with Hobart to follow on the return trip. She had signed the agreement some months back, and had well-nigh forgotten it until the manager mentioned it to her the morning after she had seen Ross Gordon.

'We shall finish our season here in a fortnight,'

the manager said to her, 'and we open at the Princess's in Melbourne first. I am very glad you agreed to go with us. We should have felt your loss very much. I was afraid the stage was going to lose you altogether,' he added with a smile.

'I had almost forgotten my agreement to go with you,' said Vera. 'I have no intention of leaving the stage at present.'

When she came to think the matter over, Vera was rather glad she was going away from Sydney. She knew she could trust Ross Gordon, and she felt it would be better and safer for him not to see too much of her at present. She wrote to him, telling him when she expected to leave, and that she hoped to see him before she left.

Ross Gordon handed the letter to Danby, who felt a strange sensation as he looked at the writing and read Vera's words of love and good wishes. He would have given all he possessed to be the man Vera Vecchi wrote such a letter to. He knew he was in love with Vera, and he hated himself for it, because she was to be his friend's wife. He must stifle his feelings at any cost, and never let either Ross or Vera suspect the truth.

'I am glad she is going away. It will be the best thing for both of you,' he said.

'I shall miss her very much,' said Ross; 'but perhaps, as you say, it is for the best. Paolo Vecchi would have made things unpleasant even if he did

nothing dangerous.   Of course I must see as much
as I can of her before she goes.'

'Can't blame you for that,' said Danby. 'But,
after all, there is a good deal of satisfaction in not
being in love.   Look how contented I am—nothing
to worry and upset me.' Yet all the time he felt a
gnawing pain at his heart, and a dreary blank spread
out before him when he realized that the one woman
he loved could never be his.

' You're a lucky dog,' said Ross, ' but I would sooner
die than lose Vera.   When you fall in love with a
woman like Vera, you will know all it means to
a man.'

Poor Danby!   His friend's words hurt him badly,
and he had to conceal the wound behind a smiling
face.   There was no more loyal and true man than
Danby Widdrington. He knew what it meant to
have a hopeless love, and through it he felt what the
love of such a woman as Vera Vecchi must be to a
man.

Ross Gordon saw much of Vera Vecchi during the
next fortnight, and Paolo Vecchi did not again
interfere. He thought, as Vera was going away for
some months, it was hardly worth while.   Besides, he
judged Vera from his own standpoint, and he fancied
she would forget Ross Gordon when away from him
and surrounded by other admirers.

It was the last night of the season at the Lyceum,
and Vera scored a triumph.   She played Fedora

with a passion and realism that electrified the house. Never had she been seen to such advantage. At her desire the season terminated with 'Fedora,' and the manager was more than content that he had granted her request. At the conclusion of the play she was recalled many times, and Ross Gordon felt proud of her success, and Danby Widdrington was unselfish enough to be glad at his friend's evident satisfaction.

Vera Vecchi was presented with a diamond bracelet by her numerous admirers, and made a speech in acknowledgment that won all hearts by its fervour and appreciation of the kindness shown her.

She felt happy in her triumph. She loved her art, as she always called it. She was never happier than when thoroughly lost in one of her best characters. But she never forgot Ross Gordon either on the stage or off.

As she played so splendidly in 'Fedora,' she imagined her lover was Ross Gordon, and she felt thrilled with a strange intense passion. Her words seemed to burn into the very hearts of her hearers, and the actors as they watched her wondered at her great power.

That night she lingered long with Ross Gordon after the play. Now that the time for parting had arrived, she felt it keenly. She clung to him, and caressed him, until he was intoxicated with her love and beauty. Vera Vecchi had the passion of the women of Southern climes, the hot blood of a race who love with an intensity that is often painful. She enchanted Ross, and held him in a bondage he had no desire to throw off. Her love was almost fierce.

Paolo Vecchi always thought she was acting when she showed any intense feeling. He was mistaken. Vera was generally in earnest—too much so to be always happy. She was never careless in the most trifling things. On the stage she would give as much earnest study to a small part as to one of importance, and it was so in her daily life.

Ross Gordon had not Vera's passionate nature, but he was capable of a strong and ardent affection. He was deeply touched by her love for him, and made a mental vow to deserve it during her absence.

'Be sure and write to me, Ross,' she said, when her feelings were calmer. 'I shall look out for your letters. They will be the joy and comfort of my life. When I read them, I shall feel you are near me, and fancy I can hear your voice. Keep away from my father. Avoid him as much as you can. Time alone can tell whether we shall discover anything about my early life. We meet with strange people when travelling: I may come across someone who has known Paolo Vecchi in another land.'

Ross Gordon promised to write frequently, and again and again assured her of his love for her.

'It will seem an age to me until you return,' he said. 'But there will be a chance of seeing you in

Melbourne. You will be there during the Cup week, and I shall be over with Danby Widdrington.'

'That will be delightful,' said Vera. 'I am glad. I shall look forward to seeing you. I had quite forgotten you might be in Melbourne.'

They talked until a late hour. Ross Gordon had ordered a supper at the Australian, and Danby Widdrington joined them there.

At first he thought of refusing to do so, but he was man enough to face his trouble.

Vera was very kind, and even affectionate towards him. Was he not Ross Gordon's best friend? That was a sufficient passport to her heart. Danby surrendered himself to the charm of her society, but he never forgot his loyalty to his friend. He thought Vera the most lovely woman he had ever seen, and probably she was.

It was a most enjoyable supper, and when it was over Danby went out to smoke a cigar. He and Ross Gordon were remaining at the hotel for the night.

At last it was time for Vera to go home, and Ross insisted upon accompanying her.

Paolo Vecchi lived at Woollahara, and Ross took Vera home in Danby's brougham.

He kissed her fondly before she got out, and seemed loath to let her go. 'Good-bye' was at last said, and Ross drove back to the Australian feeling lonely and desolate.

But he was not so lonely and desolate as Danby Widdrington. He had Vera's love to console him, while Danby had nothing.

As he sat smoking his cigar, Danby could not help thinking fate had been unkind to him. He was rich, and could afford to marry at any time, and the one woman he desired above all others belonged to his best friend, who had no money and felt he could not marry.

Clearly, there was something radically wrong in all this, thought Danby. Things were always upside-down in the world. Why could not Ross have fallen in love with some other woman? He blew a cloud of smoke, and as he looked at it, slowly hovering about him, he thought his own life was as twisted and crooked as these zigzags he had just sent up from his cigar. Gradually the smoky cloud became more even, and finally faded away into space.

' Wonder, when life is smooth to me again, if I shall vanish from the scene?' said Danby. 'What a fool I am, fretting my heart out about an impossibility! I'll try and fall in love with someone else. No, that's not possible. I think I'll try and make myself happy by putting it in Ross's power to marry Vera when he likes. I wish he would marry her. That would settle the matter at once.'

Vera Vecchi went to Melbourne by the express next day, and Ross Gordon saw her off at the station.

He watched the train until it disappeared and then

walked down George Street in a disconsolate mood. He lamented his bad luck in not having sufficient money to justify him in marrying Vera at once 'Danby rolls in money,' he thought, 'and he doesn't want to marry at all. Here am I, anxious to marry the most charming of women, and I haven't a blessed cent to call my own. Deuced mismanagement somewhere !'

'How do you do, Mr. Gordon ? You seem in deep thought. Is there anything I can fathom for you ?'

Ross Gordon looked up, and saw an open carriage drawn up at Hordern's. In the carriage was a pretty girl, and she had on a charming hat and a neat, close-fitting dress. All this Ross Gordon took in at a glance. This smiling, happy girl seemed to banish melancholy. He stepped to the carriage and took her hand.

'I am very glad to see you, Miss Heath. You are looking charming as ever. When did you return from England ?'

'Last week. We had a jolly time. We went everywhere. My father was on his best behaviour, and mother was never tired of going about. But I am glad to get home again. Dear old Sydney ! I love it. I felt inclined to jump overboard and splash about in the beautiful water when we entered the Heads, out of sheer delight at seeing it all again.'

Ross laughed as he replied :

'You are so attractive, you would have had a bevy

of sharks round you in no time. I am glad you
restrained your feelings. Are you alone ?'

'No ; mamma is inside shopping. She is being
elevated—I mean, run up and down in lifts. She
loves shops. I detest them. Mamma always goes
to a place where you get things in different depart-
ments. She says it is much more interesting. She
likes exploring,' said Nora Heath.

'I am delighted to hear your trip has not made
you forget your old friends,' said Ross. 'Mr. Widdrington will be delighted to hear you are back again.'

'Dear old Danby !' said Nora. 'Please don't call
him Mr. Widdrington ; it sounds so stiff. Not a bit
like Danby, which is not at all stiff.'

'Dear old Danby is not very much more advanced
in years than I am,' said Ross, laughing.

'That may be ; but he has a venerable way with
him. He inspires confidence. He is so different
from the general run of men. He never flirts or pays
insincere compliments, and doesn't fancy every pretty
girl is in love with him, although he is a fine, handsome man,' said Nora.

'You are quite right,' said Ross. 'He is the best
fellow I know, and he has been awfully good to me.
I've had a smash-up since you left. I had to sell all
my horses. Danby bought most of them, and has
appointed me his manager. That's his way of quietly
presenting me with a moderate income. I am living
with him at Branxton.'

' That's so like Danby,' said Nora. ' I thought you would break up in time, Mr. Gordon. Father said you were going the pace.'

' Oh, did he ?' said Ross. ' Then, he will not be at all surprised to hear I have run myself out ?'

' Not in the least,' said Nora, smiling; ' but, for all that, he is rather partial to you, Mr. Gordon. You naughty racing men have such fascinating ways with you. Danby has gone in for racing, has he ? I cannot imagine him as a naughty racing man. I hope he will have better luck with the horses than you had. Has he any really good horses ? I am as fond of horses as ever. We went to the Derby in England. It was horrid. Ascot was nice, so were Goodwood and Sandown ; but I like our own courses best. We are going to Melbourne for Cup week.'

' So are we,' said Ross. ' I think Danby ought to win the Derby with Killara. He was my horse, and he brought me to grief at Randwick ; but he ought to win at Flemington.'

' I hope so,' said Nora. ' Here's mamma.'

Mrs. Heath shook hands with Ross cordially. She liked him, and he was a favourite of hers. She was a stout, motherly woman, and it made most people comfortable and contented to look at her. Danby always said Mrs. Heath had a soothing effect upon him. He even went so far as to say he believed she would make him feel comfortable if he had the toothache.

'Do come and see us, Mr. Gordon,' she said as she got into the carriage; 'and bring Danby with you. I am sure Nora will be pleased to see him again.'

'Thank you very much,' said Ross. 'I will bring Danby over to-morrow, if that will be agreeable.'

'Yes, come to-morrow,' said Mrs. Heath. 'Bob will be at home. He'll be glad to have a chat with you. He got very tired of London at the last.'

The carriage drove away, and Ross Gordon thought :

'Now, there's a charming girl. Why the deuce can't Danby fall in love with her? I believe she is half in love with him.'

CHAPTER VIII.

PLEASANT COMPANY.

THE Heaths resided in a large house at Randwick. Robert Heath was a successful man, and head of the firm of Heath and Company, importers. He had been a friend of Danby Widdrington's father, and through his son had become acquainted with Ross Gordon. Robert Heath was partial to young men, and he was disappointed that he had no son of his own. He was devoted to Nora, and she seldom expressed a wish he did not gratify. Nora Heath

was a splendid horsewoman, and had carried off
several prizes at the Agricultural Grounds in the
ladies' jumping competitions. Mrs. Heath was a
woman easy to get on with, a good housewife, and
as hospitable as her husband. Pleasant company
could always be found at Mount Royal, the name of
their house, and it was a popular place with the
young folk of Nora's acquaintance. The grounds at
Mount Royal were not large, but there was an
excellent tennis-lawn and an abundance of flowers.
Special attention had been paid to the building of the
stables, Nora being fastidious in the matter of her
horses being properly housed. When Ross Gordon
delivered Mrs. Heath's invitation to Danby, he
accepted it with alacrity.

'I'm fond of going to Mount Royal,' he said. 'I
am glad the Heaths are home again. It is such a
jolly house; you never get bored there, and Nora is a
delightful girl.'

'She is,' said Ross; 'a more genuine, unaffected
girl it would be hard to find.'

They drove over to Randwick, and met with a
hearty reception.

'I am glad to see you again,' said Nora to Danby.
'After all, give me old friends and old scenes. We
had a good time in London, but it was rather slow.
London is such a big place, it always overpowers
me. I feel so insignificant amongst all those people.'

'You could not possibly be insignificant,' said

Danby, 'although you might feel so. Had you much riding? Did you make any purchases over there?'

'I rode in the Park most mornings,' said Nora. 'My rides in the Row were the pleasantest part of my visit. What lovely horses there are there! I felt quite envious. I should have loved to be able to take my pick out of them. I did bring something back with me that will interest you.'

'Do not keep me in suspense,' said Danby. 'What is it?'

'A dog,' said Nora, laughing. 'I know you are fond of dogs. Mother declares he is just the ugliest dog she has ever seen. I tell her the ugliness is part of the contract, and that his chief beauty lies in his ferocious aspect.'

'A bull-dog?' said Danby.

'Yes, and they told me there was only one dog in London could beat him, Barney Barnato. You ought to see Barney. He's the pet of all the ladies at the shows. He is a wonderful animal, and his owner's very proud of him,' said Nora.

'I have heard of Barney Barnato,' said Danby; 'his fame has extended to Australia. But let me see your new importation.'

Ross Gordon was talking to Robert Heath, and as Danby and Nora went out, her father said:

'Nora is going to show Danby her bull-dog. He's a fearful animal. What she sees in him I don't know, but I had to buy him. He cost as much as a racehorse.'

'Danby and dogs always go well together,' said Ross. 'He goes to the dogs his way; I have gone in my way, which is widely different.'

'Nora informed me my tip had come off, and that you had come to grief during our absence. You look well on it, I must say. It does not appear to have disagreed with you,' said Robert Heath.

'Thanks to my friend Danby, I am better off than I was before. He bought the best of my horses, and has placed them in my charge. I am going to win the Derby next month for him, I hope, with Killara,' said Ross.

'I am fond of seeing a good race,' said Mr. Heath. 'Did Nora tell you we were going to Melbourne for the Cup week?'

'She did,' said Ross. 'If you bet, have a few pounds on Killara.'

'Will he win the Cup?'

'No,' replied Ross, 'I do not fancy he will; although, of course, if he wins the Derby he will have a chance: the Derby winner always has. A mile and a half is about as far as he cares to go, and some of the older horses are very well handicapped.'

'There he is!' said Nora, when she opened the door of a loose-box, and Danby saw a splendid specimen of a bull-dog surveying him with grim looks, but with every appearance of friendliness. He patted the dog's massive head, and examined him with the eyes of a judge.

'What do you think of him?' said Nora.

'He's a splendid fellow,' said Danby. 'You will have no difficulty in winning prizes with him. What is his name?'

'I hope you won't mind,' said Nora, smiling, and with the faintest sign of a blush, 'but I have named him Danby.'

He looked at her curiously, and said : 'I take it as a great compliment. It proves to me that you consider I am your friend, and that you did not forget me when you were on the other side of the world.'

'I never forget such friends as you,' she said. 'Danby has so many good qualities, I thought there could be no harm in naming him after you. He is courageous, faithful and honest, and those are three qualities I value highly, and which I know you possess. Mother was highly indignant. She entered a strong protest against it, but I had my own way, as usual.'

Danby thought what a charming girl she was, and how travel had improved her. If he was not hopelessly in love with Vera Vecchi, he thought he might——

'What are you thinking about so seriously?' said Nora; 'I believe you are offended at my calling him Danby.'

'I was not thinking about him at all,' said Danby, smiling, 'but about you. Are you aware you have developed into a very charming young lady? I remember you when you were quite a little girl, and I have watched you grow into a beautiful woman. I mean it. I am not given to flattery. I think your trip home has done you a world of good. I mean to try a trip myself some day. I am getting old and fossilized. Travel improves the mind, and gives one broader ideas.'

'I am pleased you think I have improved,' said Nora. 'No doubt you consider there was ample room for it.'

'You were always a nice girl,' said Danby, 'even as a little mite. I never remember to have seen you with your face covered with toffy, or your hands sticky; and you always looked neat and nice, and may I say kissable?'

Nora gave a hearty laugh as she said :

'I am too big to be kissed now, except on special occasions.'

'Then, make this a special occasion,' said Danby, 'and remind me of old times.'

He took both her hands and, bending down, kissed her on the forehead.

Nora knew it was a kiss such as he would have given to his sister. She was proud of it. She knew Danby Widdrington was not given to making a show of his affection or liking for anyone. He was

6

much older than Nora, but the girl liked him better than any of her male friends.

They returned to the house, and Mrs. Heath said :

'Has Nora been to show you that horrid dog, Danby? I did my best to prevent her naming it after you. It is so frightfully ugly. I hope you boxed her ears for her impertinence.'

'No, I did not,' said Danby. 'I——' He was about to say 'kissed her and thanked her,' but, catching sight of Nora's face, and the expression on it, he said, 'I thanked her for naming it after me. I accept it as a compliment.'

'Well, I never !' exclaimed Mrs. Heath. 'There's no accounting for taste. I thought better of you, Danby.'

'I am only a very ordinary individual,' he said.

'You are a curious mixture—is he not, Mr. Gordon?' said Mrs. Heath.

'He is an excellent mixture,' said Ross. 'I can stand a lot of Danby's mixture. It does me good.'

'Well said, my boy!' said Mr. Heath. 'I knew Danby's father, and I have known Danby ever since he was a lad. The son is as honest as the father.'

'Thank you,' said Danby. 'You could not pay me a greater compliment.'

They dined at the Heaths' and enjoyed their day immensely. Vera Vecchi would have thought Ross Gordon did not trouble much about her absence.

She would not have liked the idea of her lover laughing and chatting with such a charming girl as Nora Heath. Vera was jealous, and passionately in love with Ross. The mere thought of any other woman pleasing him would have given her pain. It was her nature to live for love, and she expected Ross to do the same for her.

Ross Gordon was not disloyal to Vera, although it must be confessed he did not think much about her when at the Heaths'. He enjoyed the society of Nora Heath all the more because he felt he was safe in his love for Vera. Nora and Ross had much in common to talk about. Both were fond of horses and riding, and both had a well-nigh inexhaustible fund of high spirits and harmless chaff.

Nora Heath could talk and laugh with a man she liked without any thought of love or flirtation crossing her mind. She had not been trained to consider it her duty to look out for a husband, and appraise every man she met at his marriageable worth. She did not consider it due to her sex to dress as much like a man as possible. She detested divided skirts, and 'knickers' gave her the horrors. She preferred a horse to a bicycle, and had not the faintest interest in women's rights and ladies' clubs. Nora Heath was just verging on womanhood, and she had no ambition to divide herself, as some ladies did their skirts, and turn one half of her anatomy into a man. She thought womanly ways were best suited to a woman. She was high-spirited and courageous, and had far more 'manliness' in her than mere dress could give her. To Nora the 'new woman' was an abomination. It was Nora's womanliness that made her so attractive. There was a genuineness about her that was unmistakable.

She thought a good deal about the kiss Danby Widdrington gave her. She hardly knew how she felt about it. She confessed to herself it was a most innocent, harmless kiss, and there was an inward feeling she could not stifle, that she would have been secretly delighted had he kissed her in a different way. She had known Danby ever since she was a child. She had always regarded him as a big brother, but somehow her feelings lately had undergone a change. The more she thought about Danby, the more undecided she became as to the exact state of her feelings towards him.

As for Danby Widdrington, he thought a good deal about Nora Heath, and also of the kiss he had given her. Had he done right? Ought he to have kissed her? She had challenged him, but without any seriousness, and he had been tempted to kiss her. He ought to have remembered Nora was a woman now, not a child, and that the kisses he gave her in her young days ought not to be repeated now. He had hesitated, and finally did not say he had kissed her when he was about to do so. The look in Nora's face checked him. Why had it checked him? It

implied there was a reason for keeping that kiss a
secret between themselves.

' I am always putting my foot in it,' thought Danby.
' I should have remembered Nora is a woman. She is
a charming woman, too. Perhaps that was the reason
I felt an inclination to kiss her. I won't do it again.
I don't suppose I shall get the chance.'

Vera Vecchi's absence was a relief to Danby.
He had not got over his love for her. He thought
he should never do that. He saw Ross missed
her, and he knew he wrote to her. But Ross was
easily contented, and when Vera had been absent
a week he was as lively as ever, and took a pleasure
in writing to her and telling her all his doings. He
mentioned their visit to Mount Royal and wrote in
glowing terms of Nora.

' I think Danby is smitten in that quarter,' he wrote,
' and she would suit him admirably. She is younger
than he is, but I am almost sure she is fond of him,'
etc.

Vera Vecchi thought there was too much praise of
Nora in this letter, but the thought that it was Danby
the girl favoured, and not Ross, was a consolation to
her. She was anxiously looking forward to the time
when Ross would be in Melbourne.

CHAPTER IX.

AT THE STABLES.

DANBY WIDDRINGTON had taken convenient stables at Lower Randwick, and the horses he had bought were located there, in charge of Ross Gordon's old trainer, Mick Newton.

Ross drove to Randwick nearly every day from Branxton, and now the Heaths were home again he went round by their house, and sometimes called. One morning he was driving past, when he saw Nora in the garden, evidently intending to go out for a walk.

He pulled up and spoke to her.

'I was just going to walk to Coogee,' she said, 'to get a breeze on the beach.'

'I am driving to the stables,' he said. 'You have not seen the horses, have you?'

'No,' said Nora; 'I should very much like to do so.'

'Then, run inside and tell your mother where you are going, and I will drive you there, and on to Coogee Bay afterwards, if you wish,' said Ross.

'That will be jolly,' said Nora. 'I'll run in and ask mother.'

In a few moments she came out and said:

'Mother says I may go, but I must not stay long. She thinks Coogee Bay will be a purer atmosphere for me than the stables.'

'Jump up,' said Ross; 'I will promise not to detain you long. You can look at the horses, and then I will go to Coogee with you.'

Ross Gordon was a man, and therefore fully alive to the advantages of having a pretty girl sitting at his side.

Nora chatted gaily, and he could not help admiring her pretty face and healthy clear complexion as she looked up at him with her merry eyes.

'I could not do this in England,' she said, laughing; 'it would be against the proprieties, and no one must offend against them in that particularly proper country.'

'Then, I am glad we are in Australia,' he said, 'or I should have had to do without the pleasure of your society.'

'Would that have been a great affliction?' she asked merrily. 'Mother says I talk too much. I hope you do not think so.'

'I like girls to talk,' said Ross; 'it is rather a nuisance when you have the conversation all to yourself.'

It did not take many minutes to drive to the stables.

Nora was delighted with the horses, and took a special interest in Killara. She patted the colt's sleek neck, and he seemed proud of the attention.

'You splendid animal!' she said; 'I hope I shall see you win the Derby.'

Killara looked at her with his large, wistful eyes, and seemed to convey to her that it would not be for the want of trying if he did not.

'What grand condition he is in ! You must be proud of him,' she said to Mick Newton.

'I am, Miss Heath,' said the trainer. 'Killara is a colt worth handling. He always shows you something for the labour and trouble bestowed upon him.'

'I am glad, Danby—I mean, Mr. Widdrington— owns him,' she said.

'He had to pay a long price for him,' said the trainer. 'I am heartily glad Paolo Vecchi did not get him.'

'Who is he ?' asked Nora.

'A shady customer,' said Mick, 'and the father of Vera Vecchi, the actress. It is a pity she has such a father.'

Nora Heath had not heard of Ross Gordon's engagement to Vera, although she had heard of the actress. She did not often go to the theatre, and she had never seen Vera Vecchi act.

Ross Gordon remained silent. He did not see any necessity to enlighten Nora.

'It would have been a pity for such a horse to fall into bad hands,' she said.

Mick Newton was proud of the horses and the condition they were in, and he knew Nora Heath appreciated his work.

The stable lads gazed at Nora in admiration. She

seemed to them like a beautiful fairy flitting from box to box.

'Isn't she just lovely?' said the lad who looked after Killara, and this remark expressed the general opinion.

The inspection being over, Ross drove Nora down to Coogee Bay, and pulled up near the sea-wall.

At the hotel opposite stood Paolo Vecchi and another man.

Ross Gordon did not see him, but Vecchi caught sight of Ross and his companion as they drove past.

'That's a remarkably pretty girl with Mr. Gordon,' he said. 'Did you notice them as they drove past?'

'No,' said the man, whose name was Reuben Hide; 'Ross Gordon seems partial to pretty girls and women. I believe he admires your daughter.'

'Many men admire her,' said Vecchi. 'That is always the case with a good-looking actress. I wonder who the girl is. They are in that trap over there by the wall.'

'Can't see from here,' said Hide.

'Walk over and have a look at her, and tell me if you know her,' said Vecchi.

'You seem anxious about it. Are you on the look-out for a wife?'

'No,' said Vecchi curtly; 'but I want to know who that girl is.'

Reuben Hide walked across, and leaned against the wall.

He knew Ross Gordon by sight, and he also knew his companion as Miss Heath. He lighted a cigar, and then strolled back to the hotel.

'Well,' asked Vecchi, 'do you know who she is?'

'Old Heath's daughter. He lives at Mount Royal. She is, as you say, a very pretty girl, and, what's more, an heiress. Young Gordon knows what he's about. He's short of money, and a girl like that would set him on his feet again.'

Paolo Vecchi smiled to himself, as he thought Vera should know how Ross Gordon was occupying his time in her absence.

'Thanks,' he said to Reuben; 'I thought perhaps you would know her. She is not in very good company for such a young and pretty girl.'

'Oh, Gordon's right enough,' said the man; 'he's a fool in many matters, but he's not half a bad sort.'

'There I differ from you,' said Vecchi. 'I consider him altogether a bad lot. Come and have a drink. I don't care to talk about that fellow.'

Paolo Vecchi had only caught a passing glimpse of Nora, but he thought he would know her face again.

Ross Gordon drove Nora home in blissful ignorance of the fact that Paolo Vecchi had seen him. When Vecchi reached Sydney, he went to Falk's and asked if they had a portrait of Miss Heath. He knew Falk's took the best people in Sydney, and therefore he thought he might obtain a portrait of her.

Yes; they had taken Miss Heath's portrait before she went to England, said the assistant.

'May I see it?' asked Paolo Vecchi. He knew it would appear strange if he offered to buy a portrait, so when he saw one, and recognised it, he said:

'I am a friend of Mr. Heath's. I want you to enlarge me one of these photos. I wish to present one to him. How much will it cost?'

The girl could not give him a definite reply. She went to ascertain the price of an enlargement, taking one photo of Nora with her, and leaving three others in different styles on the table near Paolo Vecchi. He slipped one of these into his pocket unseen, and waited for the girl to return. She gave him the various prices, and he said:

'I will think the matter over, and send you word which I will have.'

He left no name or address, and went out. The girl did not miss the photo.

'This will come in useful,' he thought, as he felt the photo in his pocket. 'What a rage Vera will be in! I'm glad the girl is so good-looking; it will make the stab deeper.'

He was in a good humour at the success that had attended his efforts to procure a photo of Nora. He hated Ross Gordon, and he wished to pay Vera out for the way in which she had treated him. He meant to use this photo to the best advantage, and he knew how to do it. He was good at writing letters, especially when he had a set purpose in inditing them. When he reached home, he sat down at his desk and commenced to write. It was rather a long letter, and he took a good deal of trouble with it. He wrote a couple of sides and then read it.

'That won't do,' he said. 'It is not strong enough.'

He knew Vera's nature, and wished to wound her and make an irreparable breach between her and Ross Gordon.

At last he had written a letter that gave him satisfaction. It was an abominably clever letter, and calculated to have a decided effect upon Vera. In it he gave her to understand that Ross Gordon was paying great attention to Miss Heath, an heiress, and a very good-looking girl. He gave a graphic account of their drive to Coogee.

'He was driving her in his trap, and anyone could see how he enjoyed her society. I hear he is often at her father's house, and their names have been coupled more than once in my hearing. I am not telling you this because I detest this man Gordon. You know that without my telling you. Reuben Hide was with me when they drove past, and he knew her. I have always told you Ross Gordon was merely passing his time away with you, pretending to love you, no doubt to serve his own ends. You know what men about town—and he is one—think of actresses. He is no different from the others. No sooner are you out of Sydney than he openly pays court to a very beautiful girl and an heiress. I particularly wish to impress upon you that she is rich and he is poor. She would be a great match for him. In order that you may understand the sort of girl this Miss Heath is, I send you her photograph, which you will admire, because you have an eye for beauty. Never mind where I obtained it. It is her portrait—that I swear. If you doubt my word, write and ask Falk's, or, better still, ask Mr. Gordon if he knows it when you meet him in Melbourne. You say you love this man, and that he is your accepted husband. If you have any respect for yourself, you will cease to love him, and learn to hate him as I do. This letter may give you some pain, but as I wish to cure you of your infatuation for this man, it is necessary you should learn the truth. I swore you should never marry Ross Gordon, but I did not think he would so soon forget you. We Vecchis revenge insults, and this man has insulted you.'

Paolo Vecchi gloated over this letter. He would have been still more pleased had he known Ross Gordon had mentioned Nora Heath to Vera in his letters.

In the next letter Ross wrote to Vera he mentioned his drive with Nora. When he came to read over what he had written, something prompted him not to send it. He tore the letter up, and wrote another, in which he omitted all mention of the drive to Coogee.

'Vera is so awfully jealous,' he thought. 'She loves me so much. There is no necessity to mention it. There was no harm in it, but Vera might not like it. Hang me if I should like to hear of Vera driving out with anyone ! Of course that would be a different thing altogether.'

It was the usual man's argument. The woman must give way in all things. He posted his letter, thoroughly satisfied that Vera had no cause for un-easiness and no grounds of complaint against him. He loved Vera as much as ever. Had she been near him, he would not for one moment have thought of seeking Nora Heath's society. But he saw no harm in passing the time away agreeably during her absence.

Paolo Vecchi intended posting his letter just before Ross Gordon left for Melbourne, but he changed his mind. The two letters went by the same post.

CHAPTER X.

THE TWO LETTERS.

AWAY from Ross Gordon, Vera Vecchi was not happy. She longed for his presence, and the manager saw there was something wrong with her. She acted as well as ever, but it was off the stage he noticed a change in her.

Ross Gordon's letters were a great comfort to her, but they did not satisfy her. She wanted him to write in the same strain she wrote to him. Her letters were full of passionate, loving words. They laid bare her heart, and showed how she worshipped the man she loved. Ross Gordon's letters would have satisfied most women, but Vera was different from the ordinary run of her sex. She could not regard other men with any favour. She measured them all by Ross Gordon's standard, and of course in her estimation they fell far short of that. When he began to mention Nora Heath in his letters she became still more dissatisfied. She did not like the idea of her lover taking pleasure in the society of any other woman : she became jealous of the frequent mention of Nora's name. What right had this girl to be constantly with Ross Gordon ?

Vera Vecchi was not a woman to be won easily, or lightly loved when won. She had given her heart to Ross Gordon, and she must have his undivided love in return. Most men, and probably most women, would have called her too exacting. Her manager had once said :

'I should not care to be the man who played fast and loose with Vera Vecchi's affections. If she gives her heart to a man, she will expect his in return : nothing less will satisfy her. I do not think she is a woman born to happiness—she has too old-fashioned ideas of honour for this commonplace world. She is a noble woman, and I admire her immensely ; but for a wife I should prefer someone less exacting.'

Vera was staying at a private house in St. Kilda. She received her letters from Sydney in the afternoon, and recognised the writing on both, and wondered whose photograph her father had sent.

Ross Gordon's letter claimed attention first. She read it twice, and the faint look of disappointment noticeable when she perused his letters came into her face.

'Why am I not satisfied ?' she sighed. 'He says he loves me dearly and longs to see me again. But there is a coldness about the tone I cannot understand. If I thought he did not love me——'

A dangerous light shone in her eyes. She was not a woman to forgive easily.

She opened Paolo Vecchi's letter carelessly, but soon became deeply interested in it. Her cheeks burned, her hands shook, and she trembled with excitement. Could all this be true that he had written ? She snatched Ross Gordon's letter from the table and read it again ; there was no mention in it of a drive to Coogee with Nora Heath. It must be a diabolical plot of her father's to cause her pain, and to make mischief between them. If it were true what her father wrote, why had Ross Gordon not mentioned it ? He had always done so before. If he concealed his meetings with Nora Heath from her, he must be ashamed of what he was doing. She would not doubt him. She was miserable. She would write and ask him if what Paolo Vecchi wrote was true. He would deny it, and she would be satisfied.

She caught sight of the unopened packet on the table. Should she burn it, and not look at it ? No, she must see what this girl was like, the girl she began to feel was a rival.

It was an excellent portrait of Nora Heath, and did her justice. As Vera Vecchi looked at it she realized how beautiful Nora was, and how dangerous a rival she might be. There was something, however, about Nora's face that attracted Vera in spite of herself.

' It is the face of a good, innocent girl,' she thought. ' She does not look cruel, but kind. She will not take Ross away from me. She is very beautiful. If he is in her company constantly he cannot fail to be attracted by her. I wonder if she knows Ross is engaged to me ? He ought to have told her—

7

perhaps he has. Why did he not mention that drive in his letter ?'

She began to think what Paolo Vecchi had written was true, and it troubled her. She felt she could not write to Ross at once, she must think it over. She went to the theatre in anything but a happy frame of mind. 'As You Like It' was being played, with Vera as Rosalind and Hector St. Albans as Orlando. At any time Vera did not care to play Rosalind to the Orlando of St. Albans. She knew the actor admired her, and was in love with her, and situated as she was it made it difficult for her to act as she ought to do with him. She always felt the audience could see that Orlando's love for Rosalind was more real than feigned. As for Hector St. Albans, he was proud to act with Vera Vecchi, and he adored her with a passion he scarcely attempted to conceal. Vera was sorry for him ; she knew what it must be to love hopelessly, for she felt how it would be with her if Ross Gordon ceased to love her. She would have given much to escape acting the night she received her two letters, but there was no chance. Had it been any other play she might have endeavoured to obtain leave of absence, but she knew there was no one to take her part as Rosalind.

She went through her task, although it was bitterly hard. As usual, she tried to think Orlando was Ross Gordon, but her imagination failed her. Hector St. Albans saw there was a change in her, and that she was in trouble, and he acted as he had never done before, and wooed with such ardour that Vera was almost afraid of him. He was a fine, handsome man, much better looking than Ross Gordon, and he was a good actor. The play had seldom gone so well, and towards the close Vera seemed to forget her trouble, and to feel the delight and pleasure applause so often gives.

After the play Vera met Hector St. Albans before she left the theatre. She bid him good-night, but he stopped her and said :

' You were in some trouble to-night. I knew you were acting differently. Can I be of any service ?'

' No, thanks,' she said with a faint smile. ' I had a letter from my father this afternoon, and it did not contain very pleasant news.'

Hector St. Albans' face flushed angrily. He knew the sort of man Paolo Vecchi was, and he would have liked to kick him for writing unpleasant things to Vera.

' I am very sorry,' he said ; ' you look tired and unwell. Do let me see you home.'

She drew herself up proudly, and said : ' I prefer to go alone,' and walked out of the theatre.

He looked after her with wistful eyes. He knew why she treated him harshly. She loved Ross Gordon, and thought he (Hector) had no right to ask to accompany her.

' Lucky beggar !' he growled. ' He does not love

7—2

her as I love her—he cannot. It is torture to me to act with her. When I kiss her my whole body thrills; her mere touch makes me tremble. Things cannot go on like this: it makes me desperate. I shall do something rash, and she will never forgive me. Why cannot she be mine? We are suited, made for each other. If she were my wife we could win fame and fortune together. There is nothing I could not do with such a woman by my side.'

Everyone in the theatre knew Hector St. Albans loved Vera Vecchi, but he was popular, and therefore not chaffed about it. Had he been chaffed about his love for Vera there would have been a scene little expected.

'I was unkind to him,' thought Vera, as she drove home ; 'but he had no right to ask if he might go with me.'

Next day she wrote to Ross Gordon and mentioned that she had heard he was at Coogee with Miss Heath. 'You do not name it in your letter,' she wrote, 'so I conclude my correspondent must have been mis-informed.'

She could not wholly conceal her jealous feelings, and when Ross read her letter he saw trouble ahead.

'Why the deuce did I not tell her I went to Coogee with Nora ?' he said to himself. 'What a fuss she makes about it! She's actually jealous of Nora !'

He laughed at the bare idea, but his conscience

was not quite at ease, and he felt if Vera went about with anyone as he did with Nora, he would not be over well pleased. As usual, he went to Danby with his difficulty. Ross Gordon grew to rely upon Danby more and more. He always found Danby a sympathetic listener, and generally open to give sound advice.

'I don't see anything to make a fuss about,' said Ross, when he had explained the difficulty he was in. 'She seems to take it for granted, that as I did not mention I drove Nora to Coogee, that I did not do so.'

'I think you ought to have named it in your letter,' said Danby. 'It is always best to be straightforward in such matters. I expect Paolo Vecchi is at the bottom of this. You cannot be too careful.'

'D——n Paolo Vecchi!' said Ross.

'Quite so,' said Danby. 'Consign him to perdition by all means, but do not give him the chance of making mischief between you and Vera.'

'But what harm is there in driving out with Nora Heath?' said Ross.

'Would you care to hear of Vera Vecchi driving about Melbourne with some good-looking fellow?' asked Danby.

'Can't say I should,' replied Ross; 'but it's different with Nora. She is only a child.'

'She was a child,' said Danby. 'She is a woman now, and a very nice-looking woman, too.'

'What am I to do?' said Ross.

'Tell her the truth. Say you drove Nora Heath to Coogee, but you did not think it of sufficient importance to mention it in your letter.'

'She'll be awfully angry about it,' said Ross. 'I know Vera.'

'She may feel slightly hurt,' said Danby, 'but surely you can explain to her what an old friend Nora Heath is.'

'I shall be jolly glad when we are in Melbourne,' said Ross. 'I want to see Vera again. Letter writing is all rot : a fellow cannot explain how much he loves a woman in a prosy letter.'

'Never having written a love-letter I cannot say,' said Danby. 'I should think, however, it must be pretty easy work.'

'Why don't you begin writing love-letters?' said Ross.

'For the very good reason I have no one to write them to,' said Danby.

'Try your hand at writing one to Nora Heath,' said Ross, smiling.

'Don't be an ass, Ross!' said Danby. 'I'm old enough to be her father. You don't suppose such a girl as Nora would look twice at an old fossil like me?'

'I am sure she would,' said Ross. 'You are not more than ten or a dozen years her senior. That is a proper difference in ages. I am sure she is fond of you. The way she lingers over your name is quite sufficient, Danby. You should hear her murmur "Danby," and cast up her eyes as though "Danby" spelt "heaven." '

Danby laughed heartily. There was not an atom of conceit in him. Vera Vecchi did not love him, why should Nora Heath?

'It is no laughing matter,' said Ross. 'You are trifling with her young affections. If you do not go in for the prize you deserve to lose it. Hang me if I wouldn't cut you out myself if I had a chance, and supposing I did not love Vera.'

Danby looked at him for a few moments, and then said :

'Are you quite sure you love Vera Vecchi as she ought and deserves to be loved ?'

'Of course I'm sure,' said Ross. 'What a ridiculous question to ask !'

'Vera is a woman who will want all your love. She will not be contented with less.'

'She has all my love. I am devoted to her. Talking and laughing with Nora Heath has nothing to do with my love for Vera.'

'You mean no harm, I am sure,' said Danby ; 'but take my advice and do not give Vera any cause for uneasiness.'

'Do you mean drop calling at the Heaths' ?' said Ross.

'No,' replied Danby, 'but I should not drive Nora

about.   Does Nora know you are engaged to Vera
Vecchi ?'

'No ; I have not told her,' said Ross.

'Then I think you should do so,' said Danby.   'I
do not think Nora would have driven with you had
she known you were engaged to Vera.'

'This is a rum world,' said Ross.   'Immediately a
fellow is engaged he has to cut off all his lady friends.
Don't you consider that humbug ?'

'When a man loves a woman he ought to be true
to her in thought, word, and deed.   If I had the
good fortune to win the love of a woman like Vera
Vecchi I should——'

'Well ?' said Ross in some surprise as he noticed
the tremor in Danby's voice.

'I should love her in return with my whole soul,
and no other woman would have a place in my heart.'

Ross Gordon did not doubt for one moment the
truth of what Danby said.   He knew how faithful he
was as a friend, therefore he would be true as steel to
a woman he loved.

'We are not all built like you,' he said ; 'I wish
we were—we should be better men than we are.
You know how I love Vera, but I cannot see things
in the same light as you do and as she does.   Do you
know, Danby, I think you and Vera are very much
alike in some ways.'

'Are we ?' said Danby.   'I never noticed it.'

'Vera's idea of love is the same as yours,' said

Ross. 'I don't believe she ever gives another man a thought. I don't say this because I'm conceited, but because I believe it is true.'

'I am certain of it,' said Danby. 'You ought to be very careful of such a love as Vera Vecchi has given you.'

Ross Gordon went to the desk in Danby's den to write a letter to Vera.

Danby sat in a chair, watching his friend, and thought:

'We can't all be alike. He's a good fellow, and I'll never go back on him, but I'm a bit doubtful if he'll make Vera happy.'

CHAPTER XI.

KILLARA'S TRIAL.

Ross Gordon did not show Danby the letter he wrote to Vera. He was not satisfied with it. He felt his excuses were lame, and that Vera would treat them as such. Instead of blaming himself for his want of candour, he was cross with Vera for being so exacting. He posted the letter, and then endeavoured to dismiss it from his mind.

Next morning Danby and Ross drove to Randwick, as Killara was to be tried, and they were anxious no mistakes should be made.

Paolo Vecchi was a regular frequenter of the race-track, and took note of all the good gallops. He had become an owner of horses in order to have no difficulty about being admitted to the course. He was generally one of the first to arrive, and on this particular morning he saw Mick Newton had something on hand.

'Going to try Killara,' he thought. 'I must watch the trial closely. They are sure to run it straight. That fool of a Widdrington always does everything straight—much good may it do him!'

Ivanhoe and Marengo were both in good form, having recently won races, so Mick Newton advised Ross to try Killara with them.

As they drove up to the gate, Ross Gordon caught sight of Paolo Vecchi. He had an idea it was Paolo Vecchi who had given Vera the information about the drive to Coogee with Nora Heath, and he was anxious to pay him out.

'There's Vecchi,' he said to Danby. 'If Killara does a good trial he's sure to step in and back him. He knows the colt ought to have won the A. J. C. Derby. I'd like to put him off the scent. Would you mind me doing so?'

'You mean hoodwink him over the trial,' said Danby. 'I have no objections to keeping Paolo Vecchi in the dark, but others will suffer. No, I think Killara should be tried on his merits.'

'You can tell all your friends to back him,' said

Ross. 'It is a pity Paolo Vecchi should have the chance to win over the colt.'

Ross Gordon with some difficulty at last persuaded Danby to leave the matter in his hands. He went to Mick Newton while Danby strolled on to the track.

'I want to give that fellow Vecchi a turn,' said Ross to the trainer. 'If he has his watch on, and sees Killara win this trial he'll back him for a heap of money.'

'And if Killara shapes badly, he'll probably back his own colt for the Derby,' said the trainer.

'What do you mean?' said Ross in some surprise, 'I didn't know he owned a Derby horse.'

'He bought Burwood yesterday,' said Mick Newton, 'and gave a stiff price for him, so I hear.'

Burwood was well spoken of in Melbourne, the colt being trained at Flemington.

'That's news,' said Ross. 'Burwood .has a big chance, I hear, but Vecchi knows what Killara can do, and will back him if he wins this trial. He'll make Burwood a market horse and back Killara, and thus net money both ways. I see his little game and I will spoil it if I can.'

'What do you want me to do?' asked the trainer.

'Who rides Killara in the gallop?' asked Ross.

'I have asked Owen Cox to ride him. You said I could promise him the mount on Killara in the race, and I have done so. I expect him every minute. Oh, here he comes with Mr. Widdrington.'

'Cox says he is to ride Killara in the Derby,' said Danby.

'I asked Mick to engage him,' said Ross, 'but it quite slipped my memory until this morning.'

'I am quite satisfied,' said Danby. 'You could not have made a better choice.'

Owen Cox looked pleased.

'I want you to be very particular how you ride in this trial,' said Ross to the jockey. 'For reasons I will not explain I want Killara to be badly beaten, but at the same time I want you to exercise your judgment, and tell us if you think he could have won. With you in the saddle it will be easy to have a big weight up without notice being taken of it. Do you understand me?'

'Yes,' said Cox, 'but it would be the safer plan to ride Killara out. At all events, I can judge what he is worth if I know the weight he carries.'

'You shall know all about that,' said Ross. 'Killara is to be tried with Ivanhoe and Marengo. They are both smart, and you will have very little difficulty in being beaten. Let Killara be well beaten, but not too conspicuously.'

'I don't half like it,' said Danby. 'I would much prefer Killara being ridden out.'

Ross took him on one side, and explained how Paolo Vecchi had bought Burwood.

'If we can induce him to think Killara has gone off he'll back his own horse. I should very much like him to lose his money. He did me out of the Derby here, and I want to square accounts with him for that.'

'And for other things too,' said Danby smiling. 'Well I cannot blame you. I detest the man thoroughly. But I shall tell my friends they can back Killara if Cox gives a favourable account of him after the gallop.'

'Tell them by all means,' said Ross, 'but wait until Paolo Vecchi makes a move. If he backs Burwood, as he is certain to do, there will be a longer price about Killara.'

Mick Newton arranged the weights satisfactorily, and Killara would have been a wonder to have beaten Ivanhoe and Marengo on such a handicap.

'You ought to be able to tell what Killara is worth with that weight up,' he said to the jockey.

'I'll reckon him up all right, never fear,' said Cox.

When the three horses came on to the track it was evident the trial was looked upon with interest.

Many people did not believe in the Derby form at Randwick, and argued that Killara ought to have won. They were naturally anxious to see how the trial resulted.

'You have some good trying tackle,' said a trainer to Ross Gordon. 'There ought to be no difficulty in taking the measure of your Derby colt.'

'If he wins his trial he must have a great chance,' said Ross.

Paolo Vecchi was anxious about the result of the trial.

Ross Gordon had correctly guessed what Vecchi's intentions were. If Killara came through the test with Ivanhoe and Marengo satisfactorily, Paolo Vecchi meant to back him for the Derby and put someone in to lay against Burwood. Killara was the only colt Vecchi feared. He was anxious to see Killara beaten in the trial, but thought no such good luck awaited him. It would give him intense satisfaction to beat Killara with Burwood. He was a good judge of the work done by horses on the track, and had an idea he could easily tell the weights carried. He knew it would be rather a dangerous experiment to overload a colt with such a jockey as Cox in the saddle.

When he saw Killara go past he thought:

'There's no dead weight there. If the colt can beat Ivanhoe and Marengo this morning I'm afraid my horse has not much chance.'

'We must all pull particularly long faces after the trial,' said Ross. 'Paolo Vecchi must think we are overwhelmed at the defeat of Killara. I shall feel a great inclination to knock him down when I see the grin of satisfaction on his face, but the thought that he has fallen into the trap will console me.'

Any amount of watchers were in readiness to time the gallop, and there was quite a buzz of excitement when the horses started.

Killara kept well with his companions until they entered the straight, when he fell back a little. About a furlong from the winning post Cox brought the colt up again, and Ross could not help saying to Danby :

' By Jove! he's a good one with all that weight up.'

As they passed the post Killara looked hopelessly beaten, and rolled about a lot, as though much distressed.

The task he had been set had taken it all out of him.

Paolo Vecchi examined the colt closely as he walked in. The result of the trial was unexpected, and it gave him great satisfaction. He could not conceal his joy at such a stroke of luck.

' Must have gone off a lot,' said a man to Vecchi.

' Yes, he has,' was the reply. ' There's no doubt about it. Look at him now. He is regularly done up.'

Ross Gordon and Danby Widdrington walked down the track with the trainer, and the trio looked glum and dissatisfied.

' They've had something they didn't expect, this morning,' ' That "go" won't give them an appetite for their breakfast,' ' Not much chance for Killara in the Derby,' and such like comments were passed upon the trial.

' Look at Vecchi,' said Ross. ' He's taken the

bait all right. He looks pleased with himself. He is fairly bubbling over with satisfaction.'

Paolo Vecchi thought it would be a good opportunity to sneer at Ross Gordon, so as they passed he said :

' The defeat of Killara in the Derby was not much of a fluke. Perhaps you won't be so ready to make insinuations again, Mr. Gordon.'

Ross looked at him contemptuously, and said :

'Whatever I have said about the Derby I still believe to be true, and my opinion of you is unalterable.'

' I am glad you're beaten,' said Paolo Vecchi. ' I think I can put a spoke in your wheel—in fact, several spokes.'

There was a meaning in his tone Ross Gordon easily understood. He knew now that Paolo Vecchi had been trying to prejudice Vera against him.

' Your spoke has proved harmless,' said Ross. ' Luckily for me, you are thoroughly understood in that quarter.'

' Come along,' said Danby. ' Killara's been beaten, and there's an end of it. If Mr. Vecchi is gratified at the result of the trial, he is welcome to all the enjoyment he can get out of it as far as I am concerned.'

' You ought to get a man to manage your horses who knows more about them than Mr. Gordon,' said Vecchi.

'I am perfectly satisfied with Mr. Gordon,' said Danby. 'He is a good deal cleverer than you imagine.'

Paolo Vecchi laughed harshly as he said:

'He's a smart young man, but he has met his match. I hope he will enjoy his trip to Melbourne. I know he will get a reception he little expects in one quarter.'

He turned round to walk away, and before Danby could interfere Ross Gordon caught Paolo Vecchi by the arm and slung him round.

'You scoundrel!' said Ross. 'I know you are trying to make mischief between Vera and myself. You had better stop it, or it will be the worse for you.'

Paolo Vecchi wrenched his arm away, and said angrily:

'I'll trouble you not to lay hands on me. If you do, I shall know how to defend myself.'

'With a knife probably,' said Ross.

Paolo Vecchi turned pale as he said:

'Not with a knife. I have surer ways of ridding myself of an enemy than by stabbing him. I should not mind putting a knife into your heart in the least —the process would give me much satisfaction. To see you dead at my feet would complete a very satisfactory morning's work.'

'If you tell Vera any more lies about me I'll horsewhip you,' said Ross angrily.

'Try it,' said Paolo Vecchi. 'No man ever struck me a blow and did not suffer for it. I do not tell my daughter lies. I have told her the truth, if you care to hear it, and that is best known to yourself.'

Danby acted as peacemaker and drew Ross Gordon away.

'It will never do to have a row on the course,' he said.

Ross accompanied him to the horses, uttering all manner of threats against Paolo Vecchi.

'I wish you would control that fiery temper of yours,' said Danby. 'It is bound to get you into trouble some day.'

'How can I keep my temper when that scoundrel is trying to make Vera believe all sorts of things about me?' said Ross. 'You're such an easy-going fellow. Did you ever lose your temper?'

'Once,' said Danby, 'and I don't wish to lose it again. I made an ass of myself when I did so.'

'Which is as much as to say I have been an ass this morning. You are very complimentary,' said Ross.

'My dear fellow,' said Danby, 'I am not going to quarrel with you. I think you are anything but an ass. If you were related to that quadruped in the slightest degree I should not make a friend of you. Surely you ought to be satisfied with the trick you have played on Paolo Vecchi.'

'It is a good beginning,' said Ross. 'When he

has lost his money I shall be satisfied. There is nothing that man hates so much as losing money.'

' A grand trial,' said Mick Newton as they came up.

' Killara is a great horse,' said Cox. ' I believe I could have won with all the weight. I am glad I ride him in the Derby.'

Killara had been rubbed down, and was walking about cooling. He seemed none the worse for his gallop now.

' What do the lads think of the trial ?' asked Ross.

' They cannot understand it,' said Mick Newton. ' I think Killara's defeat has been an unpleasant surprise for some of them.'

CHAPTER XII.

ACROSS THE BORDER.

MICK NEWTON went to Melbourne, taking Killara and Marengo with him. Ross Gordon and Danby Widdrington followed a day or two later by the express.

Danby could see that Ross was uneasy about the result of his meeting with Vera Vecchi.

' See her as soon as possible,' said Danby. ' Drive to St. Kilda this afternoon, and then bring her to the theatre. I will meet you there to-night. I really do not see what you have to be alarmed about. I know your meetings with Nora Heath have been of the most innocent nature. If you wish me to see Vera I will do so, but I am sanguine there will be no necessity for it.'

Ross Gordon took a hansom and drove to St. Kilda. He found Vera at home, and she received him, as he thought, somewhat coldly. His last letter had made an unfavourable impression. It seemed to Vera that he was concealing something from her. She loved him devotedly, and in his presence could with difficulty control her feelings, but she thought it better to do so.

' You don't appear to be very glad to see me,' said Ross. ' I have been looking forward to this meeting ever since you left Sydney. What is the matter? Are you offended with me?'

' No, I am not offended, but I feel hurt, Ross. No sooner do I leave Sydney than you find someone to console you. You know how I love you. I cannot bear to think of any other woman taking my place.'

' Do not be unreasonable,' said Ross. ' Nora Heath is a mere girl. I have known her for a long time. We are very good friends, and I am sure you will like her. She will be in Melbourne for the meeting, and I want to introduce you to her.'

' I am not unreasonable,' said Vera. ' But why did you not tell me about that drive in your letter? There was no necessity to conceal it from me, and leave it to someone else to tell me.'

'Paolo Vecchi,' said Ross angrily. 'You ought to know he does his utmost to part us, and make us quarrel.'

'He was right in what he said on this occasion,' said Vera. 'It was not the drive with Miss Heath troubled me so much as the fact of your concealing it from me. Does Miss Heath know you are engaged to me?'

'No,' replied Ross.

'I thought not,' said Vera. 'She has a beautiful face, and I am sure is a good woman. She ought to have known you are engaged to me. It is not fair either to her or to me.'

Ross felt uncomfortable, and became irritable. He generally had his own way, and he did not like Vera to cross-question him.

'You make a fuss about a mere trifle, Vera,' he said. 'I met Miss Heath, after her return with her parents from London, quite by accident. She was in the carriage at Hordern's, where her mother was shopping. As I was talking to her Mrs. Heath came out, and asked me to visit them at Mount Royal, and bring Danby with me. We went, and had an awfully jolly time of it. I fail to see what harm has been done, or that you have any cause to be troubled about my conduct. You are over-sensitive. I assure you, as far as Miss Heath is concerned, she prefers Danby's society to mine.'

'It is because I love you so dearly that I am afraid

to lose you,' said Vera quietly, but with a beseeching tone in her voice that went to Ross's heart.

Vera Vecchi looked very lovely as she stood facing him, and Ross felt he had been somewhat unkind to her. In her presence she exercised a power over him he did not care to resist. He took her hands and then kissed her fondly.

'I ought to have told you about that drive,' he said ; 'it was foolish of me not to do so. Forgive me, Vera, I meant no wrong. You are the woman I love, and always shall love.'

He soothed and caressed her, and with her lover by her side Vera for the time forgot her troubles and fears.

'You said Nora Heath had a lovely face. Where did you see her ?' asked Ross.

Vera went to her desk, and, taking out Nora's portrait, handed it to Ross.

'It is an excellent likeness,' he said. 'Where did you get it ?'

'It was sent by my father. He thought, no doubt, it would not increase my happiness,' said Vera.

'It was a mean thing for him to do,' said Ross. 'He must have purchased the photograph.'

'When he wishes to obtain a thing he generally succeeds,' said Vera. 'You can imagine my feelings when I saw such a lovely face, and knew you were constantly with Nora Heath.'

'Yes ; I can understand,' said Ross. 'I know how

I should have felt had I heard you were driving about Melbourne with some good-looking fellow.'

'Such a thing would be impossible,' she said. 'I have you, Ross ; I want no one else.'

The afternoon passed quickly. Ross remained to tea and then accompanied her to the theatre. He congratulated himself that he had made it all right with Vera.

She was, however, not entirely satisfied. Ross had not appeared to advantage when making his excuses. Vera was anxious to meet Nora Heath and to find out how Nora regarded Ross. It would have been no surprise to Vera to discover that Nora loved Ross Gordon. She had a very exalted idea of Ross, and imagined him a man calculated to inspire any woman with love for him.

'How have you got on ?' said Danby when he met Ross. 'You look in excellent spirits. I suppose you have succeeded in convincing Vera you are a paragon of excellence.'

'She is quite satisfied with my explanation,' said Ross. 'There was, as you know, very little to explain.'

'Glad to hear it,' said Danby. 'I was rather afraid your task would be difficult.'

'Vecchi sent her a photo of Nora,' said Ross. 'No wonder she felt jealous. It was a splendid likeness.'

'Vera Vecchi compares more than favourably with

any woman,' said Danby. 'I don't think, Ross,
you quite understand what a lovely woman she is.'

'Oh yes, I do,' said Ross confidently. 'But a
lovely woman is generally inclined to be too exacting,
and that's just what Vera Vecchi is.'

Danby sighed. He thought if Vera loved him she
might be as exacting as she pleased.

They were standing near the door of the dress circle
bar, and two young men were smoking cigarettes and
talking near them.

'Fine actor, St. Albans,' said one.

'Yes, and a deuced handsome fellow. He's in
love with Vera Vecchi. I wonder she can resist him,
but they say she's an icicle, and there is only one man
can melt her, and that's not St. Albans.'

'Who is the lucky man ?'

'Someone in Sydney. I don't know his name—a
racing fellow, I believe.'

'If I happened to be in love with Vera Vecchi I
should not care to have a man like Hector St. Albans
always near her. It might be dangerous. Constant
love-making wears away the stoniest heart.'

Both Ross and Danby overheard this conversation.

Ross Gordon laughed as he said :

'They little imagine the " racing fellow " heard what
they said. Vera's an icicle, is she ? She is anything
but ice, I can assure you.'

'I think they were right,' said Danby. 'To any
other man but yourself she is cold and unresponsive.'

'Hector St. Albans is a splendid man,' said Ross.
'I wonder if he really is in love with Vera.'

'Shouldn't be surprised,' said Danby. 'I dare say
a good many men are in love, or think they are, with
Vera Vecchi.'

'That's the worst of being an actress,' said Ross.
'I hate the men who admire Vera on the stage, and
criticise her as though she were a horse, picking out
her good points.'

'Remember it is only what you have done yourself,'
said Danby.

'Oh, hang it all!' said Ross; 'you are always down
upon a fellow so quickly. Vera, however, is different
to many actresses. I never admired her in any other
than a respectful manner.'

As Ross Gordon watched Hector St. Albans
playing Orlando he thought how splendidly he made
love. Could it be true that he was really in love with
Vera? If so, she might be touched at the ardour of
his passion for her. Hector St. Albans was a fine,
handsome man, and he made an ideal Orlando.

Vera knew Ross Gordon was watching her, and she
played for him alone, and succeeded in making Hector
St. Albans well-nigh mad with delight. She acted so
well that St. Albans wondered if this love of Rosalind's
was merely feigned. His heart beat high with hope.
Perhaps, after all, there was a chance for him. When
Vera Vecchi was at her best her spirited acting was
contagious. She seemed to inspire others when on

the stage with her. Even the supers felt a pride in
their work when it brought them into such close
proximity to Vera Vecchi.

At the conclusion of the play Hector St. Albans
said to Vera :

'How admirably you acted to-night ! I felt your
love for Orlando was so real that I commenced to
have hopes. Forgive me for being so bold, but sometimes I feel I must speak out, or my love will kill
me.'

Vera Vecchi felt very sorry for him. She liked
him very much as a friend ; perhaps had there been
no Ross Gordon she might have loved him. She was
happy because her lover was near her, and her happiness made her considerate and kind to him.

' Please do not speak to me like this, Mr. St. Albans,'
she said. ' Try and forget me as a woman you love.
Think of me as a dear friend, one who would do much
to please and help you. It would not be right for
me to listen to you as a lover. There is only one
man I ever loved, and I have given him my whole
heart. I still have room for friendship with such a
man as you ; but you must never speak of love to me
again. It will raise a barrier between us I do not
wish to exist.'

He looked at her wistfully, his fine expressive eyes
showing the love for her burning within him. There
was a longing in his look he could not repress.

' I will try and accept your friendship in the spirit

it is offered,' he said; 'but it will be very hard work.
I cannot afford to lose your friendship as well as your
love. God knows I wish you to be happy.'

'I believe you,' said Vera, holding out her hand,
'and I trust you. Be my friend, as I will be yours.'

He stooped and kissed her hand with a grace and
dignity that well became him. His emotion was
beyond control, and Vera felt a hot tear drop on her
hand.

How sorry she was for him! Her eyes were dim,
and she sympathized with his suffering.

Ross Gordon and Danby Widdrington had come
round to the back of the stage, and saw this incident.

Hector St. Albans, when he left Vera Vecchi,
passed them with his head down. He did not see
them. His thoughts were troubling him, and he saw
no one.

Ross Gordon looked at Danby as though he
expected him to say something, but Danby maintained a discreet silence.

Vera came forward to meet them with a bright
smile on her face.

'I am very glad to see you, Mr. Widdrington,' she
said. 'I always know Ross is in good company when
he is with you.'

Before Danby could reply Ross Gordon said:

'You were in very agreeable company a minute
ago. Your cavalier was most attentive. Really, the
parting was quite romantic and affectionate.'

Vera coloured slightly, but looked Ross straight in the eyes as she said :

'It was Hector St. Albans. I will explain to you why he kissed my hand when we are alone. I am sure when you know all you will be as sorry for him as I am.'

Danby gave a sigh of relief. He had the most implicit confidence in Vera Vecchi's integrity, and was glad to hear her speak as she did.

Ross Gordon was not so easily satisfied. The conversation he overheard, and the way Hector St. Albans acted, combined with what he had just seen, made him angry. He forgot Vera had just cause of complaint against him, and that he had only recently excused his conduct to her.

Danby thought it would be better for him to leave them together, so he said :

'I merely came round to speak to you for a few moments. Ross will see you home. I am going to the club for an hour.'

Ross Gordon heard the story of Hector St. Albans' hopeless love for Vera, but he was more angry than sorry, although he concealed his real feelings from her.

'He will be a stanch friend,' said Vera. 'I can trust him. Do not be bitter against him, Ross. Love unrequited must be hard to bear. I know what it would mean to me.'

'I am not surprised at his falling in love with you,'

said Ross ; 'but he need not have told you, especially
when he knew you were engaged to me.'

'He did it on the impulse of the moment,' said
Vera. 'I am sure he will never speak of it again.'

As Ross Gordon drove back to Melbourne he
thought Hector St. Albans was not to be trusted so
implicitly as Vera said.

'I'd not trust any man who happened to be in love
with Vera, unless it was Danby.'

He laughed at the bare idea of Danby Widdrington
falling in love with Vera or any other woman.

CHAPTER XIII.

PAOLO VECCHI'S PLANS.

WHEN Paolo Vecchi arrived in Melbourne for the
Flemington meeting he began to steadily back Burwood for the Derby. After the trial of Killara at
Randwick he thought he was safe in doing so. He
had engaged Falby to ride his colt, and although the
jockey was not as sanguine as Vecchi, he knew
Burwood was a remarkably good horse. Having
ridden Killara at Randwick, he also knew Danby
Widdrington must have a chance of winning the race.

Paolo Vecchi determined to throw in for a big win
over Burwood if possible, and in addition to backing

his colt he stood in with a couple of bookmakers who had heavy volumes on the race.

Ross Gordon was delighted when he found out how completely Paolo Vecchi was in the dark as to the merits of Killara.

'It will be a hard knock for him if we win the Derby,' said Ross to Danby, 'and I think we have every chance of doing so. No horse could do better than Killara on the track, although he has put up no flash gallops.'

'I shall of course be delighted to win the race,' said Danby, 'but I wish Killara had won that trial. It is deceiving the public as well as Vecchi.'

'I'll tell you what we can do if you like,' said Ross. 'We can have another trial at Flemington, when Vecchi has all his money on, and let the public hear what Killara really is worth.'

'I should like that,' said Danby. 'It would be more straightforward.'

'If Killara does a great gallop he'll be first favourite and Paolo Vecchi will not be able to cover the money I know he has laid against him. There will be some risk in showing our hand, because Paolo Vecchi will not stick at a trifle to win the race,' said Ross.

'We shall manage to outwit him,' said Danby, 'and there will be more satisfaction in winning if I know the public are on.'

'You're a great one for the public,' said Ross. 'I

do not think they consider owners much. However, have your own way. Killara is your horse, and you can do as you like with him.'

Paolo Vecchi was constantly at Flemington, seeing Burwood do his gallops ; and he also kept a close watch upon the doings of other Derby colts, more especially Killara.

He was very much surprised, therefore, when he saw Killara and Marengo go out on to the track accompanied by Rosy Morn, a horse well backed for the Melbourne Cup.

' Going to have another trial,' he thought. ' That's curious. Perhaps they think there was some mistake about the Randwick gallop. I hope not. I shall be in a bad fix if such turns out to be the case.'

He did not at all like the idea of this trial. He knew when Rosy Morn had been borrowed for the occasion there must be more in it than he was aware of. He cursed his folly in making a move in the market so soon.

Great interest was taken in this trial, more especially by the Sydney men, who could hardly understand Killara's defeat at Randwick.

' It will be awkward for us if Killara comes well out of this "go,"' said Max Cardiff, one of the book-makers Vecchi had induced to lay heavily against Danby's colt.

' How can he come well out of it ?' said Vecchi. ' I saw the trial at Randwick and the colt was badly beaten. I never saw a horse pull up more distressed. Even if he managed to fluke home in this trial it would not alter my opinion that Burwood can beat him easily.'

'If Killara wins this morning, he'll be first favourite for the Derby to-night,' said Cardiff.

'Then we shall have all the better chance of laying against him,' said Vecchi. 'Don't be frightened, Max. I'll take good care, no matter how good Killara may be, that he does not win the Derby.'

'Of course if you can manage that, we are safe enough,' said Max Cardiff; 'but I would sooner see Killara well beaten this morning. Who is that riding him ?'

'Owen Cox,' said Vecchi; 'he rode him in the Randwick trial, so the weights will be about the same.'

Paolo Vecchi was completely out in his calculations. The weights were not the same—far from it. Mick Newton knew better than risk another gallop with such a big weight as the colt had at Randwick, and besides, there was no occasion for it, as Killara was to win, if possible. Mick had put up the colt's Derby weight, and he knew if the horse could beat Marengo and Rosy Morn the Derby was a real good thing for Killara.

'I shall enjoy this gallop much better than the last,' said Danby. 'There will be no deception about it. I see Paolo Vecchi over there, and he looks anxious.'

' If I am not very much mistaken,' said Mick
Newton, 'he will look desperate after this gallop.'

Cox went past on Killara, and Mick Newton said :

' Make the best of your way home, Owen ; Marengo
will bring you along for the last six furlongs.'

There was a confident smile on the jockey's face.
He thought Killara had an easy task before him.

Rosy Morn led Killara at a great pace for the
first six furlongs, and at this point Marengo jumped
in and the pace became even faster.

Trainers holding their watches and timing the first
six furlongs looked surprised, and their surprise increased as the horses neared the end of their journey.

As they passed, at the end of the gallop, Ross
Gordon and Danby Widdrington, who stood close to
Mick Newton, Killara finished a good length in front
of Marengo, with Rosy Morn a long way in the rear.

' That's a remarkable trial,' said Fred Otway, ' a
bit different to the one at Randwick. The change of
air must have done the colt good. He'll be favourite
to-night.'

' He has not got as much weight as he had at
Randwick,' said Mick, smiling.

' Ah !' exclaimed Otway, ' I'm beginning to see
how you have worked it, Mick. I don't fancy Vecchi
yonder will be very pleased.'

Horace Walsden came up and said :

' That's the best Derby gallop that has been seen
at Flemington for many a day. I hope you have

9

got all the money you want on, Mr. Widdrington, for he is sure to be a hot favourite.'

' I gave you the commission,' said Danby ; 'that is all I require.'

' And it is on at a fair price,' said Walsden.

'This is bad for us,' said Max Cardiff to Paolo Vecchi. 'You must have been nicely sold at Randwick. I thought you had a bit more sense than that.'

' You fellows always growl when you fancy you are going to be hit,' said Vecchi. 'Killara must have had a light weight up this morning. Cox can ride eight stone.'

' Then he must have had a deuce of a weight up at Randwick,' said Cardiff. 'It's a case of bluff, and you have been sold, my friend. As matters stand I am very glad you have such a large share in my book. It will be a case of paying and looking as pleasant as we can under the circumstances.'

' I tell you that Killara shall not win the Derby. That ought to be enough for you. This trial may be right, or it may be wrong. I am inclined to think it a fluke. If that is Rosy Morn's true form he can't have a show in the Cup,' said Vecchi.

' I do not know what your plans are,' said Max Cardiff, ' but remember, I am not going to be mixed up in any dangerous schemes. I would sooner lose my money.'

' You are a fool,' said Paolo Vecchi, ' and fools and

their money are soon parted. I am not anxious to part with mine. As for dangerous schemes, you had better not meddle with things you do not understand. I am going to prevent Killara from winning the Derby if I can, and my plans I shall keep to myself.'

'Very well,' said Max Cardiff. 'Do not get me into any trouble, and you can do as you like.'

'Take all the risk and you draw the plunder,' said Paolo Vecchi. 'No, that will not suit me. If I can stop Killara from winning, my share of your book will be larger than you anticipate. I know you, Max Cardiff, and you will do as I wish.'

Danby Widdrington was highly delighted at the result of the trial. He knew it would be wired all over the colonies, and give a correct idea of what Killara could do. At the Victorian Club the night of the trial there was quite a rush to back Killara, and he speedily became favourite at ten to one.

Next morning some of the papers made sarcastic comments about the remarkable way in which Killara had come on since his trial at Randwick. One paper in particular was severe, and the view taken of the situation made Danby wince.

'That's Vecchi's doing,' said Ross. 'He knows one or two men on that paper. I have seen him with them. You need not be alarmed. If anyone is blamed it will not be you. I can stand a lot of that.'

' I have done the best I can now to let the public know Killara's merits,' said Danby. ' It is their own fault if they do not back him.'

Paolo Vecchi knew he could rely upon Falby, and he meant that Burwood, if he could not win, should hamper Killara as much as possible in the race. He would have preferred to get at Killara before the race, but the risk was too great.

When he saw Vera after the trial he gave her his version of the affair.

' A nice man, your lover !' he said. ' A very honest, respectable man. All his conduct above-board. I'm glad you think so. Perhaps you would like to hear what he has done ?' And he handed her a copy of the paper containing the paragraph that had roused Danby's ire.

The paragraph hinted that Ross Gordon, as the manager of Mr. Widdrington's horses, was mainly responsible for deceiving the public, in order that Killara might be backed at a long price. Danby Widdrington was blamed for allowing a false trial to be run at Randwick, but the bulk of the abuse was poured upon Ross Gordon.

Vera was sensitive where Ross was concerned, and indignantly repudiated the sentiments contained in the paper.

' I believe you inspired this attack,' she said to her father, ' because it has interfered with your plans.'

' Never mind who inspired it,' said Paolo Vecchi ;

'it is true. Only a sharper would have done such a trick. I hope you are proud of him !'

'I am,' said Vera, 'very proud of him.'

'You are a confiding fool,' said Paolo Vecchi, 'and are throwing yourself away on him. He does not love you, and he will marry Miss Heath.'

'I do not believe it,' said Vera. 'He and Miss Heath are old friends. There is nothing between them.'

'If you had seen them as I saw them,' said Vecchi, 'you would have a different opinion. If he is not in love with Miss Heath, then he shams very naturally.'

'Why do you come here annoying me ?' said Vera. 'Does it please you to give me pain ?'

'I want you to learn the truth about this man. He is not worthy of you, and as your father I claim the right to come between you.'

'And I say you have no right,' exclaimed Vera angrily. 'You persecute me and annoy me. I do not believe you are my father.'

'If I am not your father,' he sneered, 'perhaps you can inform me who is ?'

'That you can do,' she said. 'I cannot prove you are not my father, but I would give much to be able to do so.'

'Some day I may tell you the story of my life and yours, but not yet. If you do not leave this man alone, if you persist in allowing him to act as your lover, I will tell him your real story. I do not think even his love would be proof against that.'

Vera turned pale, but her courage was great.

'What the mystery surrounding my birth may be I do not know. You have always overshadowed my life. There has been nothing in my own life to prevent any man loving me. You may invent vile stories against me. I believe you capable of any infamy. But let me warn you in time, you shall not take Ross Gordon from me.'

For a moment he wavered. He knew there was dangerous blood in her veins and he believed she would not hesitate to kill him if he pressed her too hard.

'I do not wish to quarrel with you,' he said, ' but I know what this man Ross Gordon is, and I have warned you against him.'

'Why do you have such bitter feelings against him ? He has never done you any injury.'

'I hate him !' said Paolo Vecchi. 'He is always thwarting me, and I brook no man's interference. Besides, he has wronged me in other ways. Before you knew him you were different to me. I have watched over and cared for you from a child. I have been mother and father to you. You were more to me before Ross Gordon stole your love. I hate him for that more than anything else.'

There was a passion in his voice that frightened her—a something she could not understand and that she had never heard before.

'I never loved you as a father,' she said. ' Ross

Gordon has made no difference to me in that respect. You have tyrannized over me from a child. I never knew what love meant until I met Ross Gordon. But I know now all that it means, and I will never let him go from me.'

'I will wait,' said Paolo Vecchi. 'There may come a time when you will look to me to help you. When that time comes I shall not fail you.'

She smiled incredulously as she said :

'I should never ask your help, even if it could save me from death.'

CHAPTER XIV.

A VILLA AT TOORAK.

THE Heaths were with friends at Toorak, Horace Plowden and his wife. They met the Plowdens in London, where they were staying at the same hotel for some considerable time. They returned on the same steamer, and Mrs. Plowden, who was a young and good-looking woman, had quietly taken a more than passing fancy to Nora Heath.

'Your friends are coming this afternoon, Nora,' said Ida Plowden. 'I shall be very pleased to see them. I have heard so much of them from you, especially about Mr. Widdrington.'

'Mr. Gordon and Mr. Widdrington are inseparable,'

said Nora ; ' and I am sure you will like them.   Mr.
Widdrington is one of father's oldest friends.'

'What a kind-hearted man your father is !' said
Mrs. Plowden ; 'and your mother always becomes a
favourite with everyone.'

'They are very kind to me,' said Nora.   'My life
has been free from trouble so far, and I hope it will
continue to be so.'

'I hope so,' said Mrs. Plowden; 'but we cannot
always have what we want.   It would not be good
for us.'

'No, I suppose not,' said Nora ; 'but still, it is very
pleasant.'

She looked at Mrs. Plowden, who was many years
her husband's junior, and wondered if her life had
always been happy.   She was inclined to think it had
not, and sometimes she doubted whether Horace
Plowden was the man to make any woman happy.

Horace Plowden was a different stamp of man to
Nora's father.   He was selfish in many things, and
thought his wife ought to find complete happiness in
ministering to his wants.

As for Ida Plowden, she had married her husband
because she wanted a home.   She was a governess at
a station in the western district of Victoria, near
Hamilton, when Mr. Plowden met her, and her lot
was much the same as that of most women in her
station of life.   She was anxious to be rid of the
drudgery and monotony of a life ill-suited to her, and

when Horace Plowden asked her to be his wife she consented. They had got on very well together so far, but Ida Plowden felt there was a good deal wanting to make her life happy.

When Robert Heath mentioned that Ross Gordon and Danby Widdrington were old friends of the family, Horace Plowden suggested that they should be invited to visit at Maldon Villa, and Ida Plowden was only too pleased to agree with him. Horace Plowden liked the idea of having the owner of the Derby favourite at Maldon Villa, and thought it would be a good thing if he could induce Mr. Widdrington and his manager to join their party to Flemington. So the gentlemen were invited and duly accepted the invitation, and Mrs. Plowden and Nora Heath were expecting them.

'I think Mr. Widdrington's your favourite,' said Mrs. Plowden, smiling.

'I am very fond of him,' said Nora simply. 'He is so different to most men.'

'Then I am still more anxious to see him,' said Mrs. Plowden. 'Men are very much alike, my dear —mostly selfish.'

'You will not find Mr. Widdrington selfish,' said Nora. 'He is the most unselfish man I know. He always appears to be devising schemes for making other people happy.'

'How delightful!' said Mrs. Plowden. 'Is he a rich man?'

'Very, I believe,' said Nora; 'but he never talks about himself.'

'And Mr. Gordon?' asked Mrs. Plowden. 'Is he a great friend of Mr. Widdrington's. I have heard of him before.'

'Mr. Widdrington is a stanch friend to him,' said Nora. 'He is more like an elder brother to Mr. Gordon.'

'Keeps him out of mischief,' said Mrs. Plowden. 'He is engaged to Vera Vecchi, the actress, is he not?'

'Who?' asked Nora, with a tone of alarm in her voice that amused her friend. 'Not Mr. Widdrington?'

'Oh dear no!' said Mrs. Plowden, laughing. 'I mean Mr. Gordon.'

'I have not heard of it,' said Nora, surprised that he had not mentioned it to her.

'But it is true,' said Mrs. Plowden. 'Horace told me so. He wondered if Miss Vecchi would accept an invitation to Maldon. My husband is rather proud of having celebrities around him. He imagines some of their glory is reflected upon himself.'

'I have no doubt she will accept your invitation if you send her one,' said Nora.

'Actresses, especially an actress like Vera Vecchi, are important personages,' said Mrs. Plowden. 'She might decline, and I should not care to have a refusal.'

'It is curious I have not heard of his engagement,' said Nora. 'Are you quite sure you are not mistaken?'

'Quite,' said Mrs. Plowden.

Nora thought Ross Gordon ought not to have kept his engagement secret from her. She would not have been seen about with him so much in Sydney had she known. She did not think it right for an engaged man to be so attentive to any other woman as Ross Gordon had been to her.

Robert Heath joined them and said:

'The gentlemen ought to be here soon, Mrs. Plowden. Where is your husband?'

'Gone to Melbourne; but he will be here in a short time. Some business matter he was obliged to attend to. He is a busy man, Mr. Heath.'

'Very,' said Mr. Heath, laughing. 'He makes business a pleasure. I am afraid I never did that.'

'Here they are,' said Nora, jumping up in delight. She had not seen either Ross Gordon or Danby since they arrived in Melbourne.

After introducing Mrs. Plowden, the conversation became general. Both Ross and Danby were good talkers when in the humour, and they felt quite at home at Maldon Villa.

Mrs. Plowden was a charming hostess, and Ross Gordon admired her greatly as she moved gracefully about the lawn. It was one of Ross Gordon's great failings that he could never help admiring charming women, either married or single. He meant no harm, but he had caused husbands many an anxious hour before this. He quickly advanced in Ida Plowden's good graces, and she thought him excellent company.

Danby Widdrington had much to say to Nora, and Mr. Heath soon went inside the house to look after his wife, who had a bad headache.

'Mrs. Plowden has told me Mr. Gordon is engaged,' said Nora.

'Yes,' said Danby; 'he is engaged to Miss Vecchi, a most excellent woman, and a lovely woman, too.'

'He did not tell me he was engaged,' said Nora.

'Ross has a habit of letting things slip his memory,' said Danby rather bitterly

'But surely he would not let his engagement slip his memory,' said Nora; 'that is not very flattering to the lady.'

'I am afraid Ross and I differ on that subject,' said Danby. 'I think when a man is engaged he should be devoted to one woman only. Ross has a tendency to be devoted to every pretty woman he meets. Look at him now.'

Ross Gordon was evidently making himself agreeable to Mrs. Plowden, who was laughing merrily at his conversation.

'Mrs. Plowden is the hostess,' said Nora. 'Of course he is quite right to be attentive to her.'

'Just so,' said Danby. 'Do you know Vera Vecchi? Have you ever met her, or seen her?'

'No,' said Nora. 'I should very much like to do so.'

'Then you shall,' said Danby. 'Your father must take you to the theatre. May I come too?'

'Of course you may,' said Nora. 'You are always welcome.'

Danby looked at her, and suddenly remembered the kiss he had given her. The more he saw of Nora the more he admired her.

'You met the Plowdens in London, I believe?' he said.

'They were at the Grand when we were there,' said Nora. 'We met in the hotel, and we returned by the same steamer. Mrs. Plowden is very nice. We are good friends.'

'And her husband?' asked Danby.

'I do not like him as well as I do his wife,' said Nora. 'He always gives me the idea that he is a selfish man. He is much older than his wife.'

'Old men ought never to marry young wives,' said Danby. 'It is not fair to the wives. I never pity the old men when such marriages turn out failures.'

'I should not like to marry an old man,' said Nora, laughing.

'There is no danger of that,' said Danby; 'too many young men are anxious to secure the prize.'

'You are quite mistaken,' said Nora. 'I have not even had an offer. I am a drug in the matrimonial market.'

'And a remarkably seductive drug, too,' said Danby. 'I believe if I did not happen to be a confirmed bachelor I should propose to you myself, and be justly snubbed for my presumption.'

Nora blushed slightly as she said :

'Are you really determined to die a bachelor?'

Danby looked at her with an amused smile as he said :

'Certainly, that is my determination at present.'

'But you may change your mind,' said Nora.

'You shall be the first to hear of it when I do,' he said, and Nora felt some faint consolation in his remark.

Meanwhile, Ross Gordon had been ingratiating himself with Mrs. Plowden, much to her satisfaction. She was fond of admiration, and she saw Ross Gordon admired her. His conversation was a decided change for the better after her husband's usually prosaic remarks.

When Horace Plowden returned home he welcomed Danby and Ross in his most cordial manner. He was rather a pompous man, and Ross muttered to Danby, when their host was out of earshot :

'I prefer the other Horace.'

'Which?' asked Danby.

'Horace Walsden,' said Ross.

Danby smiled, as he said :

'I dare say you are right. Walsden is not half a bad sort.'

'So you are going to win the Derby, eh, Mr. Widdrington ?' said Mr. Plowden.

'My horse has a chance,' said Danby. 'Do you like racing ?'

'Think it splendid,' said Plowden. 'A fine, manly sport.'

He seldom went to a race meeting, but Horace Plowden always endeavoured to suit his conversation to his company—except when addressing his wife.

'I can assure you it is not always pleasant owning a Derby favourite,' said Danby.

'Now, I should imagine it was simply delightful,' said Plowden. 'I have been envying you the honour.'

'According to some of the papers there is not much honour attaching to it,' said Danby. 'I have been abused before the race, so what I may expect after it is over I hardly know.'

'Pure jealousy,' said Plowden. 'People are always jealous of a man who owns a Derby favourite.'

'Or a pretty wife,' said Danby quite unconsciously.

Horace Plowden looked quickly at him, but Danby's face showed there was no hidden meaning in his remark.

'Quite so,' laughed Plowden. 'You own the Derby favourite, I own the pretty wife. Charming compliment.'

'And you are the luckier man,' said Danby. 'I congratulate you. I am a confirmed bachelor, and so have to be satisfied with owning a Derby favourite, and the inevitable consequences that follow.'

Ross Gordon was now deep in conversation with Nora Heath. He was explaining why he had not mentioned his engagement to her.

' I did not think of doing so,' he said. ' I fancied you knew about it. I was sure Danby would tell you.'

She did not quite believe him, and she said :

' You ought to have told me. It was your duty to do so. I should not have driven with you to Coogee that day had I known.'

' What nonsense !' he said ; ' pardon me for saying so, but it is nonsense. What difference could the fact of my being engaged make ?'

' I should not like it if I happened to be engaged,' said Nora.

' Women are all alike,' thought Ross.

They were near the gate of the entrance drive, and Ross Gordon was looking at her with an amused smile.

He put his hand kindly on Nora's shoulder and said :

' You must not quarrel with me, Nora, over such a slight matter. We always have been good friends, and I hope we always shall be. I must introduce you to Vera. I am sure you will like her.'

As Ross Gordon placed his hand on Nora's shoulder she looked down. She did not like him to do it, but she knew he was privileged as an old friend.

At that moment Vera Vecchi drove past in a carriage. She caught sight of Ross Gordon with his hand on Nora Heath's shoulder, and she recognised them.

She turned pale and gasped as though she had been hurt.

CHAPTER XV

PAOLO VECCHI GIVES ADVICE.

HECTOR ST. ALBANS was not slow to perceive that the woman he loved was unhappy. He knew Ross Gordon was in Melbourne, and that he had met Vera. Her happiness was bound up in Ross Gordon, and he put down Vera's troubles to him.

Hector St. Albans was a determined man. He had become a good actor by his own determination, and had fought his way into the front rank. He had loved Vera Vecchi from the first moment he saw her, and his love had increased until it tortured him and made him desperate. He knew he could not be a friend to Vera, as she wished, although he had promised. Friendship was impossible between them, at least on his side. He longed to ask Vera the cause of her present unhappiness, yet dared not do so for fear of offending her.

An evil chance threw Paolo Vecchi in his way when he was in a frame of mind ill-suited to combat

10

any of Vecchi's subtle suggestions. He had met
Paolo Vecchi on one or two occasions, and had disliked him.

Paolo Vecchi knew a good deal about Hector St.
Albans, and he knew he was in love with Vera.
Vecchi had a plan of his own with regard to Vera
which would have horrified her had she even contemplated the bare idea of it. Paolo Vecchi always
kept his intentions secret. He trusted no one, and
confided only in himself. His early life had taught
him that a secret, to be safe, must have only one
possessor.

A man possessed by a hopeless love Paolo Vecchi
considered easy to work upon. Hector St. Albans
was such a man, and therefore Paolo Vecchi kept a
keen look-out for a favourable opportunity to capture
him.

Luck was Paolo Vecchi's god ; he knew no other.
He worshipped luck, and so far it had favoured him.
He had never had occasion to curse this god of his,
but he frequently found occasion to rail at other
gods. Once Paolo Vecchi had been at the point of
death, but his luck did not desert him, and he recovered. The old priest who attended him on what
was supposed to be his death-bed had exhorted him
to confess his sins and die penitent. Paolo Vecchi
swore, and said he had no sins to confess ; and if he
had sinned he would not own it to a canting smooth-
faced hypocrite. The priest besought him to think

of his soul. Paolo Vecchi laughed, and said souls were all very well for priests to raise money upon, but such cant did not impose upon him. The holy man was horrified at Paolo Vecchi's blasphemy ; but he wrestled with the evil spirit in the man, and would not give up hopes of converting him.

When Paolo Vecchi recovered, the first use he made of his returned strength was to thrust the priest out of the room, and vow a terrible vengeance upon him if he returned.

Paolo Vecchi believed in nothing save his luck and himself, and he had a firm belief that, combined, the two were invincible. He used his wits upon men and women, as a skilled workman uses his tools, to fashion and mould them to his will. He had met with failure so far in regard to Vera ; but he did not blame his god of luck, but himself, and he set to work to discover where he had been at fault. In this he unconsciously set an example to far better men, who are apt to cast the blame of their own misdeeds and failings upon the God they worship instead of seeking the fault in themselves.

When Paolo Vecchi met Hector St. Albans he at once set to work to create a favourable impression, or, more correctly speaking, to remove the unfavour-able impression he divined Hector St. Albans had regarding him. He found this an easier task than he expected.

Deftly he, to all appearances, allowed their conver-

sation to drift towards Vera, when all the time he had
guided it in that direction.

'I should like to have a talk with you about Vera,'
he said. 'Come and lunch with me, if you have no
other engagement.'

Hector St. Albans was deeply interested in anything
concerning Vera, so he accepted the invitation, and
lunched with Paolo Vecchi.

It was an excellent lunch, such as Vecchi, who was
epicurean in his tastes, knew how to order, and he
suited his conversation to his guest.

Hector St. Albans began to think he must have
been mistaken in the estimate he formed of Paolo
Vecchi's character. He tried to discover some likeness to Vera in him, but failed to do so. There was
not the slightest personal resemblance between father
and daughter, nor did they speak or think alike.

'I should never take you to be Vera Vecchi's father,'
he said during a pause in their conversation.

Paolo Vecchi hated to be reminded of the difference
between himself and Vera. It did not suit his plans.

'If Vera were more like me she might take more
notice of my advice,' he said ; 'I think you are aware
she considers herself engaged to Ross Gordon, but it
is without my consent.'

'She has chosen the man she loves best,' said
Hector St. Albans with a sigh.

'She does not love him,' said Vecchi.

'Not love him !' echoed Hector St. Albans.

Then he laughed aloud, a noisy, hysterical sort of laugh. The bare idea of Vera Vecchi not loving Ross Gordon appeared to stagger him.

'You may laugh,' said Paolo Vecchi; 'but it is true. She may be infatuated with him, but that is not love. If her eyes were opened, and she saw this man as he really is, she would despise him, and hate him for playing with her feelings. I know my daughter better than anyone. She comes of a race that revenge themselves for injuries. This man, Ross Gordon, is unworthy of her. He deceives her, and merely passes the time with her to amuse himself. He is courting an heiress, a beautiful girl, who is more than half in love with him, which is a pity for her. I have sworn my daughter shall not marry this man.'

'Why do you tell me this?' said Hector St. Albans. 'What is it to me if your daughter loves this Ross Gordon?'

'It is much to you,' said Paolo Vecchi; 'because you love her. I admire you, and I hate Ross Gordon. You see I am candid with you. I will help you to win my daughter. The task ought not to be difficult. You are a handsome man, and women are susceptible.'

'She has no love for me,' said Hector St. Albans. 'She offered to accept my friendship, which is a certain proof she has no love for me.'

'And do you always take a woman's word? I tell you her infatuation for Ross Gordon shall pass away. It must. I will have it so,' said Vecchi.

'You are a strange man,' said Hector St. Albans. 'How can you rule a woman's will?'

'I have ruled men and women before,' said Paolo Vecchi, 'and I can do it again. This man Ross Gordon shall not have my daughter. If you can win her I will give her to you, and I will help you to win her.'

Paolo Vecchi's eyes gleamed, and had Hector St. Albans noticed him he would have been surprised at the look upon his face. It was the look of a man determined to obtain possession, not to help another man to win—a strange look for a father to have when talking and thinking of his daughter.

'Come, will you let me help you?' said Paolo Vecchi.

'I love your daughter,' said Hector St. Albans. 'I would do much to win her, but I will only win her openly. If you can help me I shall be glad. But you are mistaken in Vera. Once she loves she will always love. Is it true this man deceives her?'

'It is,' said Vecchi; 'and I have given her the proofs.'

Hector St. Albans clenched his hands, and, rising from his seat, strode rapidly up and down the room, his face working with excitement.

'She loves him and he deceives her,' he said. 'What does such a man deserve?'

'Worse than death,' said Paolo Vecchi. 'He should be unmasked. You ought to be the man to do it.'

'I!' exclaimed Hector St. Albans. 'I have no right to interfere.'

'Do you not love her?' asked Vecchi.

'With all my heart and soul,' said Hector.

'Then your love ought to protect her from disgrace,' said Vecchi.

'Disgrace and Vera are far apart,' said Hector; 'where Vera is there can be no disgrace.'

'You little know the man she has put her trust in,' said Paolo Vecchi. 'He is a libertine, a man without scruples where a woman is concerned. I am not always near her to protect her. You travel with her, and are constantly near her. Watch over her and guard her honour as you love her.'

'You talk strangely for a father,' said Hector. 'You cannot doubt your daughter's honour?'

'No,' said Paolo Vecchi; 'but no woman's honour is safe with such a man as Ross Gordon. Vera is very innocent in many things. He could easily persuade her to go through a mock marriage ceremony. It has been done, and cleverer women than Vera have been deceived.'

'By Heaven, if he dared such a monstrous sin I would kill him!' said St. Albans. 'Why do you say these things to me?'

'Believe in Ross Gordon, then,' said Paolo Vecchi, 'and stand quietly by and see Vera's life ruined.'

'You are her father,' said Hector. 'You can save her from this man, and it is your duty to do so.'

'That may be,' said Vecchi; 'but I want help. I offered you my help to win Vera. Give me your help to save her from this man, and you have advanced the first step towards winning her yourself.'

Hector St. Albans looked hard at his companion. He did not like Paolo Vecchi's face. As an actor he was a close student of men, and a good judge of character. He wondered if Paolo Vecchi had any ulterior motive underlying his intentions. Would it be fair to Vera to accept, as it were, the guardianship of her honour, for such Paolo Vecchi's proposal amounted to? What right had he to undertake such a task, more especially when he was in love with Vera himself? He would not be disinterested, as he ought to be, if he accepted Paolo Vecchi's proposal literally.

Paolo Vecchi studied Hector St. Albans as closely as the actor did him.

'He doubts me,' thought Vecchi. 'Always acting himself, I suppose he fancies I am acting. He is right, but he must not know it. I think I should have made a good actor.'

'I know no man,' said Paolo Vecchi, 'I would sooner trust Vera to than yourself. I have not known you long, it is true, but I have heard of you very often from Vera. Before she met Ross Gordon there was no one like you. If she had never met him you would have had no rival. Now that you have a rival, beat him and win the stakes. There is nothing dishonourable in such a rivalry. A man has the right to love where he pleases. No one can control love. It is a free agent and wanders about at will. Many men, and a few women, have tried to control it, but have failed miserably. Your love is an honourable love, and therefore you must fight to win. Women love more easily than men. They are courted and flattered, and love comes to them readily. There are heroic women who sacrifice all for love. Vera is not heroic. She is too sensible to be heroic. It is the fashion nowadays to write down men and hold up women as models of virtue and truth. Being a man, I think differently. Believe me when I tell you it will do Vera a great kindness to separate her from Ross Gordon. Have you never thought what might have happened had she not met him ?'

'I have,' said Hector. 'I believe I could have won her had he not come between us.'

'Then win her still. Think the matter over. I will help you at the proper time. Meanwhile, Vera is jealous of the girl Nora Heath. A jealous woman can always be persuaded,' said Vecchi in his most insinuating tones.

'If I can win Vera honestly I will do so,' said Hector ; 'and I shall, in that case, not forget your offer to help me.'

When the actor had gone Paolo Vecchi gave vent to his real feelings.

'He's a fool !—an honest fool, which is the worst fool

of all. There is a good deal more honesty in this world than I imagined. I think this honest fool can be tempted. Vera is an enticing bait to a man in love with her. He will be useful to play off against Ross Gordon. When she is in sore trouble and doubt my time will come. Then I can step in and play my part. Then she shall hear the story of her life and mine. She will not like it, but it will tell in my favour. As for the honest fool, perhaps he will turn knave; and the other one, Ross Gordon, perhaps he will marry the heiress. This is becoming interesting. Where do I come in? I think I know. Yes, I can assign my position to a certainty.'

CHAPTER XVI.

VERA'S INVITATION

MRS. PLOWDEN wrote a courteous note to Vera Vecchi, asking her to visit them at Maldon Villa, and also requesting her to make one of their party to the races.

'I know you by reputation, and have often been charmed by your acting,' wrote Mrs. Plowden. 'Mr. and Mrs. Heath and their daughter Nora are staying with us. They are friends of Mr. Ross Gordon and Mr. Danby Widdrington, who visit here.

Knowing the intimate relation in which you stand to Mr. Gordon, I have ventured to ask you to join our race party, and to visit us at Maldon Villa, in order that we may all become acquainted before Derby day. You have, no doubt, many calls upon your time, but I trust you will be able to accept my invitation, which I can assure you is cordially given. You will be charmed with Nora Heath. She is a most lovable girl, and a great heiress, which surrounds her with a golden halo of attraction for young men who have more good looks than cash. I admire your choice of a husband exceedingly. Mr. Gordon is a fascinating man, and there is a charm about his conversation I appreciate. Mr. Widdrington has persuaded me, but not by arguments, that there is one thoroughly unselfish man in the world—himself. But come and judge us all for yourself.'

Vera recognised the cordial tone of the letter, and it gave her pleasure. Had she not witnessed the little incident between Ross Gordon and Nora Heath she would have accepted it without hesitation. This incident, trivial though it would appear to most people, was of vast importance to Vera. She could understand Ross Gordon talking with Nora Heath ; but why did he place his hand upon her shoulder in such a protecting manner ? It was construed by Vera almost into an embrace. She was anxious to meet Nora Heath, and yet dreaded to do so. Nora Heath was an heiress and Ross Gordon was poor.

Vera herself was rapidly accumulating money, but she could never hope to be as rich as the millionaire's daughter. Since she had begun to doubt Ross's love for her she had been miserable. Why could she not believe in him, and trust him ? A thought flashed across her mind, ' If it was Danby Widdrington you could trust him.' She knew the sterling worth of Danby's character. It compared more than favourably with that of Ross Gordon. A lover's faults are, however, seldom seen, and when seen not acknowledged by the woman who loves him. Gloss over Ross Gordon's faults as she might, Vera could not help acknowledging that he was fickle and inclined to admire other women.

She had not seen Ross since his visit to Maldon Villa. After much consideration she decided to accept Mrs. Plowden's invitation, and wrote accordingly. She anticipated meeting both Ross and Danby there, and then she could judge for herself as to which Nora Heath favoured.

Mrs. Plowden was delighted at Vera's acceptance of her invitation, and Mr. Plowden beamed with satisfaction at the mere thought of having the celebrated beauty and actress and the owner of the Derby favourite on his coach. He shut his eyes and smiled placidly as he inwardly thought how people would level their glasses at the occupants of the coach, and sigh with envy of his good fortune.

' I am pleased she accepted,' he said to his wife,

'but of course there was no doubt about her doing so.'

'I took some trouble over the letter,' said Mrs. Plowden. 'I thought she would be pleased with it.'

'Of course you mentioned I should be charmed to welcome her here ?' said Mr. Plowden pompously.

'Yes, dear,' said Mrs. Plowden, who had not named him in her note.

Ida Plowden was beginning to feel somewhat disgusted with this rich, self-complacent husband. She constantly compared him with Ross Gordon, and sighed at the result. She was a very pretty woman, and she knew it. As for Mr. Plowden, he knew she was fair to look upon, but he considered himself entitled to have beauty bestowed upon him. Her commercial value was *nil*, so it was only right she should bring good looks into the Plowden circle to make up for this deplorable deficiency.

There are many conceited old men like Horace Plowden, and it is not pleasant to contemplate them. They marry young wives, and expect them to lavish their affections upon them at a time when they ought to be on the look-out for a professional nurse to see them safely out of the world. Horace Plowden, however, looked tough, and not at all given to dying. He was on the wrong side of sixty, but wished to be thought fifty. His wife owned to five-and-twenty and did not look more. Horace Plowden thought his wonderful vitality and personal attractions fully

entitled him to the possession of Ida Plowden and
her twenty-five years. She thought differently, but
carefully concealed her thoughts.

Ross Gordon and Danby Widdrington were invited
to meet Vera Vecchi at Maldon Villa.

'Haven't seen Vera for two or three days,' said
Ross. 'I'm awfully glad she is to be there.'

'Takes it coolly,' thought Danby. 'If I happened
to be in his shoes I should not allow three days to
elapse without seeing her.' To Ross he said :

'I am afraid you are rather neglectful of Vera.
Are you quite sure you are as fond of her as ever ?'

'Of course I am,' said Ross. 'What an old
croaker you are. Surely you do not expect me to be
tied to Vera's apron-strings because I happen to be
in love with her ?'

Danby saw it was useless to argue with him, so he
made no further remark.

Vera Vecchi was anxiously expected at Maldon
Villa.

Nora Heath wished to know Vera because she was
engaged to Ross Gordon, and Mrs. Plowden was
interested in many ways, but chiefly because she had
a desire to attach Ross Gordon to herself in a purely
platonic way.

Danby Widdrington and Ross Gordon arrived
before Vera.

When Vera Vecchi was announced her name
caused quite a flutter of excitement. Mrs. Plowden

greeted her cordially and introduced her to Mr.
Plowden and the Heaths.

Vera was looking her best; she desired to create
a favourable impression and at once did so. She
was completely at her ease, and greeted Ross Gordon
with a kindly smile of welcome that effectually concealed her thoughts. She was anxious to talk to
Nora Heath, and the opportunity quickly came.

'I have heard so much of you from Mr. Gordon,'
said Vera, 'that I was quite anxious to make your
acquaintance. I seldom visit, but I felt I must
accept Mrs. Plowden's invitation when it gave me
the opportunity of meeting you.'

Nora felt gratified, and confessed she had been
quite as anxious to meet Vera.

'I think Mr. Gordon did not tell you he was
engaged to me?' said Vera, after a short pause.

'No,' replied Nora, 'but I think he ought to have
done so, and I told him as much.'

'He is an old friend?' said Vera.

'I have known him for some years, but he is
not such an old friend as Mr. Widdrington,' said
Nora.

'They are great friends,' said Vera. 'I am glad
Mr. Widdrington is his friend.'

'I am sure he could not find anyone so stanch and
true as Mr. Widdrington,' said Nora.

Vera was looking at Ross Gordon, who was paying
marked attention to Mrs. Plowden. Danby Widdring-

ton felt things were slightly out of joint. Ross Gordon
ought to have been with Vera, he thought.

The garden gate clicked, and Vera started to her
feet with an exclamation of surprise and alarm as
she saw a man walking up the pathway. It was
Paolo Vecchi, scrupulously dressed and evidently
making no mistake as to the house he was coming
to. Ross Gordon and Danby Widdrington also saw
him, and looked at him in amazement.

Paolo Vecchi was always well prepared when he
undertook any task. He had ascertained who Mr.
Plowden was, and where he could be seen, and had
watched for him, and studied him, so that he had no
difficulty in recognising him again. He went straight
to Mr. Plowden and, lifting his hat, said :

' Pardon my intrusion. My name is Paolo Vecchi.
My daughter is here. I have something of importance to communicate to her, so I took the liberty
of calling.'

Mr. Plowden shook Vecchi by the hand, and said :

' Delighted to see you, I am sure. You are
welcome to Maldon Villa. Allow me to introduce
you to my wife.'

He moved across the lawn to where Ross Gordon
stood with Mrs. Plowden. Ross felt inclined to
knock Vecchi down. He wondered at the man's
impertinence and audacity.

' Ida ! this is Mr. Vecchi, Vera's father,' said Mr.
Plowden.

Mrs. Plowden welcomed him and Ross Gordon

slightly inclined his head and then walked away. The direct cut he gave Paolo Vecchi could not fail to be noticed.

'Mr. Gordon and I are not the best of friends,' he said. 'I do not approve of him as a husband for my daughter, but I suppose a wilful woman must have her way. I will speak to my daughter now if you will excuse me?'

'What are you here for?' said Vera when he came up to her.

'For a purpose of my own,' he said. 'I shall not remain long. I have informed Mr. Plowden I came to see you on important business. I wish you to keep up this mild deception, that is all.'

'I shall do nothing of the kind,' said Vera.

'You must,' said Vecchi. 'If you do not, I shall know how to act. It's not much I ask.'

'But why are you here?' said Vera.

'I thought it would be to my advantage to know the Plowdens,' he said coolly.

Vera flushed angrily as she said: 'And you have become acquainted with them through me in this underhand manner? It is shameful!'

'It is all for your good,' he said. 'There are many things I cannot explain to you at present. When I do so, you will understand my conduct.'

'You have come here because Mr. Gordon is here,' she said.

'That is one reason. I do not trust that man, and

you know I have sworn he shall not marry you. He does not love you. Look at him now with Mrs. Plowden. I think Horace Plowden had better take good care of his wife,' said Vecchi.

Vera Vecchi doubted Ross Gordon, so she could hardly wonder at her father doing so.

'Leave me,' she said. 'Do not remain long, and I will conceal the real object of your visit.'

'Thank you,' said Paolo Vecchi simply, and in a much kinder manner than he usually spoke to her ; and Vera noticed it.

Paolo Vecchi remained long enough to see that Ross Gordon did not speak to Vera, but paid much attention to Mrs. Plowden. He laughed to himself as he thought how easily Ross Gordon was playing into his hands. He believed in his heart that Ross loved Vera better than any other woman, but Paolo Vecchi also believed that no man was true to one woman.

Mr. Plowden thought Paolo Vecchi a most agreeable man. With his usual tact Vecchi had flattered Mr. Plowden, and praised everything he saw at Maldon Villa, including Mrs. Plowden. Horace Plowden loved to hear his wife praised. It satisfied him that he had not made a bad bargain when he married her.

'Perhaps you will join our party to the races, Mr. Vecchi ? Your daughter has accepted,' said Mr. Plowden.

Danby Widdrington heard the offer, and waited with an amused smile for Paolo Vecchi's answer. The notion of Paolo Vecchi accompanying the Maldon party to Flemington tickled Danby immensely.

'Will he have the cheek to accept?' he thought.

Paolo Vecchi exulted at this invitation, but he declined it.

'I am very sorry I cannot accept, Mr. Plowden,' he said, 'but I have a prior engagement. I hope, however, to have the pleasure of joining your party at Flemington for a short time.'

'Certainly,' said Mr. Plowden in his most pompous manner; 'we shall be most happy to see you.'

Paolo Vecchi congratulated himself on the success of his call at Maldon Villa.

'Plowden is a pompous ass,' he thought. 'I shall be able to work him to a profit. I have a speculation or two on hand that I should like him to invest a few of his thousands in. There's no chance with old Heath; he's too wide awake. I dropped into the midst of that party with much the same effect as a bombshell. Vera was frightened; I saw it in her face. She is half inclined to believe all I tell her about Ross Gordon. Mrs. Plowden will help me along. She is infatuated with Gordon. What the women see in him puzzles me. Hector St. Albans will have more chance with Vera. I must contrive to make Mr. Ross Gordon jealous. But Vera is not for Hector St. Albans. I have other plans for you, my sweet Vera. All these men and women are merely assisting me to gain my own ends.'

When Paolo Vecchi left, Ross Gordon said to Vera:
'Why did he come here? Beastly impudence, I call it.'

Vera did not like his tone, and she said haughtily:
'You have no right to speak to me like that. I do
not know his real reason for coming.'

'He said he came to see you on business,' said
Ross. 'I should have liked to knock him down.
Vera, that man, your father, is the cause of this
coolness between us.'

'Not entirely,' said Vera. 'It is partly your own
fault. Oh, Ross,' she said, with a sudden burst of
feeling she could not suppress, 'you are not the lover
you were in Sydney a few weeks ago. Something
seems to have changed you.'

'I have not changed,' he said. 'You misunderstand
me. I do love you dearly, Vera.'

'I will try to believe it,' she said slowly.

He turned away, and again began to talk with
Ida Plowden.

CHAPTER XVII.

AT FLEMINGTON.

IT was a splendid morning for the opening day of
the V R. C. Spring Meeting, and, as usual, there was
a vast amount of excitement over the Derby and the
probable winner. Despite the trial done at Flemington by Killara, Paolo Vecchi's colt ran him a close
race in the betting for favouritism. Vecchi showed

his confidence in Burwood by steadily supporting the colt, and the boldness with which he put on his money inspired confidence. Racing men knew when Paolo Vecchi put his money down in earnest he generally had a good thing on.

Ross Gordon could not understand Vecchi's game. He had not anticipated, after the Flemington trial, that Vecchi would still continue to back his colt. Danby Widdrington took very little notice of the betting. It mattered little to him whether Killara maintained his position as favourite or otherwise. What he desired was to see his horse win, and if the win benefited the public and his friends, so much the better. He knew hardly anything of the shady side of the turf, and had not been through the mill like Ross Gordon.

The night before the Derby he had not even gone to the Victorian Club; but Ross Gordon was there and saw how heavily backed Burwood was. Next morning the papers gave Burwood the position of favourite at a point shorter odds than Killara.

'There's something wrong,' he said to Danby as they sat at breakfast. 'What it is I don't know, but you may depend upon it that fellow Vecchi has something up his sleeve. He has backed Burwood to win a heavy stake, and he will not stick at a trifle.'

'If Killara is the better horse,' said Danby, 'as I sincerely hope, Burwood cannot win.'

'You forget,' said Ross, 'that Killara would have won at Randwick except for Paolo Vecchi.'

'But there is no danger of Owen Cox being got at,' said Danby.

'Cox is to be depended upon,' said Ross, 'but Falby is not. There is some scheme afloat to keep Killara out of it. I hear there will be ten runners, and I am afraid two of them, besides Burwood, will try and keep Killara out of it.'

'I hardly think Vecchi will go as far as that,' said Danby. 'If Killara is as good as we fancy, there will not be much chance of blocking him.'

'The Derby is such a peculiar race,' said Ross. 'As a rule, the horses are all well together. Sometimes one is put on to make a pace, but in the straight the bulk of the runners are pretty well alongside each other.'

'We will not anticipate any bad luck,' said Danby. 'Cox must keep a sharp look-out, and not throw a chance away.'

Ross Gordon drove the Maldon party to Flemington, and Vera Vecchi occupied the box seat at his side. To this she demurred, but Mrs. Plowden insisted upon it, although she would have much preferred being alongside Ross Gordon herself. They were a merry party, and Vera was in excellent spirits. She determined to enjoy herself and believe in Ross Gordon's love for her. Mr. Plowden was very proud of his turn-out, and noticed the company on his coach attracted much attention.

After luncheon, Paolo Vecchi came up with Hector St. Albans, and introduced him. Vera could not understand the sudden intimacy between her father and the actor, but she made no comment upon it. Having introduced Hector St. Albans, Vecchi made his excuses, and left the actor with the Plowdens. Ross Gordon went to look after Killara, and when he left Hector St. Albans attached himself to Vera.

They were a handsome pair, and, being well known, were watched by many people as they promenaded the lawn.

'What a brilliant scene!' said Hector St. Albans. 'I confess Flemington cannot be beaten when the spring meeting is on.'

'That is a great concession for an Englishman,' said Vera. 'I always thought racing in England was perfection.'

'Did you?' said Hector. 'Then I can undeceive you. It is anything but perfection. There is nothing like the comfort at home we get out here. Have you any wagers on the Derby?'

'Mr. Widdrington has put me five pounds on Killara,' said Vera.

'Your father tells me his colt Burwood will win,' said Hector.

'Have you backed him?' asked Vera.

'Yes, I have put a few pounds on. I like to have an interest in the race,' he said.

'How long have you known my father?' asked Vera.

'I have known him for some time,' said Hector, 'but have become more friendly with him since I met him in Melbourne this time.'

'You never mentioned to me that you knew him,' said Vera.

'I thought he would have named it,' said Hector.

'My father tells me very little about his friends. Many of them I prefer not to hear about,' said Vera.

'I hope I am not one of those friends,' said Hector.

'No, you are not,' said Vera candidly. 'Here are Nora Heath and Mr. Widdrington. Is she not a charming girl?'

'Considering I only met her a few minutes ago, I will not venture an opinion,' said Hector, smiling. 'Personally she looks charming.'

'Mr. Widdrington appears to think her attractive,' said Vera; and she felt relieved at the thought.

'They are well matched,' said Hector.

He looked at Nora with interest. This was the girl Paolo Vecchi said Ross Gordon wished to marry. Had Vecchi made a mistake? and was it Danby Widdrington she favoured?

'How is the betting?' asked Hector St. Albans. 'I have not been in the ring yet.'

'Nor have I,' said Danby; 'but Ross tells me Burwood is favourite.'

'I have a trifle on him,' said Hector; 'but I must save on Killara. Miss Vecchi fancies your horse will win.'

'I hope he will,' said Nora. 'We are all anxious to see Killara win.'

Ross Gordon was busy looking after the finishing

touches to Killara in the paddock, when Owen Cox came across from the direction of the jockeys' room.

'You look serious, Owen,' said Ross. 'Anything the matter?'

'I don't fancy I shall have a very pleasant ride,' said the jockey.

'What have you heard?' asked Ross quickly.

'Bray, who is riding Kangaroo, has heard Killara is not to win. He asked me about it,' said Cox.

'Not to win! But who is going to stop him?' asked Ross.

'I do not care to make accusations,' said Cox; 'but I hear Falby and Jones were talking rather big the other night, and Falby said he was sure Killara would not beat Burwood. You know what he is. He has been up before the stewards more than once, and has twice been suspended for foul riding. Jones is a friend of his, and rides Dingo, a horse with no chance, and started, I am afraid, to hamper me if he can.'

'Vecchi is at the bottom of this,' said Ross. 'You must try and keep a clear course. Do not get on to the rails if you can possibly help it. They will block you if they can, or knock you on to the rails.'

'I'm not afraid of them,' said Cox; 'but I am anxious about the race. I want to win it for Mr. Widdrington.'

'He will not blame you, whatever happens,' said Ross. 'Do your best, and keep a sharp look-out. If you are hindered from winning, we shall know how to act.'

'Falby's a bad lot,' said Cox, 'and he is in Paolo Vecchi's clutches. He will have to ride to orders.'

'I am glad you told me of this. I will let Mr. Widdrington know. I think he ought to take some action before the race,' said Ross.

'No,' said Cox; 'not before the race. I may have been misinformed, and I do not care to make complaints at any time when they can be avoided.'

Paolo Vecchi was busy in the ring backing Burwood again, and his lead was followed by many sharp people.

Burwood became an even-money chance, and Killara had gone back to three to one. Kangaroo was a good third favourite, and occasional investments were made on the remainder at long odds.

Mr. Plowden and Mr. Heath came across Paolo Vecchi in the ring.

'Do you still fancy your colt?' said Horace Plowden.

'I think he will win,' said Paolo Vecchi; 'but he is at a very short price. If you have not backed him I will let you stand in with me for what amount you care to invest.'

'Much obliged to you, I am sure,' said Horace Plowden. 'I will have twenty pounds on with you at the best odds you can lay.'

'Do you wish to back my colt?' said Vecchi to Mr. Heath.

'No, thanks,' said Robert Heath; 'I have already backed Killara. I do not care to back two in the race.'

'I am afraid you will lose your money,' said Vecchi.

'How is it Killara has gone back in the betting?' asked Horace Plowden.

'That is not for me to say,' said Vecchi. 'I know what I think.'

'Tell me what you think,' said Horace Plowden.

'Killara ought to have won at Randwick,' said Paolo Vecchi; 'but he did not. Some people say Falby pulled him; I do not believe it, and that is why I have put him up on my colt. I do not think Mr. Widdrington has anything to do with it, but there is something wrong about the way Killara goes in the market to-day.'

Robert Heath did not like Paolo Vecchi, and he said: 'If Killara is the best colt he will win—that is, if nothing unforeseen occurs to prevent him.'

Paolo Vecchi did not like the tone of this remark, and soon left them.

'I prefer the daughter to the father,' said Mr. Heath, as he looked after Vecchi.

'Seems to me a shrewd man,' said Horace Plowden.

'Too shrewd for my fancy,' replied Mr. Heath.

The horses were saddled and walking about the paddock when the two gentlemen entered the gate. Ross Gordon spoke to them and inquired where Danby was.

'With the ladies,' said Mr. Plowden. 'He is quite a ladies' man.'

Ross laughed as he said: 'He is not generally

considered so, but I suppose he does not wish to desert them.'

'Hector St. Albans is with them,' said Mr. Plowden. 'He appears to be a great friend of Miss Vecchi's.'

Ross Gordon did not relish the idea of the handsome actor being Vera's companion. He remembered the incident he had witnessed at the theatre, and the remarks he overheard there.

'We met Paolo Vecchi in the ring,' said Mr. Heath. 'He is confident about his colt. What do you think of the race? Killara has gone back to three to one.'

'That is the only thing I cannot quite understand,' said Ross. 'Vecchi has backed his horse for a lot of money, and he will win if he possibly can. I have an idea he knows why Killara has gone back in the betting.'

'He said there was something wrong about it,' said Mr. Plowden.

'Did he? Very kind of him, I am sure. Perhaps he informed you what it was?' said Ross.

'You need not lose your temper over it, Ross,' said Mr. Heath, smiling. 'I know what value to put on Mr. Vecchi's insinuations.'

'He made no insinuations,' said Mr. Plowden. 'I did not understand him to do so. I think you are both prejudiced against him.'

'There's the bell,' said Ross. 'We shall soon see if there is any reason for Killara going back in the betting. I'll join you when I have seen Cox in the saddle.'

When Ross Gordon had seen Killara safely out of the paddock he made his way through the ring to the stand where the Plowdens were. As he came through the crowd the roar of the ring surged in his ears, and he heard the odds of four to one shouted against Killara.

' I'll take five to four.'

It was Fred Otway's voice, and Ross Gordon stopped to speak to him : ' What is the meaning of this ?' he said. ' Can you understand it, Fred ?'

' Blest if I can,' said Otway. ' All I know is I shall be pretty hard hit if Burwood wins. There has been a ton of money going on him ever since we reached the course. Is anything the matter with Killara ?'

' No,' replied Ross, 'book me four fifties about him.'

' Right, sir,' said Otway, and his clerk pencilled the wager down. ' If there happened to be any other jockey in the saddle I should say he had been got at,' said Fred Otway to his clerk. ' Cox will ride straight, safe enough, and that's why I can't make it out. I'm anxious to see this race. Come along.'

He went towards the terrace, followed by the clerk, and looked at the horses as they swept past in the preliminary canter.

On the stand the Maldon party had obtained a good position, and as Ross Gordon joined them Killara went past with Cox up in the sky-blue jacket, white sleeves and cap of Danby Widdrington.

'Goes well,' said Ross. He saw Hector St. Albans next to Vera and resented it.

'Splendid,' said Danby. 'Mick has put a grand polish on him.'

'Killara's at four to one in the betting,' said Ross. 'It is a false price. He ought to be favourite. I shall be glad when the race is over.'

Vera was looking at him and he went to her. She introduced him to Hector St. Albans. They eyed each other in anything but a friendly manner.

The horses were walking back past the stand to the starting-post, and the sky-blue jacket stood out conspicuously.

'What pretty colours Mr. Widdrington has !' said Vera Vecchi.

'And they are carried by a good colt,' said Ross. 'I am sure Killara will win if he gets fair play.'

'You do not anticipate foul play, surely?' said Vera.

'The betting puzzles me,' said Ross. 'Killara ought to be favourite, and he has gone back to four to one. Burwood is at slight odds on. Your father has backed him for a lot of money.'

There was a hidden meaning in his tone, and Vera Vecchi turned a shade paler. She put her hand on his arm and said : 'I hope Killara will win. If he does not I shall think I am always bringing trouble upon you.'

'It is not your fault, Vera,' he said kindly. 'True, Paolo Vecchi is your father, but you are not in any way connected with his actions.'

'But it is through me he has such animosity against you,' she said.

'The possession of your love, Vera, is worth more to me than anything in the world. Paolo Vecchi's conduct makes me more determined than ever that he shall not come between us,' said Ross.

'How good you are, Ross!' she said. She was happy again, and forgot all her doubts and fears.

But there was no more time for talking. The horses were off, and the race for the Derby had commenced.

CHAPTER XVIII.

FOUL RIDING.

WHEN the horses had galloped a couple of furlongs Cox saw Jones on Dingo and Falby on Burwood were shepherding him closely. Kangaroo held the lead and Cox kept Killara well on the outside. He knew, however, that it would not increase the colt's chance of winning if he kept him on the outside all through the race. As they entered the back stretch the pace was slow, but Cox did not care to take Killara to the front so far from home. Jones had brought Dingo on the outside, and Killara was now racing between the outsider and the favourite.

Ross Gordon watched the race closely through his glasses and saw this move on the part of Dingo's rider. He knew it was a bad position for Killara to

be in, between this pair, but he consoled himself by
the thought that there was plenty of time for him to
get clear. There was some bumping at the far corner,
and the horses were all well together. As they neared
the home turn into the straight Dingo swerved onto
Killara and knocked him back, and then left the
favourite with the lead.

Ross Gordon muttered something which, to Vera,
did not sound polite.

' Anything the matter ?' she asked anxiously.

' Dingo has knocked Killara right back,' he said.
' I think Jones did it on purpose. Hang me if the
fellow is not boring Killara on to the rails now! He'll
have both horse and jockey over if he does not stop !'

Dingo had not fallen out of the running when Jones
pulled him on to Killara, and he was now crowding
Danby's horse onto the rails.

' Pull out, you'll have me over !' shouted Cox.

The words were no sooner uttered than Cox felt
Killara's legs slipping from under him, and at the
same time the jockey's leg was crushed violently
against the rails.

Cox did not lose his presence of mind for one
moment. He saw Jones intended to keep Killara out
of the race if possible. He kept Killara on his legs
by a great effort and then steadied him. It was a
narrow escape. An inch or two more and both horse
and rider would have been down. The pain in Cox's
leg was intense, and he saw blood upon his breeches.
He did not think of himself: his whole thoughts,

were concentrated on how he was to beat Burwood.

Falby looked over his shoulder with a malicious grin on his face and thought : ' Jones did his work better than I expected. It makes it all the easier and safer for me. He'll get into a mess. There's one comfort, he'll have more chance of pulling through than I would.'

Ross Gordon could hardly control his feelings.

' It is scandalous !' he said. ' Did you notice it, Danby ? That fellow Jones on Dingo deliberately tried to knock Killara over the rails.'

Unobserved by Ross, Paolo Vecchi had joined the Plowdens, and was sitting just behind him. He heard the remark passed by Ross, and said in an undertone to Mr. Plowden : ' Did you hear that ? Rather a serious accusation to make against a jockey. There's no accounting for what some men will say when they are beaten.'

Horace Plowden took very little notice of Vecchi's remark. He was too excited over the race. Paolo Vecchi had laid him a good wager about Burwood, and the colt looked to be winning easily.

Danby heard Ross Gordon's remark, and said quietly: ' I am afraid that little manœuvre of Jones's cost us the race.'

The ladies were all excitement. Nora was quite pale. She knew what horse-racing was, and also how horses should be ridden, and she felt that Dingo's jockey had been guilty of foul riding.

Danby Widdrington caught sight of Paolo Vecchi's face, and the look of cunning delight on it irritated him. It was not often Danby desired to throttle any-one, but his fingers itched to catch Paolo Vecchi by the throat and shake him. He knew very well who had put Jones up to this little game.

When a Derby favourite has a lead of four or five lengths, and is going strong and well about a couple of furlongs from the winning post, there is some justification for jubilation on the part of his backers. Hundreds of people had money on Burwood and rejoiced accordingly, and the name of Paolo Vecchi's colt was shouted loudly as the winner. But there were hundreds of people who had backed Killara, and naturally they had watched the colt all through the race. When Dingo bored Killara on to the rails and nearly brought Danby's colt to grief there was an angry murmur.

'That's foul riding, or I'm no judge of a race,' said Fred Otway.

'Dastardly, I call it,' said Horace Walsden, who was standing near him. 'I think the betting market clearly indicated there was something wrong.'

'And the worst of it is,' said Otway, 'the favourite will win, and there'll be no chance of a protest.'

'The swindle has been cleverly worked, Fred,' said Walsden; 'but the race is not over yet,' he added excitedly. 'By Jove! look how Killara is making up his ground! Cox is riding splendidly. There's a chance yet.'

'Too far behind,' said Otway. 'You can't expect Killara to make up all that ground. It's asking too much. I only wish he could. I hate that —— Vecchi.'

All over the course a wave of intense excitement was passing. It commenced gradually, and with a dull murmuring sound, which swelled until it became a prolonged roar. The huge crowd on the hill above the grand stand surged backwards and forwards in a tumult of excitement.

The crowd which thronged every part of the grand stand caught the infection, and commenced to add to the general uproar. On the flat hundreds of people were yelling themselves hoarse and endeavouring to catch a glimpse of the horses. The man at the winning-board, who had picked out Burwood's number to be in readiness to put up as the winner, dropped it in his excitement and gazed at the horses. Even the judge, calm and cool in his box, felt his pulses tingle as he looked up the straight.

Paolo Vecchi swore under his breath and bit his lips. He threw a look of eager expectancy upon the faces of those around him.

Danby Widdrington suddenly grasped Nora Heath by the arm and said with a gasp : ' I believe Killara will win after all.'

This was just it, the identical reason that had driven thousands of people wild with excitement—such tumultuous feelings as only a well fought race can call forth.

'I believe Killara will win after all,' exactly expressed the opinion of hundreds of people.

Ross Gordon almost shouted for joy. Defeat had, he thought, been certain, and here was a chance of recovery.

Owen Cox felt when he pulled Killara together that the horse was not beaten. He looked ahead, and saw what a tremendous advantage Burwood had obtained. This did not daunt him. He meant to win if possible, even though it was only a forlorn hope.

He nursed Killara for a few seconds, until the horse was fairly into his stride again, and then commenced to ride the colt and to get every ounce out of him. There was a strange numbness in his leg, but he heeded it not. He seemed to have only the use of one limb, and he could not ride as determinedly as he ought to have done. But his head was as clear as ever, and his hands as firm and yet light. Cox had wonderful hands. Horace Walsden, who was a good judge, said Owen Cox 'talked to a horse with his hands.' Killara seemed to understand what his rider required of him. The noble animal did his best. He strained every nerve to win. There was no need for whip or spur, Killara was extended to the utmost. It was with a wild beating of the heart that Owen Cox saw the gap between Killara and Burwood gradually reduced. It was a question of time and distance. He felt Killara would beat Burwood if he could only get the colt on terms with him.

Falby heard the shouts of 'Burwood wins!' and

felt the race was as good as over. He was not prepared for that sudden revulsion of feeling from the
crowd which denoted the race was not yet over. It
startled him, and he looked anxiously round. Coming
at a great pace on the outside he saw a sky-blue
jacket and a horse's dark bay head. He was a good
jockey, although not a straight one, and he knew
Burwood would have to be ridden hard to win.

'D——d if he shall win!' snarled Falby. 'I'll run
him into the judge's box first.'

Roar after roar from the vast crowd proclaimed the
excitement. It was a magnificent struggle, a grand
exhibition of pluck and endurance, a combination
that never fails to win admiration.

As Killara neared the leader Cox saw with dismay
and anger that Falby was riding Burwood wide and
keeping Killara out of his track. It was impossible
for Cox to change his course. He must keep Killara
on the outside or lose the race.

'Keep straight!' he shouted with all his might, but
Falby took no notice.

Burwood was galloping at an angle with the judge's
box, and it was impossible for Killara to pass him.
Angry shouts came from the crowd. Some people
thought Burwood was beaten and Falby could not
keep him straight. Others realized that Falby was
deliberately hindering Killara, and preventing the
colt from getting on terms. The judge, as he looked
at them, began to think there was every prospect of
one of the horses running into his box.

Cox was certain it was a deliberate attempt on the part of Falby to do Killara out of the race.

Amidst a scene of intense excitement the two horses passed the winning-post close under the judge's box, and Burwood was nearly a length to the good.

'My horse won,' said Paolo Vecchi exultantly.

Ross Gordon heard him, and, forgetting in whose company he was, turned round on him savagely.

'Won, you confounded scoundrel!' he said. 'You've not won yet. We'll see what the stewards have to say about it.'

'Come, come, Mr. Gordon,' said Horace Plowden; 'you are forgetting yourself. Remember the ladies.'

Ross Gordon glanced at the speaker angrily and then said: 'I beg your pardon, ladies. In the heat of the moment I forgot myself. Come, Danby, you must lodge a protest against the winner.'

'That's how such men take a defeat,' whispered Paolo Vecchi to Mr. Plowden. 'My horse was distressed, anyone could see that. No real sportsman would put in a protest. I must go and lead my horse in.'

'Surely you are not going to lodge a protest against Burwood?' said Mr. Plowden to Danby.

'If he takes my advice he will,' said Ross, 'and he will get the race.'

'I strongly advise you to protest,' said Mr. Heath. 'I never saw such a barefaced thing in my life.'

'Shameful!' said Nora, and then, seeing the pained

look upon Vera's face, she said to Danby: 'We are forgetting Miss Vecchi is here. It is not kind to discuss the affair before her.'

Danby beckoned to Ross, and as he was about to step over to him Vera said : 'I do not know much about racing, but I think the race throughout was a most unfair one for Killara. I hope you will protest against the winner.'

'We shall,' said Ross. 'I am sorry for your sake it has happened, Vera, but Danby must do what is right. Hark !'

From all parts of the course were heard loud cries of 'Protest !' 'Have him up !' 'Warn him off !' 'Protest, protest !'

These cries were redoubled as Burwood came into the enclosure, and Falby dismounted to weigh in. The jockey did not seem at all put out, and coolly took the saddle on his arm.

When Danby Widdrington and Ross Gordon reached the enclosure there was a cheer. Cox still sat on Killara, and Ross said : 'Why don't you dismount ? I suppose you think we ought to protest.'

'Most decidedly !' said Cox in a weak voice. Then, bending down, he said : 'I cannot get off alone, I must have help. I believe my leg is smashed. I was jammed onto the rails.'

Ross Gordon saw the blood slowly trickling down the jockey's boot, and said : 'I'm awfully sorry, Owen, but they shall suffer for this. I'll obtain permission from the stewards to assist you to weigh in.'

The requisite permission was readily granted. The crowd which had gathered round the fence saw Cox slowly assisted out of the saddle and carried into the weighing-room by Danby Widdrington and Ross Gordon.

The rumour quickly spread that Owen Cox had been forced on to the rails and had his leg smashed.

Anxiously the vast crowd waited to see the flag go up, denoting whether it was 'all right' or 'protest.' The jockeys weighed in correctly, and a minute or so afterwards it was known all over the course that Danby Widdrington had lodged a protest against Burwood, and rumour further said he had complained of foul riding on the part of Jones, the jockey of Dingo.

CHAPTER XIX.

THE PROTEST.

'I'LL bet on the protest!' shouted the members of the ring, anxious to square their books, which were bad against Burwood. There was almost as much excitement now as before the race. Backers of the favourite saved themselves by investing on Killara. The general opinion seemed to be that Killara would get the race. Burwood's backers, however, were very indignant, and declared no protest ought to have been made.

Paolo Vecchi was excited, and raved about the

unsportsmanlike conduct of Danby Widdrington, and cursed Ross Gordon as the instigator of the proceedings. He expressed his opinions freely, and in no complimentary terms. For once, he appeared to have lost control over his temper, and he said many injudicious things. The bookmakers who had stood in with him were anxious Burwood should get the race. They knew well enough Killara had not been fairly treated, but the money they had at stake counted more than fair play. Max Cardiff called Falby a blundering idiot, and Paolo Vecchi was designated in stronger terms.

'Bah!' sneered Vecchi. 'You have no pluck! There is no danger. They will not disqualify a Derby winner. The colt was dead beat, and swerved across the course from sheer distress.'

'That tale is all very well until another is told,' said Cardiff. 'All stewards are not blind, and some of them know as much about racing as we do. That idiot Jones will be sure to let something out; he is such a confounded ass.'

'But there is ample evidence to prove Burwood was struggling home. Falby will swear to it, and the trainer will say he never handled a horse more distressed,' said Vecchi. 'Max, my boy, you ought to be making picture-books for children, not making a book in the ring.'

Although Paolo Vecchi tried to treat the matter lightly, he was very uneasy. He sought out Horace Plowden, and induced him to do what he could to influence Danby Widdrington.   Then he tried Vera.

'I want you to ask Mr. Gordon not to press this business,' he said to her. 'You seem to think he will do anything for you. Try him.'

'I shall do nothing of the kind,' said Vera. 'You deserve to lose the race. I am ashamed of my name when I remember how you disgrace it by your mean, contemptible actions. I hope Killara will get the race.'

'If Burwood is disqualified, I know whom to blame for it,' said Paolo Vecchi angrily. 'Ross Gordon will wish he had not interfered if my horse loses the race, but it will be too late then.'

Vera was always alarmed at Paolo Vecchi's threats. She had an unaccountable dread of what he would do. She was, however, determined not to interfere in the matter.

When Cox had weighed in, the doctor examined his leg, and found it was broken below the knee. He admired the jockey's pluck for riding such a desperate race with a broken limb.

The stewards took Cox's evidence first, as the doctor wished him to be removed to the hospital as soon as possible. Although in great pain, Owen Cox gave his evidence clearly and to the point.

'Let him tell his story his own way,' said the senior steward.

Cox then described what occurred.

'I noticed early in the race that Jones kept Dingo dangerously near my mount, and I spoke to him once or twice, but he took no notice. At the back of the course he cannoned against me, but it did not throw Killara out of his stride. When we were fairly in the straight I was making a run to get on terms with Burwood, when Jones deliberately crushed me onto the rails. It was not accidental; I am certain of that, because I called out to him that I should be over, and he laughed. Killara very nearly lost his legs, and I was crushed against a post and had my leg smashed. I was in great pain, but in the excitement of the race I almost forgot it. I steadied Killara, and got him into his stride again. Dingo fell back, beaten, and I went after Burwood at top speed. Killara's a good 'un, one of the gamest colts I ever rode. The bumping had taken a lot out of him, but he answered to every call I made upon him, and was fast catching Burwood. When Falby looked round and saw me coming he pulled his horse to the right. There is no mistake about this, for I saw him do it. The nearer I got to him, the wider he rode his mount, and bored me over towards the judge's box. I called out to him, but he took no notice. I had no possible chance of passing him, and only just missed the judge's box. He bored me right across the course. I do not think Burwood was beaten, nor did he swerve from distress. I think Killara would have won had he had a straight course to finish on, because he was going much faster than Burwood and I was catching Falby easily at every stride. Killara is a much better finisher than Burwood. I have

ridden both colts and therefore I know. I advised
Mr. Widdrington to lodge a protest because I believe
but for Falby's running me out of my course that
Killara would have won. I have no animus against
either Jones or Falby, but I must do my duty by
Mr. Widdrington. I believe there was a dead set
made at Killara during the race, and that had there
been no foul riding he would have won comfortably.
Under the circumstances the colt ran a splendid race.'

Cox answered several questions put to him by the
stewards, and was then carried to the ambulance and
removed to the hospital.

Falby had heard what Cox said and also Jones,
but the questions they put to him did not tend to
shake the evidence against them.

Danby Widdrington gave his version of the race,
but did not unduly press any charge of foul riding or
intentional interference on the part of Falby. He
thought, however, that if Burwood had taken a
straight course at the finish Killara would have won.

An adjournment was made until the next race was
over, and then Ross Gordon made his statement.

He said he had received a warning before the race
that Killara would be interfered with.

'You ought to have reported the circumstance
before the race,' said one of the stewards.

'I wished to do so, but Cox begged me to remain
silent as he did not wish to make any unfounded
complaints against jockeys. I know, however, that
he was very uneasy, not on his own account, but

because he feared he would be hindered from doing his best to win on Killara. I watched the race closely, and I am convinced that Jones deliberately tried to knock Killara over the rails.'

' That is a malicious lie !' said Paolo Vecchi.

' If you do not remain quiet I shall order you out of the room,' said the chairman. ' We cannot permit such remarks here.'

Vecchi scowled, but thought it better to hold his tongue.

' Regarding Falby's riding of Burwood,' continued Ross, ' I prefer to leave it to the judgment of the stewards. I have my opinion upon it, but as Falby and myself had some differences over his riding of Killara at Randwick I prefer to remain silent. I most strongly urged Mr. Widdrington to enter a protest because I do not think he has had fair play.'

The judge was called, and gave it as his opinion that Burwood's running wide interfered with Killara's chance of winning, but he declined to say whether he thought Falby guilty of intentional interference. Pressed to give a decided opinion, he said emphatically : ' I think the course Burwood took lost Killara the race.'

The last race was run and the stewards had not yet heard the evidence on the other side. The majority of those present left the course, but hundreds remained behind waiting for the result.

Paolo Vecchi gave his evidence well. He disclaimed all knowledge of any plot to prevent Killara winning.

As to the running of Burwood, he placed great confidence in Falby, and thought the swerving across the course was the result of the severe race the colt had run.

'Burwood finished a length in front of Killara,' said Vecchi, 'and I did not see any interference. I have been told Mr. Gordon threatened what he would do if Killara lost the race. He has been an enemy of mine for some time, and I believe he induced Mr. Widdrington to bring this protest to gratify his personal spite.'

Ross Gordon denied Paolo Vecchi's statement, and said the animus was all on the other side.

'Personal matters, I need hardly say, we shall give no weight to,' said the chairman. 'We are merely calling evidence to hear what explanation is offered. The stewards saw the race for themselves, and can form their own opinion. Still, we are desirous of ascertaining if there was foul riding, as it is a serious matter, and we are determined to put a stop to it.'

Falby was quite at his ease. He had been before the stewards on previous occasions. He denied any wilful interference with Killara's chance, and said Burwood would have won under any circumstances. It was not true that he and Jones had agreed to stop Killara if possible.

Jones gave his evidence in a somewhat halting manner, and kept constantly looking at Paolo Vecchi, much to his disgust.

He said he heard Cox call to him to pull out, but he could not do so as Kangaroo shut him in. Had no intention of injuring Killara's chance, and was sorry for what had occurred. Had never been up for foul riding before.

' Not in New Zealand ?' asked one of the stewards.

He had forgotten about that, it was such a long time ago. He was on that occasion suspended for six months.

The stewards were a long time coming to a decision, and the crowd anxiously waited for the result. It was growing dark, and lights commenced to appear in the bars and on various parts of the course.

The Maldon party had left, Ross Gordon and Danby Widdrington remaining behind. Hector St. Albans accepted a seat on the coach, and Thomas Heath handled the ribbons, Mrs. Plowden sitting alongside him, and Vera Vecchi against Hector St. Albans.

Ross Gordon saw them drive off, and was annoyed to see Vera had changed her seat. He soon forgot it, however, and anxiously awaited the result of the protest.

' I think you are sure to get the race,' he said to Danby.

' I shall be very pleased to defeat Paolo Vecchi's plans,' he replied ; ' but I should have preferred to see Killara first past the post.'

' That's where he would have been,' said Horace Walsden, 'if Burwood had not blocked the way. You deserve the race, Mr. Widdrington, even on a protest.'

After an hour's delay the stewards gave their decision. They disqualified Burwood and awarded the race to Killara, placing Kangaroo, who had run third, second. They suspended Jones and Falby during the pleasure of the stewards, and stated it was their intention to further inquire into the allegation that the endeavour to prevent Killara winning had been prearranged.

The decision was popular and not unexpected, and Ross Gordon was delighted. Danby Widdrington was heartily congratulated, although he protested and said there was not much cause for congratulation when he only won the race on a protest.

Paolo Vecchi was in a terrible rage. He accused the stewards of partiality, and vowed vengeance against Ross Gordon.

'You'll have some nice accounts to settle, my friend, after the meeting,' said Cardiff. 'Mind, I hold you responsible for a heavy share in my book.'

'D——n your book !' said Vecchi. 'What is your paltry book to me ? It is not the money I care about, it is being done by such a parcel of fools.'

'Well, I'd sooner be a fool than a rogue,' said Cardiff.

'What do you mean ?' asked Vecchi.

'What I say. You ought to understand what a rogue is,' said Cardiff.

'And you ought to understand that if I am a rogue I use other rogues for my tools,' said Vecchi. 'You happen to be one of them.'

The news of the race being awarded to Killara was well received at Maldon Villa. Mr. Plowden thought it hard lines for Paolo Vecchi, but congratulated Danby on the success of Killara.

Nora Heath was delighted and showed it, and Danby thought it was worth while to have won the race, even on a protest, in order to be congratulated by Nora in such a charming way.

When Vera heard the news at the theatre she felt a vague feeling of alarm. She was glad Killara had got the race and yet dreaded the result to Ross Gordon. Paolo Vecchi, she knew, would not tamely submit to it. He would be revenged for his supposed wrong. All she could do was to pray and hope that Ross Gordon would be kept from all harm.

CHAPTER XX.

AFTER THE MEETING.

THE stewards' decision over the Derby made a vast difference to many people. Burwood had been so heavily backed that the majority of bookmakers were glad Killara had got the race. They also preferred parting with their money to Danby Widdrington rather than to Paolo Vecchi. As far as the double event betting, on the Derby and Cup, was concerned, Burwood and Killara were equally bad for the layers.

Paolo Vecchi, when he came to total up his losses,

13

found they amounted to a lot of money. It was annoying to him to think that Burwood beat Killara and yet did not receive the stakes. On Cup day he plunged heavily, in order to recover his losses, but matters went from bad to worse, and when an outsider at a hundred to three won the Cup he cursed his luck at last. It was the first time he had blamed his luck for what had occurred. On the Thursday and Saturday he again tried to win back a portion of his losses, but failed. After the meeting he had to confess it would be a very hard matter to meet his liabilities.

When he returned to Melbourne after the last race on the Saturday he found a letter waiting for him, and on opening it gathered that more misfortune had overtaken him. A mine in which he had invested largely had closed, and the company was to be wound up. His liabilities in the matter amounted to several thousands of pounds.

Paolo Vecchi was not easily daunted. He had faced far greater troubles than this and come out of them well. But he required time to think, and so on the Sunday morning, when the church bells were ringing and people flocking to the various places of worship, he shut himself in his room and held council with his own evil spirit. The sound of the bells jarred upon his nerves, and he cursed them and all connected with churches.

Vera, he knew, had saved money. She must have several thousands, he thought. It was no good asking her to lend it him, she knew him too well. Could he force her to lend it him? He went to his desk, opened it, and took out a small dark-coloured bottle. There was writing on it in a foreign language which few people could have deciphered. It was a relic of days gone by, when he had waged war against society and had been the leader of a savage gang of brigands in Smyrna. The drug in this bottle was one he valued greatly. It produced a curious effect upon the person to whom it was administered. It was a concoction made from various herbs, and he had never known it to fail. It was a source of intense satisfaction to him now that he had retained this drug. Its effect he knew well. A few drops changed the person taking them completely, and made the mind subservient to the will of another. He had often wondered at the subtle power of the drug. He remembered how on one occasion he had given a few drops to an unfortunate lady who had fallen into the clutches of his band. The effect had surprised himself. The unfortunate woman fancied herself madly in love with him, and he had taken full advantage of it. On recovering her senses she had gone mad and killed herself by leaping over a precipice. Paolo Vecchi was brutal enough to smile even after this lapse of time as he thought of it.

'This must be my friend,' he thought; 'but how am I to use it? Perhaps there will be no necessity for it. Vera may consent without. No, she will never do that; she little knows who she is—a beautiful woman, a very beautiful woman,' he said, as he looked at a photograph of Vera he had taken from the desk.

'No, I am not your father,' he went on, talking to the picture. 'I am more than a father to you. I love you, my beautiful Vera. Not as other men love you, but savagely, and I love you for your beauty. You will be rich some day, when I care to make known the secret of your birth. Why should I not marry you, Vera? True, you have looked upon me as a father, but there is no reason why you should not regard me as a husband. You have been in my care ever since you were captured by the band, and your father and mother were—well, what matter? —I did not slay them. But I must have money at once. How to obtain it from her?'

He thought for a long time and then appeared to have decided upon his course of action.

In the afternoon he drove out to St. Kilda and called upon Vera. She was not at home.

'I will wait until she returns,' he said.

The woman of the house knew him as Vera Vecchi's father, and made no demur.

He had a long time to wait. It was late when Vera returned home. She had been at the Plowdens', and had met Ross Gordon, and had spent a pleasant afternoon. She entered the room, and a look of vexation passed over her face when she saw her visitor.

'You here,' she said, 'and at this hour?'

'Business of importance,' said Paolo Vecchi, 'or I would not have troubled you.'

'What is it?' she asked wearily.

'I want money. It is settling day to-morrow. Will you let me have some?'

She made no answer and he went on : 'I have had heavy losses, not alone over the races—I could have pulled through over them—but a mine in which I am deeply involved has gone wrong, and the company is to be wound up,' he said.

'You have no claim upon me,' said Vera.

Paolo Vecchi fingered the small bottle in his waist-coat-pocket as he said :

'I have a claim upon you, Vera, that you little understand. Will you let me have some money?'

'How much do you require?'

'Two thousand pounds will tide me over settling-day, with what cash I have,' he said.

'I can let you have no such sum,' she replied.

'You mean you will not let me have it,' said Vecchi.

'Put it that way, if you prefer it,' said Vera. She rang the bell and asked for a cup of coffee. 'Excuse me a few moments,' she said to him ; 'I will take off my things. Perhaps when I return you will have found it convenient to leave the house.'

She swept out of the room, and Paolo Vecchi sat down and waited.

'I will not be thwarted,' he said savagely.

The servant brought in the coffee. Paolo Vecchi took the small bottle from his pocket and dropped a few drops into Vera's cup. Then he sat down with a smile upon his face.

' Not gone ?' said Vera when she returned. ' It is useless your remaining ; I shall not change my mind.'

' I think you will,' he said.

She sipped her coffee and looked at him. He remained perfectly still, and watched her.

' Why do you look at me like that ?' she said.

' Because you are very beautiful. I never knew you were so beautiful before,' he said.

Vera laughed scornfully.

' Flattery from you is wasted,' she said. She put her hands to her eyes, and rubbed them gently. She felt a peculiar sensation in her head, as though something was slipping away from out of her memory.

' How long are you going to remain ?' she asked.

' Until you change your mind,' he said.

' About what ?' she asked.

' Have you forgotten ?' he said, watching her intently. ' The drug's working,' he thought.

She made no reply, but sank back in her chair and fell sound asleep. He touched the bell, and when the servant appeared, said : ' My daughter is tired, and has fallen asleep. I will remain with her until she wakes. You need not wait up.'

For two hours Vera slept soundly ; then she stirred uneasily, and finally awoke. She looked about her, and her eyes rested upon Paolo Vecchi.

' You have been asleep,' he said. ' I have waited to ask if you will oblige me by letting me have a cheque for the amount I wish to borrow from you ?'

She looked surprised.

'I do not remember anything about it,' she said.

He explained to her, watching her steadily all the time, and then said :

'Can I get your cheque-book for you ?'

'Thank you, I will get it myself,' she said, and rising, unlocked her desk, and took out the book.

He placed a pen and ink before her, and said, 'Write what I tell you,' and dictated the filling-in of the cheque for £2,000. She signed it boldly, and in her usual hand.

'Thank you,' he said. He looked at her again and stepped towards her.

Vera did not move, but gazed at him in a frightened way. He took both her hands and then kissed her. She was unresponsive, and he knew the drug would soon cease to have effect. He was interested in the experiment he had tried, and remained watching her.

'I think l shall go to bed,' said Vera. 'I am very tired. Good-night.'

He did not detain her, and she left the room.

Paolo Vecchi managed to settle next day at the club, and in the afternoon he again went to see Vera. He found the manager of the theatre there. Vera had written to him, stating she was too ill to appear that night.

'She seems very strange,' said the manager. 'Her mind wanders a little. I fancy she is feverish.'

Vera was on the couch, and Paolo Vecchi went across to her. 'I am sorry you are ill,' he said ; 'I trust you will soon recover.'

'The cheque was all right?' she asked.

The manager looked at Paolo Vecchi, who explained : 'My daughter was good enough to advance me £2,000 last night. I had a heavy settling to-day.'

When the manager left, Vera Vecchi turned suddenly to Paolo and said : 'What have you done to me? I know I gave you a cheque last night; I saw the counterfoil. I remember writing it. You forced it from me against my will. I feel ill, too. Tell me! what have you done?'

He looked surprised as he replied :

'I have done nothing. I am very much obliged for the cheque. What is the matter with you?'

'Tell me what you did to force me to give you that cheque and I will make you a present of the sum,' she said. There was a look of terror in her eyes : she seemed to dread something she should hear.

'I tell you, Vera, I did nothing,' he said. 'You gave me the cheque of your own free will.'

'It is false!' she cried. 'You drugged me. You practised some of your devilish knowledge upon me. What else did you do to me! Speak, man!—speak!'

'If I knew what to say, I would speak,' he said. 'I did nothing to you, Vera. I thought you were more attached to me than usual, because you kissed me before I left.'

Her eyes burned and her cheeks flushed. 'You mean you forced me to kiss you,' she said. 'I know you now, Paolo Vecchi. You are not my father. I know who and what you are. I know you drugged me.   There is the proof of your guilt.'   She flung a small label on the table.

Paolo Vecchi started.   It was the label off the bottle in which he had the drug.   It must have been loosened by the heat of his vest-pocket, and come off when he took it out.

'What is this?' he asked, recovering himself. 'What has it to do with me?'

'Much,' she said.   'Read the inscription.'

'Can you?' he asked hurriedly.

'I can, and I have,' she said.

'Ah!' said Paolo Vecchi.   'And has it reminded you of anything?'

'Many things,' she said.   'First of all, of your infamy.'

'So you really believe I drugged you?'   He laughed uneasily.

'I know you did,' she answered.   'Tell me all that happened when I was under the influence.'

'You recollect giving me a cheque,' he said, 'therefore you can remember all.'   He emphasized the last word.

'I only remembered it when I saw the counterfoil,' she said.   'The finding of the inscription explained why I signed it.'

'Then you regret it?' he said.

'I will give you double the amount if you will tell me the true story of my life,' she replied.

'You have said you remember who and what I am,' he said ; 'in that case, you remember all.'

'No, I do not,' she said. 'It is all very indistinct. I think the drug recalled memories that were dead.'

'It has that effect sometimes,' said Paolo Vecchi.

'Then you did drug me?'

'I did.'

'Why?'

'You need not look frightened,' he said. 'I did nothing terrible. I wanted the money: you refused it. That was the only way of obtaining it. You looked so beautiful I could not help kissing you. That is all that happened.'

'Will you swear it?' she said.

'I swear it,' said Vecchi.

'And you are not my father?'

'No.'

'Who is my father?'

'I cannot tell you,' he said.

'You can, and you must,' she said. 'I will know the secret of my birth.'

'On one condition,' he said.

'Name it,' she replied.

'That you consent to become my wife,' he replied calmly.

CHAPTER XXI.

VERA IN PERIL.

VERA was startled when Paolo Vecchi asked her to become his wife, but she had half expected some such answer to her question. She looked at him

steadily for some moments, and then said calmly :
'So this is what you have been scheming and
plotting for, to make me your wife. There must be
some very strong inducement. I hardly expected
such an offer from you on my own account. In
order to ascertain who I am you wish me to become
a Vecchi in reality. You are very much mistaken if
you think to succeed. I shall find other means of
ascertaining the truth. You are perfectly aware that
I despise you. I have long ceased to think of you
as a father, and merely tolerated you in order to try
and obtain the history of the past from you.'

'And in all these years you have not succeeded,' he
said. 'How do you expect to do so without my aid.'

'I feel I shall succeed,' she replied ; 'but even if I
knew I should fail your conditions would still be
hateful to me.'

'My dear Vera,' he said ; 'you would do well to
consider my power. I have the means of forcing you
to do as I wish.'

'But you will not again have an opportunity of
carrying out your plans. You will never be able to
use that drug upon me again.'

'We shall see,' he said. 'I am not at all afraid.
The opportunity will present itself, and be sure I
shall take full advantage of it.'

She knew the desperate nature of the man, and
that so long as he had the drug in his possession she
was in peril. Vera Vecchi was brave, but her courage
almost failed her as she thought what might happen

if Paolo Vecchi used this drug upon her again. 'Why do you wish to marry me?' she asked. 'Have I a fortune you wish to share with me? I know you are too selfish to care for anyone but yourself.'

'There you are wrong,' he said. 'I care for you, Vera. I have watched you grow up from a mere child. I have seen you develop into girlhood, and then grow into a beautiful woman. I have watched and longed for the time when all those expanding charms should be mine. It is because I desire you above all other women that I hate Ross Gordon and have tried to make a tool of Hector St. Albans. I never meant you to marry any other man but myself. If I have been stern with you it has been for your own good. I have had you in my power all these years. Think how I might have used that power. The drug I have had always in my possession, but you have never felt its power until now. You are the woman I have vowed to make my wife, and I shall keep my vow.'

'You are an unscrupulous villain!' she said. 'I would sooner die than wed such a man. How dare you make such a vile proposal to me! You have been regarded as my father; think what my position would be as your wife. It is too horrible to contemplate.'

'You are madly in love with this man Gordon,' he said. 'I will give you the opportunity of testing his love. He shall hear from me what you are, and what you have been to me.'

' You will tell him——' gasped Vera, shuddering.

'I will tell him many things. I will tell him I am not your father, and that you are no relation to me. He shall know that you have lived with me for years, not as a daughter, but as my——'

Before he could say the word, Vera Vecchi, her eyes dilated with horror, rage, and agony, at the mere thought of what this man suggested, caught up a small dagger which she used as a paper-weight and book-cutter, and threw herself upon him. He narrowly escaped a serious wound in the side of his neck, but he was too quick for her. Paolo Vecchi had been accustomed to sudden attacks in his brigand days, and he was prepared for Vera's. He seized her by the wrist, but not in time to prevent the dagger inflicting a slight wound on his cheek. He wrenched the dagger from her hand, and put it quietly on the table.

'I do not think you will attempt that again,' he said coolly. ' There is your dagger.'

He took out his handkerchief, and pressed it to his cheek. A few spots of blood showed upon it. He looked at the stains, and gave a savage laugh. The sight of blood acted upon Paolo Vecchi with much the same effect as on a wild beast. Blood always infuriated him, and rendered him merciless. He had been baptized in deeds of blood, cowardly, murderous attacks.

' First blood to you,' he said. ' Now it is my turn.'

The savage look of the man turned Vera cold, and

she trembled violently. She was weak and ill from the effects of the drug, and powerless to resist. What little strength had remained to her she had expended when she attacked him. He saw her helplessness, and gloated over it. He was utterly cruel now, and had no more mercy for her than a lion for a lamb.

'Call for help, utter one cry,' he hissed, 'and it shall be your last.'

'Those words,' she said suddenly. 'I remember, I remember! Those were the very words.'

He laughed fiercely. 'They were words often uttered in a different tongue in years gone by,' he said. He took her by the wrist and forced her on to the couch.

She seemed paralyzed with fear, and Paolo Vecchi stood over her like a demon of another world.

'Hear me out,' he said, 'I have no mercy to show you now. Ross Gordon shall learn from me what you are, what I intend to make of you.'

She shuddered and said hoarsely: 'He will not believe you. He will know it is an infamous lie.'

'It shall be no lie,' hissed Vecchi, and he took the small bottle from his pocket again.

The sight of this, and the knowledge of what the drug was capable, roused Vera to make an effort to save herself. She attempted to cry out, but Paolo Vecchi stifled the sound by pressing his hand over her mouth.

'You shall drink it all!' he hissed. 'Then you are mine to do with as I will.'

She struggled desperately, but he stifled her, and in her weak state her strength soon gave way. In a few moments she had fainted.

'Good!' muttered Paolo Vecchi, looking at her. 'Now for it.'

He took up a glass, poured out a small quantity of water and emptied half the contents of the bottle into it. He then forced open Vera's lips and poured the liquid down her throat.

'I will leave her now,' he said.

He rang the bell violently.

'My daughter has fainted,' he said. 'Please see to her at once. I will go for the doctor.'

He left the house, gloating over his hideous work like a fiend. He thought it better to call upon a doctor, and asked him to go round at once and see Miss Vecchi. Dr. Grainger, when he saw Vera, came to the conclusion it was a severe fainting fit, and at once took measures to restore consciousness. In this he quickly succeeded. The drug had not yet taken effect, and he saw nothing unusual about the symptoms.

Vera was relieved to find Paolo Vecchi had gone. She thanked Dr. Grainger, and said she did not think he need trouble to call again.

'Be sure and send for me at once,' he said, 'if you require me.'

Vera went to bed, her maid attending her.

'Please remain with me until I go to sleep, Annie,' she said. 'I feel nervous and upset.'

The girl, who was very much attached to Vera, sat down in a low chair by the bedside and watched her mistress. Vera quickly fell into a deep but restless sleep. She talked in a rambling way, and sometimes in a language the girl had never heard.

Annie remained with Vera all night and had very little sleep. In the morning she brought Vera her breakfast, and noticed how pale and strange her mistress was. Vera, however, talked rationally when spoken to, but appeared to have some difficulty in remembering several things Annie mentioned to her. She came downstairs about noon and seemed much brighter and more cheerful.

To return to Paolo Vecchi. Next morning he met Danby Widdrington at the club. He had made up his mind to try and impress Danby first, because he did not think Ross Gordon would listen to him. He knew Ross would pay attention to Danby, and therefore he spoke to him.

Danby Widdrington was rather sorry for Paolo Vecchi, scoundrel though he thought him. It was not in Danby's nature to bear animosity against any man. He might feel angry and aggrieved for a time, but the feeling quickly passed away. He knew Paolo Vecchi had paid his bets in full, and he admired him for it. ' He can't be quite such a bad lot,' thought Danby. ' I know some men who would not have acted as promptly.'

When Paolo Vecchi said ' Good-morning ' to him, Danby returned his salutation.

'You settled promptly, Vecchi,' he said. 'I hope it caused you no inconvenience. You ought not to have put Falby up. You knew the sort of reputation he had. I am sorry there was any necessity for a protest, but I think the stewards' decision just.'

'It is over and done with,' said Vecchi. 'It was a severe blow to me, but I am glad I got over it. Vera helped me. She's a real good sort.'

He knew his man, and thought it best to be candid with him.

'So hard hit as that?' said Danby. 'Rather rough on Miss Vecchi, is it not?'

'She knows I shall pay her back,' said Vecchi. 'Mr. Widdrington,' he added, as though he had taken a sudden resolution, 'I think it is time certain matters should be explained.'

'What do you mean?' asked Danby.

'Well, to put it plainly, the world has been deceived for many years about the relations existing between Vera and myself.'

Danby Widdrington shook his head. 'I fail to comprehend your meaning,' he said. 'Put it plainly.'

'To be as brief as possible,' Vecchi said, 'Vera is not my daughter.'

He thought Danby would be startled, surprised, but was not prepared for his answer when he said: 'Well, do you know, Vecchi, I have often thought she could not be your daughter.'

Paolo Vecchi weighed his answer before he said:

14

' Perhaps it would be as well for Mr. Gordon to know the real state of affairs.'

' I think it would,' said Danby. Then it suddenly occurred to him to ask : ' Miss Vecchi thinks you are her father ?'

' No,' said Paolo Vecchi, ' she does not.'

' Ah, then you have told her ?' said Danby.

' I think you hardly understand me,' said Vecchi. ' There was no necessity for me to tell her I was not her father. She knew it.'

'You are mistaken,' said Danby. 'She doubted sometimes whether she was your child, but she acknowledged the relationship to Mr. Gordon and myself.'

' That was part of the deception,' said Paolo Vecchi. He did not quite know his man, after all. He did not know Danby Widdrington was in love with Vera.

Danby turned upon him, and said : ' Explain what you really mean.'

' I mean that it was necessary to keep up appearances, living together as we were, and the father-and-daughter relationship seemed the easiest way out of the difficulty,' said Paolo Vecchi.

Danby Widdrington was furious, but he concealed his feelings. He leaned across the table, and said to Vecchi in a low voice : ' If we were not in this club I would ram that black lie down your throat ! You are a greater scoundrel than I imagined !'

Paolo Vecchi was surprised, but he said : ' I have told you the truth, Mr. Widdrington, and I think you will be sorry for those words.'

'Never !' snapped Danby. 'I do not believe you !'
'If you will go with me now to Vera's house, you shall hear the truth from her own lips,' said Paolo Vecchi. He spoke with such an air of confidence that Danby wavered. 'Will you go with me, and hear what she has to say ?' he asked. 'I wish you to do so in order to tell Mr. Gordon the truth. I would rather he heard it from you.'

'I will go with you,' said Danby, who looked like a man stunned by a heavy blow. 'I will hear her denial from her own lips. Then I will deal with you. Will you undertake the risk ?'

'I will,' said Paolo Vecchi ; and they left the club together.

CHAPTER XXII.

DANBY AND VERA.

DANBY was not inclined to talk to Paolo Vecchi as they drove to St. Kilda. The communication Vecchi had made to him weighed like lead upon his mind, but he refused to admit the possibility of Vera being such a woman as the man sitting beside him insinuated. He placed such absolute faith in Vera. She was the one woman he loved above all others, and his love burned the more fiercely because he was bound in honour to his friend to hide it. The drive seemed very long, and Danby wished it at an end. The thought that troubled him was, What motive

14—2

could Paolo Vecchi have in taking him to Vera if she would not corroborate his story? At last the cab pulled up at the house.

Vera was sitting on the couch, and went to the window when the cab stopped, and saw Paolo Vecchi and Danby Widdrington alight. She felt no fear, nor had she any dread of approaching danger. She had completely forgotten the incidents of the previous day. As she shook hands with Danby, he looked at her wonderingly. The quick eyes of love noticed a change in her. Danby noticed things connected with Vera that Ross Gordon would not have discerned.

'You look ill,' said Danby anxiously.

'I have not been very well,' said Vera, 'but I am much better now.' She did not inquire after Ross Gordon, and he thought it strange.

'She does not know why I have brought you here,' whispered Paolo Vecchi to Danby. 'I shall have to drag it from her, I expect.' Danby would have liked to knock him down, but he wished to get at the bottom of this mystery. 'Do you know why I brought Mr. Widdrington here?' asked Vecchi.

'No,' said Vera; 'but I am very glad to see him. I am always pleased to meet Mr. Widdrington. He is a true friend.'

Her tone melted Danby's heart. There was a weary pathos in it, a sadness he could almost feel. He knew she was suffering, and he pitied her.

'I have thought fit to explain certain matters to Mr. Widdrington,' said Paolo Vecchi. 'I wish him to understand the relationship in which we stand to each other. I thought it better to speak to him, so that he could tell Mr. Gordon.'

Vera bowed her head, and answered mechanically, ' Yes, it is better so.'

' You know I am not your father ? you have known it for years ?' said Vecchi.

' Yes,' said Vera, ' I have known it.' She did not look at Danby, but kept her eyes on Paolo Vecchi.

' I do not wish to hurt your feelings more than I can possibly help,' said Vecchi ; ' but Mr. Widdring- ton must understand the truth. We have lived together as friends—have we not ?—nothing more ?'

' Friends !' said Vera. ' Oh yes, we are friends.'

' And you have consented to become my wife at last ?' said Paolo Vecchi.

Danby Widdrington hung upon Vera's answer as though his life depended upon it. Was this some horrible dream ? Vera Paolo Vecchi's wife! The mere idea appalled him. Vera did not answer imme- diately, and Paolo Vecchi trembled for the success of his diabolical scheme.

' You have consented to become my wife ?' he said in a commanding tone.

' I have,' said Vera, with an effort.

' I hope you are satisfied,' said Paolo Vecchi, with a malicious smile.

Danby Widdrington was stunned and bewildered by what he had heard. He sat as one stupefied. His brain was confused, and he could not grasp the full import of Vera's confession. Mechanically he rose and left the room with Paolo Vecchi. Vera sat and wondered why he had not said good-bye, but it did not affect her much. The drug still held her brain in subjection. Paolo Vecchi had administered a strong dose.

' Are you satisfied ?' asked Vecchi, when they were outside the house.

' Leave me !' said Danby hoarsely. ' Leave me, or I shall kill you, you devil !'

The words were so fierce and full of passion that Paolo Vecchi thought it best to go. His plot had succeeded so far, and he was satisfied. Vera would be his, for when she recovered she would realize that marriage with him was her one hope of escape from utter degradation.

Danby Widdrington walked on to the esplanade and then on to the pier. He went to the far end, and stood looking out across the bay. People saw him, and wondered at the wild look on his face, his strange, fierce manner. Gradually he calmed down, and began to think. The more he thought, the more terrible all he had heard seemed to him. He thought of Vera as he had first seen her, and as the woman beloved by and loving his best friend. He had re-garded Vera as a type of all that was good, and pure, and true, a woman incapable of deceit, whose very name seemed symbolical of truth. Now his faith was shattered. She had confessed herself all that was vile and deceitful. She had acknowledged she was

about to marry a man who had been regarded as her
father. She had deceived Ross Gordon. Her love
for him was the passion of a wanton. Oh, it was
horrible! And amidst all this chaos and wreck of
truth and honesty Danby Widdrington was tortured
with the knowledge that he loved this woman with a
love that could never be quenched. He knew he
would have rejoiced to take her in his arms—ay, even
now, with all her sins and imperfections on her head
—had she not been bound to his friend, the man he
had said he would stick to through thick and thin.
And he had to tell this friend a story so full of
shameful wrong that he shuddered at the mere
thought. Why had this burden been put upon him?
What had he done to deserve it? Deep down in his
heart he heard, as it were, a voice saying, ' And your
friend will not feel it as you do. He will rave and
rant about his wrongs, and the deceitfulness of
women, and he will console himself elsewhere.'

Danby knew what this silent voice said to him was
true. He had never been blind to Ross Gordon's
faults, but he liked him as a friend, and to Danby
that meant being true to him, no matter what he did
or what happened. A hero, this blunt, manly Danby
Widdrington; made of the sort of stuff that conquers
nations and explores wild, savage countries—a man
who would lay down his life to save a fellow-man,
and think he had done no more than his duty; who
would face any danger bravely, knowing what the
peril was he had to meet; the man to lead men on to

victory, and turn the tide of defeat into a glorious triumph; and yet a man who would have failed miserably over an army examination-paper, and been completely routed by a mild question in Greek or Latin grammar. Yet it is to such men as Danby Widdrington that England and her colonies look in time of danger. These are the men to man ships, to storm forts, to ride with the dashing bravery that distinguishes many a crack cavalry regiment of the British army: who prefer to hurl bullets at their foes instead of expletives, classical or otherwise, and have more courage in their little fingers than a host of men who pick holes in their grammar.

Danby roamed up and down the pier until it was dark. He remembered how Vera had answered Paolo Vecchi's questions as though she were overwhelmed with shame and remorse. The sadness in her voice he still remembered, and it pained him. Could such a woman be wholly false? Had this wretch Paolo Vecchi bewitched her? No, there was no loophole of escape. And yet, if he told Ross Gordon, what would happen? Ross, impulsive as he was, would accept Danby's statement, and never see Vera again. That Danby thought a very probable result. Then a wild desire seized upon Danby to save Vera from Paolo Vecchi's clutches. He was certain Vecchi was forcing her to marry him, and her life would be one long misery. But what could he do? He was powerless. Clearly his first duty was to break the news gently to Ross Gordon. There

was no backing out of it; it was a duty he owed to
Ross. After he had told him he would defend Vera.

Danby arrived home late, and found that Ross had
already come in.

'Wherever have you been?' said Ross. 'You look
bad. Are you ill?'

'I'm all right,' said Danby. 'A bit hipped. I'd
like a glass of champagne.'

Ross rang the bell. 'A bottle of the best champagne, waiter; extra dry. That's the advantage of
wallowing in riches; you can always order what you
require, regardless of cost.'

'Have you been out?' said Danby.

'Yes; drove over to see Vera——' said Ross; then
stopped suddenly.

Danby jumped from his chair, breathless with excitement. 'You've been to see Vera!' he exclaimed.

'Yes. What the dickens has come over you?
Nothing very remarkable in that, is there? It's my
opinion you have been dining, not wisely, but too well.'

'Did you see her?' gasped Danby, only partially
recovered from the shock.

'I was about to explain when you interrupted me
in such an unceremonious manner,' said Ross, 'that
Vera was ill, and had gone to lie down. They thought
it best not to disturb her, and I thought so too. I
went round to the Plowdens. Old Plowden was out,
the Heaths were out, Ida—I mean, Mrs. Plowden—
was in. She is a charming woman, and we get on
very well together.'

' That's just the sort of woman he will console himself with when he hears about Vera,' thought Danby. ' He'll be mad enough for anything. Ought I to tell him ? I am sorry you did not see Vera,' said Danby, ' but I'm hardly surprised.'

' I wasn't much surprised,' said Ross ; ' I knew she was unwell.'

' I have seen Vera to-day,' said Danby.

' *You !*' said Ross Gordon in genuine surprise. ' Well I'm blest !'

' I went with Vecchi,' said Danby hurriedly. ' He told me something at the club, and said, if I didn't believe him, he would take me over to see Vera, and hear what she had to say. Of course, I did not believe him, and so I went.'

' Then she was well enough to see you ?' said Ross.

' We saw her, but I should say she was far from well,' said Danby. ' Ross, old fellow, I have something to tell you—something that will hurt you very much ; you must take it calmly. It will be an awful blow to you, because you love her so.'

' What's the matter ?' said Ross. ' She's not— not——'

' No, not dead,' said Danby—' worse.'

Ross Gordon looked bewildered, and said : ' For Heaven's sake, tell me what you mean !'

Then Danby Widdrington told his story. He spared Ross Gordon and he spared Vera. It was agony for him to tell the story of the shame of the woman he loved to his friend who loved her.

Ross Gordon sat crushed under the blow, but he did not feel it as keenly as Danby. He was built on different lines to his friend, and his feelings were not so acute. After sitting silent for some time, he said : 'I think I'll have some champagne now, Danby. It will revive me a little. Marry Paolo Vecchi—well, I wish her joy of him ! This is your immaculate, your spotless Vera, Danby ; the woman you thought too good for me, your friend. Don't deny it ; I know you thought so. The hypocrite ! Oh, what an accomplished liar she is !'

'Hush, man,' said Danby. 'As there is a heaven above us, I am certain she loves you—has always loved you. She will never live to marry Vecchi. The thought of it will kill her. Pity her, Ross—God knows she needs it !'

'Pity her ?' said Ross ; 'I have no pity for such women. I loved her, but I love her no longer. I will never speak to her again.'

'There may be some explanation,' said Danby. 'Perhaps things are not as black as they look. You ought to see her.'

'I tell you I will never speak to her again,' said Ross ; 'not if she lay dying.'

'You do not know what love is,' said Danby quietly.

Ross looked at him in surprise. 'Do you ?' he asked.

'Yes,' said Danby, and his face glowed. 'I know what love is. Love believes and hopes when there is no hope ; it trusts when trust is dead ; it is blind to faults and sins ; it has but one thought—to love the loved one for ever.'

Ross Gordon came across to Danby Widdrington, and then saw how he had altered. The past few hours seemed to have aged him years. A light broke in upon Ross Gordon, and before its shining rays he stood abashed. 'Danby, you love this woman?' he said.

' God help her—I do !' he said. His prayer was for her, not for himself.

'You are a noble fellow,' said Ross, with a quiver in his voice. ' I do not deserve such a friend. How true you have been to me and to her, I alone know. I am not worthy to clasp *your* hand, Danby, for, had I been tempted as you were, I should have fallen.' He put his hand on Danby's shoulder, and said : ' Good-night, old fellow. God help you, too !'

CHAPTER XXIII

VERA'S DESPAIR.

WHEN Vera recovered from her stupor and lapse of memory, she was not aware of what had taken place. She had a faint, hazy notion that Danby Widdrington had been there with Paolo Vecchi, but did not know how she had placed herself in a false position. She recovered sufficiently to go to the theatre, but her acting seemed to have lost its charm. Hector St. Albans was surprised and troubled. Something, he

felt sure, had gone wrong with her. Perhaps she had
discovered that Ross Gordon was faithless, and if so
he might have a chance of winning her himself.

For a whole week she saw neither Ross Gordon nor
Danby Widdrington, and she wondered at it. What
was the reason of their keeping away from her? She
had an indefinable dread of something about to
happen. Perhaps Paolo Vecchi had blackened her
character. She must see him and learn the truth.
Paolo Vecchi was waiting for her summons when it
came. He at once called upon her.

'You have sent for me and I am here,' he said.
'What can I do for you?'

'I have not seen Mr. Gordon for a week,' she said;
'and Mr. Widdrington I have not seen since he was
here with you.'

'Oh! you recollect our visit?' said Vecchi. 'Do
you know what occurred at that time?'

'I only know Mr. Widdrington came here with
you, to inquire after my health,' she said.

He laughed harshly, and said: 'Mr. Widdrington
heard a good deal that surprised him when he was
here. I expect that is the reason he did not call
before he returned to Sydney with Mr. Gordon.'

'Ross gone back to Sydney!' exclaimed Vera, 'and
without saying good-bye to me. I do not believe it!'

'It is true,' said Paolo Vecchi; 'and he will never
speak to you again.'

'What has happened?' said Vera. 'Tell me what
you have done!'

' There is not much to tell,' said Paolo Vecchi. ' I asked you to be my wife, and in the presence of Mr. Widdrington you said you would marry me. Naturally it was a shock for him, and no doubt he told his friend, Ross Gordon. Can you wonder at their departing without seeing you? Vera, you are mine now. I have waited for you long. You shall know the secret of your birth soon.'

She looked at him wildly. She only vaguely understood as yet the terrible nature of his words.

' You may as well hear the whole story,' he said. ' I told Mr. Widdrington at the club that you were not my daughter, and that we had lived together for years on terms of friendship. I said we adopted the relationship because it was respectable, and kept up appearances. He refused to believe me. I offered to let him hear from your own lips that such was the truth, and that you were about to become my wife. He came here with me, and you corroborated all I had said. Can you wonder at his surprise?'

Vera was in despair. She could not believe this horrible story. It was a vile invention of Paolo Vecchi's.

' Have you dared to tell this infamous story about me ?' she said.

' I have,' he replied calmly ; ' and you corroborated it to Mr. Widdrington.'

' *I* corroborated it !' she said. ' That is not possible.'

' You are completely in my power, Vera,' he said. ' Your only course is to marry me, and do what you can to save your tarnished reputation.'

'I will never marry you,' she said. 'I would sooner die!'

'You do not know all,' he said. 'When you fainted on that sofa I drugged you again. It was under the influence of the drug, and my will, that you told Mr. Widdrington the story I have related to you. In this room you confessed to him you had lived with me on intimate terms, and had consented at last to marry me. He believed you. How could he do otherwise? You will never be able to speak to them again. Your only chance now is to consent to my proposal and become my wife. You shall be my wife even against your own will, but I would rather not employ force.'

'Is this true?' she asked in a hollow voice.

'Yes,' he replied. 'You must now see how hopeless it is to resist me.'

Crushed and overwhelmed by the terrible injustice that had been done her, Vera for the time was incapable of action. She hardly realized the full extent of the injury Paolo Vecchi had done her.

'I will leave you to think over all I have said. You must see there is no chance of escape for you. I have had you all these years, and I am not going to part with you now,' said Paolo Vecchi as he left the room.

Vera's despair was pitiable; her anguish was intense. She felt that Paolo Vecchi had for once told the truth. Out of her own mouth she had condemned herself. True, she was under the influence

of a drug ; but would anyone believe so improbable
a story ? No one would credit her statement. She
had confessed to Danby Widdrington, Ross Gordon's
best friend, that she had been guilty of the vilest
conduct. She knew what the effect of such a confession would be upon a man like Ross Gordon. He
would have no pity for her. He had thought her the
best of women, and she had confessed she was one of
the most degraded. To a pure, sensitive woman
such as Vera, the thought was too horrible to bear.
Knowing herself innocent, she had been compelled
by a stronger will than her own to confess an
imaginary guilt. She saw the use Paolo Vecchi
would put such a confession to. She was an actress,
and the world was only too ready to impute evil to
a woman in her position. To be thought guilty
of such conduct was to Vera a fearful punishment.
Danby Widdrington and Ross Gordon had left her
without a word of farewell. If such friends deserted
her and believed her guilty, upon whom could she
rely ? She was alone, friendless, her lover gone from
her, and in the power of the vilest man on earth. In
vain she tried to think how she could save her good
name and prove her innocence. This to Vera meant
everything. She had lived a pure, unsullied life,
amidst temptations that would have proved fatal to
many women. To Ross Gordon she had given her
love, the first love of her heart. Strange to say, at
this moment of greatest peril and dark despair, it
was the name of Danby Widdrington that gave her

some slight ray of hope. She knew what such a man could be if his friendship was assured. She felt she could fight, to restore her lost honour, with Danby Widdrington more successfully than with Ross Gordon, because she was not in love with him. With Ross she would plead ; Danby she would convince. Danby had heard her strange confession, extorted from her when she was unconscious of what she said. He must have noticed something peculiar about her. Happily, she had retained the label of the bottle in which Paolo Vecchi carried the drug. This would be useful to her.

It was to Danby Widdrington Vera at last made up her mind to apply for help. She knew he was to be trusted. Her only fear was that he might decline to assist her. There was not a moment to be lost. The mere thought of having Danby Widdrington to help her nerved Vera to strive to outwit Paolo Vecchi before he did her an irreparable injury.

' I will wire to him at once,' she said. ' He will not refuse to help me. He will do it, if only for the sake of his friend.'

She went to the telegraph-office and sent a wire to Sydney, and returned home, where she anxiously awaited the result.

Danby Widdrington and Ross Gordon had re-turned to Sydney without seeing Vera. Ross was determined he would not see her, and Danby felt afraid to do so. Since their return, Danby had been

15

more unhappy than Ross Gordon, and he was restless and uneasy. He knew Ross Gordon had received a letter from Ida Plowden, and he dreaded what might come of it. Danby had none of the new-fangled notions which seem to be fashionable in these days, that married women should have single men as their lovers. To Danby the wife of a friend or acquaintance was sacred. He gave Ross plainly to understand that Horace Plowden's wife had no right to correspond with him. Ross handed him the letter, saying : ' Read it for yourself. There is nothing in it old Plowden himself might not read.'

Danby read it, and acknowledged such to be the case, but he did not approve of it.

' That is her first letter,' he said. ' If you keep up a correspondence, there is no telling what it will end in. Stop it, Ross, before any harm is done.'

Ross growled out an unsatisfactory reply, and then went to write to Mrs. Plowden.

A telegram was delivered to Danby at Branxton about three o'clock. He opened it, and read :

' Can explain all. Am in great danger. Will you help me ?—VERA.'

' Is the messenger gone ?' he asked.

' No, sir.'

' Tell him to wait. There is an answer.'

He wrote on a telegram-form :

' Leave by express this afternoon.'

He surprised Ross Gordon by saying in an off-hand manner: 'I am going to Melbourne by the express to-day. I may be away two or three days or more. You will manage without me.'

'I suppose I need not expect you to tell me why you are going?' Ross said.

'I have a telegram of importance,' said Danby. 'I don't wish to raise false hopes, Ross; but I believe I am on the track of a discovery that will make everything right between you and Vera again.'

Ross Gordon gave an impatient exclamation, and said: 'If that is the object of your journey, you are going on a fool's errand.'

'I do not think so,' said Danby. 'At all events, it is worth trying for.'

'Don't be fooled by a woman as I have been,' said Ross.

Danby smiled as he said: 'I hope to show you I am not a fool, or a man easily fooled. I have not lost faith in Vera yet, and I believe she will prove herself a true woman. Then you will be happy again, old fellow.'

'I never met such a man,' said Ross with a sigh, as he waved his hand to Danby as the train steamed out of the station. 'It takes a lot to shatter his faith in anyone. I wonder if Vera sent for him. She knew better than to send for me. She will have a difficult task to convince even Danby that her conduct has been beyond reproach.'

Danby, as he travelled towards Melbourne, felt a

sense of satisfaction in the fact that Vera had tele-
graphed to him and asked him to help her. It showed
she trusted him, and did not know his secret. There
was some strange mystery about her conduct he could
not fathom. Why had she confessed to such deception if untrue? Paolo Vecchi was at the bottom of
it. Could the man have terrified her into making
such damaging admissions? If Vecchi had done her
some grave injury, Danby felt he could make it exceedingly unpleasant for him. He was doing this for
Ross Gordon's sake as well as Vera's, and all his
efforts would end in bringing Ross and Vera together
again, thus placing an impassable barrier between
himself and Vera. But Danby thought very little of
this. What he wanted to do was to serve his friend
and the woman he loved. In securing their happiness, he knew it would bring happiness to himself.
Had the step he was taking entailed the utmost
misery upon him, he would not have shirked it.
When he reached Melbourne, he drove to Menzie's
Hotel, and then went on to St. Kilda. The servant
opened the door, and he noticed the frightened look
on her face. 'Is anything the matter?' he asked.

'I'm afraid so, sir. I'm glad you've come.
Mrs. —— is out. You came with Mr. Vecchi before.
He's upstairs now, with his daughter in the drawing-
room. I heard a noise like two persons struggling,
and went upstairs. The door is locked, sir. I am
sure there is something wrong.'

Danby strode past the frightened girl and went up

the stairs two at a time. He knocked at the drawing-room door, but got no answer. 'Open the door,' he said, 'or I will burst it in.'

Paolo Vecchi gave an exclamation of baffled rage as he recognised Danby's voice. He was struggling with Vera. He had his hand on her throat, and she could not cry out, and in his other hand he held the small bottle containing the terrible drug.

Vera had been struggling with him for some minutes and was well-nigh exhausted, but desperation gave her strength. She was fighting for something dearer to her than life, for Paolo Vecchi had threatened what he would do. When she heard Danby's voice she gave way. The revulsion of feeling at knowing help was near overcame her. She staggered backwards, and fell half fainting on the couch.

At this moment Danby burst open the door and rushed into the room. He took in the situation at a glance, and, catching Paolo Vecchi by the throat, flung him savagely backwards. He fell against the table, breaking it with a loud crash, and sprawled upon the floor.

CHAPTER XXIV

DANBY'S WRATH.

PAOLO VECCHI, partially stunned by the fall, was some minutes before he recovered. He staggered to his feet and looked fiercely at Danby. Vera, now the strain was over and she felt safe, wondered what would happen. She saw Paolo Vecchi meant mischief, but as she looked at Danby she was not alarmed for his safety. As for Danby, he took very little notice of Paolo Vecchi. At present his thoughts were for Vera, and he meant to deal with her assailant later. He felt satisfied, from what he had seen, that Vera was resisting Paolo Vecchi's advances to the utmost of her power. When he heard her explanation of the struggle that had taken place, he thought it would lead up to a complete exposure of this man's conduct.

'You shall answer to me for this,' said Paolo Vecchi, white with rage.

'Leave the room,' said Danby, 'or I will shake the breath out of your miserable body.'

'I remain here,' said Vecchi. 'You must go.'

'Let him remain,' said Vera to Danby. 'He ought to hear what I have to say to you.'

'As you wish,' replied Danby; 'but, remember, when his presence becomes undesirable, you have only to give me a hint, and he will go quickly.'

'You arrived just in time,' said Vera. 'God knows what would have happened to me had you not come! When I heard from his vile lips yesterday all he had done, and all I had said to you, I felt I must ask your help.'

'Do you mean you were unconscious of all you said to me the last time I saw you?' asked Danby, amazed.

'Did you believe what I said?' asked Vera quickly.

'I could hardly do otherwise when I heard it from
your lips,' said Danby ; 'but since I have thought over
it, I believed there might be a possible explanation.'

'There is,' said Vera, 'a full and complete explanation. I was in that man's power when he forced the
words from me against my will. It may appear
incomprehensible, but I had no idea, until he told me
the wretched truth, what I had said ; then I fully
understood why Ross and yourself left for Sydney
without saying good-bye.'

'She is acting,' said Vecchi—'acting better than
she ever did on the stage.'

'I am not acting,' said Vera, 'and you know it.'

Then she told Danby the story of Paolo Vecchi's
villainy, and how he had drugged her, in order to
separate her from Ross Gordon and ruin her reputation.

'He holds the secret of my birth,' said Vera, 'and
it must be wrung from him by force. I am not his
child. He has kept me with him under that delusion
all these years for some purpose of his own. Perhaps
I am entitled to wealth, and if so, his avaricious nature
will in a great measure account for his conduct. When
you arrived here,' she went on to Danby, 'he had
threatened to force me to take the drug again, and to
marry me when under the influence of it. I resisted
with all my strength, but he overpowered me, and in
a few more moments it would have been too late.
You have saved me from a terrible fate, Mr. Widdrington, and I thank you for it with all my heart. As for
you,' she said, suddenly turning upon Paolo Vecchi,

'you shall answer for all you have done. I am not devoid of means, and I will use all I possess to bring you to justice, and drag the secret of my early days from you.'

Paolo Vecchi sneered and said: 'You talk well, but no one will believe you, except the infatuated fool who is in love with you—Danby Widdrington.'

Danby grasped him fiercely by the arm, and said in a low voice vibrating with passion: 'Leave the room, or I will not be answerable for myself.'

Paolo Vecchi looked at him and saw danger in Danby's face. He thought the wisest course he could take would be to go; but he did not mean to give up Vera and all the possession of her meant to him. Without another word he left the room.

Vera looked at Danby timidly. She wondered if Paolo Vecchi's words were true. She had never contemplated the possibility of Danby being in love with her, but now she recalled many actions on his part which suggested such might be the case. The thought that Danby loved her caused a peculiar sensation to Vera for which she could not account. If he loved her, as Paolo Vecchi said, how nobly he had acted, and how stanch he was to his friend, her accepted lover!

Danby appeared to divine what passed in her mind, and it troubled him. He must deceive her as to the real state of his feelings at any cost to himself. He had told Ross Gordon he would do his best to bring about a reconciliation with Vera; at the same time, he doubted whether Ross was over-anxious for such a reconciliation. Clearly, it was his duty to do all he could for his friend. The best way, he thought, would be to ignore Paolo Vecchi's remark and Vera's evident trouble and surprise.

'I am glad I have heard your explanation,' he said. 'What an infamous scoundrel Vecchi is! He must suffer for all he has done. I will help you in any way you please. Do you know of any means by which he can be forced to confess the truth?'

'No,' said Vera, deceived by Danby's manner into believing Paolo Vecchi's assertion that he loved her to be false; 'but I am sure he is a fugitive from justice. Where he came from, or where I came from, I have only a very dim recollection. I have very little doubt he was a brigand, the leader of a desperate gang of men, and that he either murdered my parents or kidnapped me.'

'In that case there will probably be a reward for his capture,' said Danby.

'It is so long ago,' said Vera. 'We have been in Australia almost since I can remember.'

'I do not think it safe for you to remain alone in Melbourne,' said Danby. 'Cannot you throw up your engagement and return to Sydney with me? I will ask your manager about it if you wish; I think I can persuade him to let you off.'

'It is very good of you,' replied Vera. 'I am afraid it will mean a serious loss to him if I refuse to carry out my engagement. I confess I am terrified at the thought of being at the mercy of Paolo Vecchi again.'

'That you shall not be,' said Danby. 'I wish you to return to Sydney and see Ross again. You will convince him of your innocence, as you have convinced me.'

Vera sighed. She wondered at Ross Gordon's lack of faith. Danby did not doubt her, of that she felt sure, and the thought comforted her. She was anxious to see Ross again, for she still loved him, although, strange to say, an almost imperceptible change was coming over her. She was not passionately in love with him, as she was at the time she told him her dreams and hopes and fears in Sydney. Then he was to her as a god to be worshipped, but he had shattered some of the faith she had placed in him. His flirtations with Ida Plowden had given her pain, although she concealed it, and he had deceived Nora Heath about his engagement. Almost unconsciously she compared Ross with Danby, and the latter's conduct gave him a decided advantage over his friend. As to putting another man in Ross Gordon's place in her affections, such a thought never occurred to her, and had it done so, it would have been scouted as unworthy.

'I will return to Sydney with you,' she said, after a pause, 'if the manager will allow me to cancel my engagement.'

'That's right,' said Danby heartily. 'I am glad you have come to this decision; it will be the best for you. I will see your manager myself and arrange everything for you.'

'I must compensate him in some way,' said Vera. 'I do not know what value he will place upon my poor services.'

'If you are not afraid to remain here, I will go and see him at once,' said Danby.

'Oh no, I am not afraid,' said Vera. 'I do not think Paolo Vecchi will venture to return.'

'He might if he knew I had gone,' said Danby. 'Do not venture outside. If you are wanted at the theatre, I will come for you.'

Vera thanked him, and Danby went to attempt his task with the manager. He knew there would be some difficulty, but he thought the compensation he was prepared to offer would be adequate. In this he proved to be right, for although the manager said Vera's absence meant almost ruin to him, he was not able to withstand the temptation of the cash-down offer Danby made him. Vera was relieved at his success, and amazed at the modest sum the manager expressed himself willing to accept.

'I have given him a cheque for the amount,' said Danby. 'You can repay me at your convenience.'

They arrived safely in Sydney, and Danby took Vera to the Australia, where she engaged rooms.

'Ross will not expect to see you here,' said Danby. 'It will be a pleasant surprise for him.'

'I hope so,' said Vera doubtfully.

Danby drove to Branxton, and found Ross was out. He went into his den and sat down to have a think. He was troubled about Vera. He did not think she had quite forgiven Ross for doubting her, and for his flirtation with Mrs. Plowden.

'When he hears her story he will believe it,' said Danby. 'To many people it would appear improbable, but strange events happen every day. I wonder where Ross can be?'

Nero, the huge St. Bernard, lying at Danby's feet, looked up into his master's face with his large liquid eyes, as much as to say : 'What does it matter where he is? Haven't you got me?'

Danby patted the dog's head, and said : 'You're a faithful friend, Nero. I do not think there is much fear of our quarrelling.'

It was late when Ross Gordon returned to Branxton.

'Back again, Danby?' he said. 'You have soon done your business.'

'Yes, and been successful,' said Danby. 'Vera is in Sydney, and waiting to see you.'

Ross did not seem over-pleased at the announcement, and said : 'Has she offered a satisfactory explanation of her conduct?'

'To me, yes,' said Danby ; 'and I am sure you will be satisfied when you hear her story. It is an extraordinary story, and Paolo Vecchi is a desperate villain. I should like to shoot the blackguard.'

'You are seldom bloodthirsty,' said Ross, smiling. 'He must have done something outrageous.'

'He has,' said Danby. 'There is nothing more despicable he could have done. He has tried his best to ruin a pure, innocent woman, and he has failed. Had I arrived a few minutes later, he would have accomplished his purpose.'

Danby then related to Ross what occurred when he burst open the door and found Vera struggling with Paolo Vecchi. 'Her own story you had better hear from herself,' he added.

'I will see her to-morrow,' said Ross, in an off-handed way. 'By-the-by, the Plowdens are in Sydney. Did you know they had come over?'

'No,' said Danby. He was sorry Ida Plowden was in Sydney at this particular time.

'They are staying with the Heaths,' said Ross. 'They are going to Rosehill races on Saturday. Will you come? You have three horses entered, so it will give you an interest in the sport.'

'All right,' said Danby; 'I will go. Perhaps you will ask Miss Vecchi to go, too.'

'I'll see about it,' said Ross. 'Are you quite sure, Danby, old fellow, she has not deceived you?'

'Certain of it,' replied Danby warmly. 'She is an ill-used woman. I'll wring the secret of her birth from Paolo Vecchi somehow.'

'Then she is not his daughter?' said Ross.

'No; that part was true. She has been deceived by him for years. But the danger is not over yet. He is a determined, desperate man. He has some powerful reason for retaining his hold over her. She needs a protector, and no one can keep her from danger better than a husband. If you love her, Ross, marry her. That will deal Paolo Vecchi a blow he will never get over.'

'l did love Vera,' said Ross. 'I think I love her now. When I see her again, I will think over what you have said.'

'If only I had his chances!' thought Danby with a sigh.

_____

CHAPTER XXV.

AT ROSEHILL.

ROSS GORDON saw Vera, heard her explanation, and doubted her no longer. His faith in her renewed Vera's love for him, and she determined to do all in her power to please him.

'You are not safe, Vera,' he said. 'You ought to have someone to protect you from Paolo Vecchi. If you are willing, we will be married as soon as possible, and then I shall know how to protect my wife.'

At first Vera demurred, but eventually gave way, and it was decided that they should be married by special license the following week.

'And you must give up the stage,' said Ross. 'You will promise me that?'

It was a struggle, a great sacrifice, for Vera loved her profession, but she gave way and agreed to leave the stage.

Ross mentioned the proposed party to Rosehill races, but Vera asked to be excused. She did not feel equal to it after all she had recently gone through,

Ross was disappointed at her disinclination to join them, but did not press the matter. Seeing, however, that it would please him if she decided to go, Vera changed her mind, and was rewarded by seeing how pleased he was.

Paolo Vecchi returned to Sydney as soon as he heard Vera had left Melbourne. Ross Gordon made no secret of his forthcoming marriage, and consequently Vecchi heard of it. How to prevent it was the thought that occupied his mind. Even if he could not get Vera for himself, he was determined no other man should have her. He had his own reasons for wishing to make her his wife, and, as usual, they were purely selfish.

As Paolo Vecchi thought over his defeat, and racked his brain for some means of revenge, he tore in strips the sheet of paper he held in his hand. It happened to be a printed list of the Rosehill entries, and his eyes caught sight of the welter handicap for amateur riders. He had a horse entered, and so had Danby Widdrington, and he remembered he had heard at the club that Ross Gordon was to ride Danby's horse. Paolo Vecchi was a good horseman, and had been an amateur rider for some time, although he very seldom rode in a race. The thought occurred to him that he might possibly make use of this opportunity. Many things happened in races, and he was bold enough to risk a good deal in order to injure Ross Gordon. Why should he not ride in this race himself? Very little notice would be taken of it, although some people might think it strange he had decided to appear in the saddle again. It mattered little to him what others thought, but if anything happened in the race, and he was the cause of it, or reputed to be the cause, comments might be made about his riding in this particular event.

'I must risk it,' he said to himself. 'It will not be my fault if Ross Gordon does not come to grief. There is generally an opportunity in a race, if a fellow has only pluck enough to seize it.'

He went over to the Rosehill office, and saw the secretary, who said he did not think there would be any difficulty about his riding, more especially as he had formerly ridden at Randwick. The committee met that afternoon, and he would place the matter before them.

The same evening Paolo Vecchi received a note from the secretary stating that they had granted him an amateur rider's license to ride at Rosehill. He went to the club and talked about the race. As a rule, not much interest was taken in these races before the course was reached, but the members of Tattersall's were never averse to making sporting wagers when an opportunity offered.

'I'll bet you a level fifty you don't get a place,' said Fred Otway.

'Perhaps you think I have forgotten how to ride?' said Paolo Vecchi. 'You are very much mistaken. I'll take you five hundred to fifty I win the race.'

'Bravo, Vecchi!' shouted several men who heard the offer.

'I'll lay you,' said Otway. 'I consider it an easy way of picking up fifty.'

'You'll change your tune when the race is over,' said Vecchi. 'I haven't got a bad mount, remember.'

'What, old Snip!' said Fred Otway. 'He's no chance of beating Marengo at the weight, and Ross Gordon is a much better horseman than you are.'

'We shall see about that,' said Vecchi. 'He is younger, but I doubt if he rides better.'

Ross Gordon was in the club-room, and Fred Otway crossed over to him and said: 'I have just made a fancy wager with Vecchi. He is going to ride his horse Snip in the amateur welter on Saturday. I've laid him five hundred to fifty against his mount. He has no chance with you. I suppose you ride Marengo for Mr. Widdrington?'

'Yes,' replied Ross. 'He has a big weight, but he ought to win. I'll go you halves in the wager if you like. If you can lay Vecchi a level hundred that Marengo beats Snip, do so for me. I wonder what the deuce he wants to ride his own horse for; it is a long time since he had a mount.'

'He's a bit flash,' said Fred Otway. 'I think someone must have been taunting him about getting old, and being unable to ride, or something of that kind.'

'Very likely,' said Ross. 'He's a conceited fool at the best of times.'

When Ross told Danby of Paolo Vecchi's intention to ride Snip, Danby said : 'He means mischief, depend upon it. You will have to watch him. He'd risk his own neck if he thought he could break yours.'

' I'll give him a clear berth,' said Ross. ' Snip will not have much chance with Marengo.'

'There is a lot of difference in the weights,' said Danby. ' He will hardly dare do anything very dangerous at Rosehill.'

' I am not at all alarmed,' said Ross. All the same, he felt a trifle uneasy, for he knew the sort of man he was pitted against.

Rosehill Races are always popular, and as most of the leading sporting men had returned from the Cup meeting, there was an enormous crowd present. The Heaths and Plowdens were there, and Vera accompanied them. She knew Paolo Vecchi was riding in the welter race, and felt a strange feeling of fear, and a presentiment that something would happen to Ross. She would not persuade Ross to let someone else ride Marengo, because it seemed cowardly. Paolo Vecchi did not speak to her, although she had caught his eyes fixed upon her once or twice with a malicious expression in them. Mr. Plowden, unaware of all that had taken place, chatted with Paolo Vecchi, who had given him the straight tip to back Snip.

' You ought to have won your money on Burwood,' said Vecchi. ' I'll take good care you win it this time.'

There were ten starters for the amateur welter, and two of the horses carried extra weight in order to have the services of professional jockeys. One of these men Paolo Vecchi had been able to speak to before the race, and promised him a twenty-pound note if Snip won.

'The only one I am afraid of is Marengo,' said Vecchi. ' You have no chance, but you might get in Marengo's way by accident.'

' My mount cannot win,' said the jockey, ' so I'll do what I can to help you to win, Mr. Vecchi; but I'm not going to deliberately block any horse.'

' I didn't ask you to block Marengo,' said Vecchi. ' I said you might get in Marengo's way by accident.'

Marengo was restless and caused a good deal of trouble at the starting-post. ' That will take something out of him,' thought Vecchi with satisfaction. He had made up his mind what to do and where to do it, if he had an opportunity.

At last, after considerable delay, they were off, and, as usual with the machine, it was a good start. Ross meant to ride Marengo a waiting race, as he knew the horse had a fine turn of speed that would serve him well at the finish. This suited Paolo Vecchi's plan, and he gave an inward chuckle of satisfaction. All went well until they were rounding the bend and approaching the straight for home. Ross felt Marengo going well under him, and knew he had a good chance of winning. Vecchi on Snip was close behind Marengo, and as they rounded the bend he gradually drew level. There were four horses in front of Marengo and Snip,

and four behind them. What really happened Ross
Gordon did not know. He heard Vecchi shout, 'Look
out, mine's bolted!' and then felt Marengo swerve,
scramble and strive to recover himself, and then roll
over. Something struck Ross a tremendous blow on
the head, and he became insensible. When Vera
saw Ross fall, she gave a slight cry of pain and sank
back onto the seat.

Danby muttered an oath, and said : 'I knew something would happen.'

And something had happened, more than Paolo
Vecchi expected. He had broken a stirrup-leather,
and his horse had swerved on to Marengo before he
was ready for it. By a great effort he retained his seat
in the saddle, but the reins were loosened, and Snip,
feeling his head free, and being excited by the fall of
Marengo and the bumping he had received, bolted
in real earnest. Paolo Vecchi knew he had to look
after his own safety now. Ross Gordon had fallen,
and Vecchi hoped, even at this time of danger to
himself, that he had received severe injuries. There
was no lack of a sort of desperate pluck about Paolo
Vecchi. He stuck to Snip and endeavoured to
control him. He knew if he could master his horse
the bolting would be all in his favour, if it came to an
inquiry into the cause of the spill.

Snip galloped down the straight at a great pace,
and even Danby had to acknowledge the horse had
bolted and it was no sham. Snip passed the judge's
box first, and then made for the side-fence. Paolo

Vecchi had, however, got him under control again, and succeeded in getting off with a few slight bruises to his leg, caused by running up against the fence. As he rode Snip back into the enclosure he was cheered for his pluck, for although unpopular, the public would not withhold what was justly due to him, and, moreover, Snip had started favourite and won. Down the course a small knot of people had collected, and were looking at Ross Gordon as he lay insensible on the ground.

'He's been struck on the head—galloped on,' said a man; 'he looks uncommon bad.'

The ambulance waggon came up, and Ross Gordon was carefully lifted into it. Danby Widdrington was anxiously awaiting its arrival. The waggon passed through the gate and was driven to the casualty-room. Ross Gordon was lifted tenderly out and placed on a camp-bed, and Dr. Ransom, who was in the paddock, came to him at once. Danby stood looking down at his friend with a great fear in his heart. Ross looked so lifeless, and there was a nasty gash in his head, and the mark of a horse's hoof was plainly visible on the sky-blue jacket, across the breast.

'Clear the room,' said Dr. Ransom. 'Keep them away as much as possible. Ah, is that you, Mr. Widdrington! This looks serious. Poor young chap! A fine young fellow!'

Danby could not speak. His mouth felt parched and dry, and he simply looked at the inanimate form of Ross Gordon helplessly. Dr. Ransom made a careful examination of the wound on Ross Gordon's head. Then he stripped down the jacket and looked at the dull blue mark on his chest.

'He's in a dangerous state, Mr. Widdrington,' he said. 'He had better go to the hospital at once.'

This roused Danby. 'Will he recover? he asked.

'I cannot tell,' said Dr. Ransom. 'He's suffering from concussion of the brain, and has serious internal injuries as well. It was a nasty fall, and he's been galloped on.'

At this moment the door flew open, and Vera came in with a wild look on her face. She flung herself beside Ross Gordon, and, burying her face on his body, said piteously : 'He's killed him ! Oh, my love, my love, I am the cause of all this !'

Danby put his hand on her shoulder and said firmly : 'You must be calm. He is in danger. Try and save his life.'

'Is there a chance?' she said, looking up quickly, hopefully.

'Yes,' said Dr. Ransom, 'there is a chance ; but you must be very careful. He needs nursing, and he must be kept quiet. Will you promise to control your feelings?'

'Oh, yes, yes!' said Vera ; 'I will be brave ; I will do anything you tell me. Only save his life. Give him back to me. I love him so.'

'I will do my best,' said Dr. Ransom, thinking what a beautiful woman she was.

'How she loves him !' thought Danby. 'I must help to save him for her if I can.'

CHAPTER XXVI.

SUSPENSE.

ROSS GORDON was conveyed to Paramatta Hospital in charge of Dr. Ransom. Danby borrowed a horse and buggy and followed with Vera, as she insisted upon being taken there. The injuries Ross had received were more serious than Dr. Ransom anticipated from his necessarily hasty examination on the course.

Ross did not recover consciousness until late at night, and Danby remained with Vera at the hospital. They were sent for, as they had requested, and went at once to Ross. He recognised them, but only for a few moments, when his mind began to wander and he talked incoherently.

' It will be a fight to pull him through,' said the house-surgeon, and Dr. Ransom gave a silent acknowledgment.

' May I remain to nurse him ?' said Vera.

' It is against the rules,' said the surgeon ; ' but perhaps we can arrange it, as he is in such a dangerous state.'

Vera thanked him with a look that made his pulses tingle. Vera had a way of attaching people to her, and the house-surgeon felt it would be a pleasure to serve her.

' You can get a bed in the town,' said Dr. Ransom to Danby. ' It will not do for you to remain here.'

' Very well,' replied Danby. ' I will come up first

thing in the morning. If you want me during the night, send to the White Horse.' He spoke a few words of encouragement to Vera, and then left.

It was an anxious night for Vera, a terrible strain upon her; but she bore it bravely, hoping against hope, and trying to believe the man she loved would be spared to her. She had never loved Ross as she did now when she felt he might be taken away from her by death. She hardly realized what it would cost her to bid him farewell for ever; she dare not think of it. The nurse who remained with her watched her with wondering eyes. She was a pretty, sympathetic woman, and realized for the first time what it meant to a woman when she was under the spell of a passionate love.

Vera watched her as she moved about quickly, yet silently, and touched everything with a firm and gentle hand. When Ross moaned or moved restlessly, the nurse's hand soothed him more than Vera's. It was the touch of a woman who knew how to control men in their sickness. There was a calm courage about this woman that Vera envied.

' How noble it is to nurse the sick !' thought Vera. ' Surely there can be no nobler work than this.'

She was about to speak, but the nurse, divining her intention, put her finger warningly to her lips, and Vera remained silent. Through the long night the two women watched by Ross Gordon's bedside, noting every change, every movement—Vera watching him with the eyes of love, her heart-strings strained, her mind stretched to the utmost tension; the nurse alert and active, watching him as only a well-trained woman can. When the daylight came, as it did, with a suddenness almost startling, the change seemed to rouse Ross Gordon, who had been slumbering fitfully. He opened his eyes and looked vacantly around, and Vera saw with a pang he did not recognise her. The nurse gave him some medicine, and in a short time he slept again.

Danby came to the hospital early, and Vera went to meet him.

'How is he?' he asked anxiously.

'Sleeping,' said Vera. 'The nurse said he has had a good night. Oh, this suspense is terrible!'

She seemed to cling to Danby, as though all hope of saving Ross rested with him. He soothed her and talked to her calmly and naturally, and all the time his heart was full of a desperate love and pity for her and for his friend. Danby was not what the world would call a religious man. He never entered a church, and he seldom looked at a religious book; but he believed in God, and he prayed that Ross Gordon might be spared to make Vera happier. He went to Ross Gordon's bedside, and as he stood there with Vera the injured man opened his eyes and looked straight at Danby. A faint smile spread over his features.

'It's all right, old fellow,' he said almost in a whisper. 'I shall pull through. I know you'll stick to me through thick and thin.'

Danby's favourite expression, and as he heard it he felt glad; but before he could reply, Ross was rambling again, and the nurse bade them begone.

'He did not recognise me,' said Vera sadly. 'Your friendship is more to him than my love.'

'You are mistaken,' said Danby quietly. 'He saw me as he opened his eyes, and there was a faint sign of recognition. He was wandering again in a moment. He did not see you.'

But Vera knew how great must be Danby's love for his friend when the wandering mind clung to him and relied upon him.

It was a fortnight before Ross Gordon was pronounced out of danger, but he could not yet be removed to Branxton. Vera remained with him, and watched over him, and cared for him, until Ross recognised how good she had been to him. Danby came to see him constantly and brought him the news.

'There has been an inquiry into the cause of the accident,' said Danby. 'Paolo Vecchi has been exonerated from blame. I fail to see how it could have been otherwise, considering the evidence. Snip bolted with him, and he lost a stirrup-leather. He nearly came to grief himself.'

'I recollect he called out to me his horse had bolted,' said Ross; 'but I believe he brought me down on purpose.'

'Probably,' said Danby; 'but there can be no doubt about the horse bolting after the spill. I saw it myself.'

'What happened after Marengo fell?' asked Ross. 'I don't recollect anything. I must have been stunned by the fall.'

'It was a nasty spill,' said Danby. 'How you escaped being killed is marvellous; Marengo slipped under the rails, and got on to his feet on the other side. You fell right in front of the horses behind you. They jumped you, but one of them struck your head, and put one hoof on your breast. He was too near to clear you. I thought you were smashed all to pieces, and it was a terribly anxious time for all of us. But you'll pull through all right now, Ross, and you know the fate in store for you when you are quite recovered,' he added, smiling at Vera.

Ross looked at her lovingly as he said : 'She has been an excellent nurse, Danby. She has brought me back to life. I shall owe her a lifelong debt.'

Vera bent over him and kissed him as she said : 'You must not give me all the credit, Ross. There is one here who nursed you far better than I could have done—Nurse Nicholson.'

The nurse smiled as she said : 'I did my best—I always do—but Miss Vecchi has been an excellent nurse. You owe her much, Mr. Gordon.'

'More than I can ever repay,' he said.

'I am more than repaid by your love,' said Vera.

Danby stood watching them, and thought how happy they were. Again he felt that longing for Vera he tried so hard to check. 'I shall live it down,' he thought to himself. 'When they are married and happily settled I shall be contented.' Then he thought how lonely it would be at Branxton without Ross Gordon, and as he was thus thinking, Nora Heath came into the room.

'Father had to come to Paramatta,' she said, 'so I persuaded him to bring me. I was determined to see how you were, Mr. Gordon.'

She was heartily welcomed, and looked so young, fresh and bright, and rosy with health, that Danby held her hand for a moment, and seemed unconscious of what he was doing. Nora blushed faintly as she felt the pressure of his hand. She was always happy when near Danby. He was so big and strong and faithful that she wished she could always have him near her.

Vera and Ross exchanged glances. They thought it was a self-evident fact that Nora Heath was in love with Danby, and that he was too genuinely unaffected to realize it.

When Ross had sufficiently recovered he was removed to Branxton, and Danby was glad to have him in the old place again. Paolo Vecchi heard of Ross Gordon's removal to Branxton, and cursed his misfortune.

'I wish he had died in the hospital,' he said to himself. 'But I'll have Vera in spite of them all. I kidnapped her when she was a child; I'll do it again now she is a woman. She will venture a good deal to learn the truth about herself. Natural curiosity, of course. That will be the bait to tempt her with. Gordon is safe. He cannot help her, and I have only that fool Widdrington to fear.'

Although he called him a fool, Paolo Vecchi knew Danby was more than a match for him if it came to a trial of strength. The difficulty was how to get hold of Vera without Danby's knowledge. If he wrote to her she would consult Danby. He must see her and tempt her to go with him to learn the secret of her birth. He had one small bottle of the drug left. If he could find the means to use it, all might yet be well with him. ' That old witch of the mountains knew too much for this world,' he said as he looked at the tiny bottle and held it up to the light. ' She hasn't been clever enough to return to earth and wreak her vengeance upon me for causing her death. How the old hag screamed before—— Bah ! I'm a fool. Why do I think of such things ?' He unlocked a small box with heavy iron clasps on, and took out a magnificent pearl necklace. He handled it carefully and examined the small gold clasp at the back, on which were the words ' Aidée Calve. A love-token.' A diamond star glittered in the box, and several rings. One ring, a man's, had a plain circle of gold with a fine diamond set in it. He read the inscription on the inside : ' Enrico Francesci. A love-token.'

' And I took their first love-token from them when they were married,' he said, ' and helped myself to these gems also. They'll come in handy to prove the claim. Count Enrico Francesci. Every year for the last score years or more has the reward been offered for the stolen child. He knows she is not dead. I have managed that skilfully, I think. But I could not claim the reward. It would be too risky. Married to the daughter of Enrico Francesci I could make my own terms. It shall be done. Vera Francesci, it shall be done.'

He next took out a couple of official-looking papers. One was the marriage certificate of Aidée Calve and Enrico, Count Francesci. The other was a miniature of a beautiful child about two years old, or perhaps a year more. On the back of the miniature were the words ' Vera Francesci.'

' Proofs. No stronger proofs than these are needed. The mother is dead. She was very beautiful. Perhaps the shock killed her. The Count was a brave man. How he fought! A man worth fighting against. But he had no chance. We were too many for him. What am I thinking about ? I must have Vera here, and then all will go well. I'll drug her again and take her to Queensland. We can be married in Brisbane, and then away to sunny Italy.'

Vera was still at the Australia, and she was not surprised when Paolo Vecchi called. She received him, knowing herself safe in the hotel, and listened attentively to all he had to say.

' And you promise to give me the proofs, unmistakable proofs of my birth, if I come to you,' she said. ' It is a large sum you demand.'

'They are worth it,' he said. 'They will make you a rich woman.'

'Why not bring them here?' she said.

'If you want them, you must come to me for them,' he said, 'and alone. I will have no spies round my house.'

'It is not safe,' said Vera. 'I will not go.'

'Then, by God, I will burn the proofs,' said Vecchi in a rage.

'No,' said Vera; 'I will come.'

'Alone!' he said.

She hesitated, and he went on: 'At the first sign of treachery, if you have brought anyone with you, I will burn the proofs before your eyes.'

Vera knew the risk was great, but she must obtain the proofs.

'I can protect myself,' she thought. 'I will not go unarmed.'

Aloud to Paolo Vecchi she said: 'I will meet you as you desire. To-morrow night at nine I will come to your house.'

'It is well,' he said. 'You shall have the proofs.'

'And you shall have the money,' she said haughtily.

'She is mine,' muttered Vecchi, as he went along the street. 'I do not want her money, I want herself; and I will have her. Once in my power, I can snap my fingers at such men as Ross Gordon and Danby Widdrington.'

CHAPTER XXVII.

IN SELF-DEFENCE.

IT wanted two hours to the time when Vera was to meet Paolo Vecchi and buy the secret of her birth from him. The sum he asked was two thousand pounds, which, in addition to a similar sum already obtained from her, drained her resources considerably. Paolo Vecchi had no desire to sell his proofs, but she was unaware of this. She knew he was an avaricious man, and thought the sum demanded would satisfy him.

Vera had no intention of trusting herself unarmed in Paolo Vecchi's house. She stood in her room watching the clock impatiently, and from time to time examining a small but efficient revolver which she had that morning purchased. It was a six-chamber Colt's, and a deadly weapon, although it looked like a toy as it lay on the table. It was loaded in all the chambers, and as she placed it in her jacket pocket Vera felt it would be a trusty friend in case of need. She did not mean to use it unless forced to do so, for she had no wish to maim Paolo Vecchi, or bodily injure him in any way. She drove in a cab to Vecchi's house, which she reached shortly before nine.

'Return for me at ten,' she said to the driver, and then knocked at the door.

It was opened by Paolo Vecchi himself, and she surmised he must be alone in the house. She asked the question, and he replied : ' I thought it better to send the servants out. They have an order for the theatre, so we shall be safe from interruption.'

She followed him into his private room at the rear of the house. He motioned her to a seat, intimating it would take him a considerable time to explain matters to her. It was his intention to tell her the facts connected with her birth, and then inform her he meant to detain her and marry her, in order to secure his own safety and her money.

'The proofs are in this box,' he said, as he placed it on the table; 'but first let me tell you my story: it will then be time to produce the evidence for my assertions.'

Vera expressed her willingness to hear anything he had to say.

'I will pass over the time when I led a rough life with a gang of men near Smyrna,' he said. 'The place became too hot for us, and we shifted our quarters to Italy. Your father and mother resided at a villa about twenty-five miles from Rome. It was a secluded spot in the midst of a lovely country, such as Italy alone can boast of. There were ten of us in the band, and I was leader. I arranged to make an attack upon the Villa Foggia, and this was agreed to by the band. It was risky work, but we knew the Count had great wealth, and the house contained much of value to such men as composed the band. In order to cut my story as short as possible, I will simply state that we succeeded in

17

plundering the villa and in capturing the child—
yourself. With our treasure we fled to the mountains,
but we knew the pursuit would be hot, so we determined to move to another quarter as soon as possible.
This was easier said than done, for the passes were all
watched, and the Count had appealed to the Govern-
ment, and soldiers were in pursuit of us. After
several weeks, during which we were hunted from
place to place, we were so hard pressed that we had
either to fight for our liberty or surrender. We
agreed to fight. Seven of the band were killed, and
I succeeded in escaping with you after a ride for life
I shall never forget. The Count, your father, was
wounded severely, and I saw him fall from his horse.
Your mother never recovered from the shock of
losing her child, and died. The Count recovered,
and is alive now. I know this to be true, for he has
regularly advertised and offered a large reward for
his child every year since you were stolen. Through
my brother he has been frequently informed by
sundry mysterious letters that his daughter is alive,
and that when the proper time arrives he will see her
and the man she has married.'

Vera started, and said: 'Married! I am not
married. What do you mean?'

'You will hear in time,' he said. 'You have often
imagined scenes of bloodshed and riot in your childhood's days, and you were right. There was ample
foundation for that imagination. You were a mere
child when the fight took place during which the

Count was wounded ; but you saw it and were terrified. I had to cut my way through the soldiers, with you in front of me on my horse; and that saved me, for they were afraid to fire, for fear of killing you. I beat them all, as I always beat people who attempt to thwart my plans.' He went on speaking proudly : ' I was tracked, but soon put them off the scent, and went to my old haunts near Smyrna again. There we lived for two years with another wild band. During that time several captures were made and heavy ransoms obtained. I formed a plan which I have steadfastly carried out up to the present time. I became tired of the men I was associated with, and left them, taking you with me to the coast. Many a time have I saved you from those brutal men, who respected neither women nor children. I was an adept at disguising myself, and we journeyed to Constanti-nople as wandering peasants, and your dancing earned money, which we did not need, but it was safer. From Constantinople we sailed to London. We remained a few weeks, but I saw no chance for myself there. We then sailed to South Africa, and from the Cape went to Australia. I had money, and you received a good education, and I saw you had great ability as an actress from the way you recited at the convent schools. You were trained for the stage, and I watched you grow into a beautiful woman, not with the love of a father, but with the passion of a lover.'

' We need not allude to it,' said Vera haughtily.

Paolo Vecchi's eyes flashed, but he continued calmly : 'You soon made a name for yourself on the stage, and I was proud of your success.'

'And glad of my earnings,' interrupted Vera.

'They were used to your advantage,' he said. 'All went well until the man Ross Gordon fell in love with you, and you became foolishly infatuated with him.'

'We will leave that out of the question,' said Vera. 'I have the money in notes. Where are the proofs ? What is my real name ? Who is my father, and who was my mother ?'

'Your father is the Count Enrico Francesci. Your mother before he married her was Aidée Calve, a renowned Italian singer. You inherit your talent for acting from her.'

'I am very glad,' said Vera. 'The Count will not be displeased that I have been an actress. Where are the proofs ?'

'Here is the marriage certificate of Enrico, Count Francesci, and Aidée Calve,' he said, handing it to her and watching her read it.

'This may be a forgery,' said Vera.

'You know it is not. Examine it closely.'

He handed her the pearl necklace and the ring and the miniature of herself as a child. She looked at them with glistening eyes, and a fierce desire for vengeance upon this man, who had robbed her of her parents' love, rose in her heart. She kept it in check, however. She must get safely away with the proofs before she attempted to bring him to justice.

'There is the money,' she said, as she put the jewellery back into the box and turned the key. 'Our bargain is completed and I will go.'

'I have more to say,' replied Paolo Vecchi; 'and the bargain is not completed.'

He went to the door, locked it, and put the key in his pocket. Vera placed her hand on the revolver in her jacket pocket and waited to hear him. She was not in the least afraid. She meant to use the weapon fearlessly if necessary. It was a quarter to ten by the clock, and the cab would return soon.

'What more have you to say?' she asked.

Her calmness exasperated him. She showed no sign of fear.

'You are in my power again,' he said. 'This time there will be no one to help you. Do you think I am going to part with you and those proofs for these paltry notes? I have carried my plan out so far, and I mean to carry it to the end. I have brought you up from a child, watched over you, and cared for you, because I determined, when the time came, you should be my wife. With you as my wife, Vera Francesci, I can defy my enemies in another land. Count Enrico Francesci is all-powerful, and will protect the husband of his child. You thought to marry Ross Gordon. It is a pity he did not die in the hospital, for it would have saved trouble. You must marry me after this night. Here you remain, and if you do not consent I will force you to it. I have a powerful weapon at my command, as you know, and

it is not all used. Do not force me to use the drug
again, but I swear I will do it if you still refuse to
marry me. You must decide quickly before the
servants return.'

'I have decided,' said Vera. 'I hate and loathe
you. I look upon you as a vile wretch, a murderer,
and God knows what else. How wicked you are you
alone know. Unlock that door and allow me to go.'

He smiled sarcastically as he said : 'Let the bird
out of the cage now I have trapped it again ! That
is not my way.'

'Will you open the door?' she said with a slight
tremor in her voice.

'No,' he replied. 'You remain here until I take
you out to marry you. This will persuade you, I
think.' And he held a small phial up to her tauntingly,
and then placed it in his watch-pocket again.

Vera pulled her revolver out, and, aiming at the
lock of the door, fired and shattered it. Then she
turned upon Paolo Vecchi, who was surprised at her
action, and said : 'There are five shots left. I am
going.'

She opened the door and he rushed forward, but
paused, as she levelled the revolver at him.

'Stand back, or I will shoot you,' she said firmly.

'You dare not,' he shouted. 'I am not afraid of
a woman.'

He stepped forward again. She knew if he caught
her by the arm he would quickly wrench the revolver
from her grasp and overpower her.

'It is in self-defence,' she thought.   'I must fire.'

'Stand back,' she said.

He smiled at her sarcastically, and said : ' Put that toy down.   I have faced too many dangers to fear that.'

He watched for an opportunity, and, thinking to get under her aim, ducked, and then sprang upon her. Vera noticed his movement, and as he sprang forward fired point-blank at him.   With a groan Paolo Vecchi fell forward on his face, shot through the heart.   Vera was terrified at what she had done.   She stooped and pulled him over on to his back.   He gave her a look of intense hatred and ferocity, and then with a convulsive shiver of the body life left him.

'Dead,' said Vera, 'and by my hand.   It is fate. It was in self-defence, for my life and honour.   I can justify the act, and I will face the consequences.'

She took the cloth from the table and threw it over him.   Then she left the house, locking the hall door after her.   She did not think of the servants returning to the house, nor did she know Paolo Vecchi had discharged them in order to be safe in carrying out his plan.

'Thought I heard shots,' said the cabman suspiciously.   'Has anything happened?'

'Drive to Branxton, Mr. Widdrington's house,' said Vera, in a voice that showed she was determined.

'Can't be anything wrong if she's going to Mr. Widdrington's,' thought the cabman ; ' but I'll swear I heard two shots.'

It was eleven when the cab drove up to Branxton. Vera, telling the cabman to wait, rang the bell. Danby was just going to bed, and was about to put out the hall-lamp.

'Wonder who this is,' he thought. 'Lie down, Nero!'

He opened the door, and when he saw Vera's white, scared face he staggered back, exclaiming: 'Good God, Vera! what is the matter?'

She came inside, shutting the door after her. Then she took hold of Danby's arm, and in an awe-struck voice said: 'I have killed Paolo Vecchi!'

CHAPTER XXVIII.

A SENSATIONAL TRAGEDY.

SOME time elapsed before Danby fully realized the force of what Vera had told him. 'I have killed Paolo Vecchi.' The words rang in his ears and clanged through his brain.

'This must be kept from Ross, if possible,' he said. 'He is not strong enough to bear it. Good God, Vera! do you realize what you have done—in what a terrible position you have placed yourself?'

'I am prepared to face the consequences,' she said. 'I acted purely on the defensive. I fired the shot to protect my honour and my life. I had no intention of killing him.'

'I understand,' he said, 'and Ross will understand,

but other people may think differently. Why did you venture to his house alone ? You must have known it was unsafe to do so.'

'That was why I purchased the revolver. Here it is. Two shots were fired. With the first I shattered the lock ; with the second I killed Paolo Vecchi,' she said.

Danby handled the revolver carefully and looked at it curiously. 'Was it possible such a tiny weapon could be so deadly ?' he thought.

'What do you advise ?' asked Vera.

'There is only one thing to be done,' said Danby. 'You must inform the police what has taken place. I know Inspector Forrest, and I will go with you.'

'When ?' asked Vera.

'The first thing in the morning—early ; not after eight,' said Danby. Then, as he looked at the woman he loved, the thought of what might happen to her almost stunned him.

'Will they lock me up ?' asked Vera.

'Yes,' said Danby. 'There will be an inquest, and meanwhile you will have to remain in custody. If the verdict is against you, you will be sent for trial. Can you bear all this, Vera ?'

'Yes,' she said calmly. 'I have nothing to fear when I have such friends as yourself to stand by me.'

He saw Vera to her hotel, and left her with a great sadness at his heart. He drove back to Branxton, but he could not rest. All night long he paced his room, a prey to bitter thoughts and regrets for Vera's rash deed. He knew why she had killed Paolo Vecchi, but others would be hard to convince of her innocence. The whole story would be dragged to light in open court, and the newspapers would make capital out of the sensational tragedy. In the morning he told Ross he had an appointment, and must be in Sydney before eight. 'There's one blessing,' he thought: 'there will be nothing in the morning papers.' He called for Vera and took her direct to Inspector Forrest, who was naturally surprised at such an early call from unexpected visitors.

'Forrest,' said Danby in a voice that betrayed his emotion, 'there has been an unfortunate accident, and this lady is concerned in it. You know her, of course?'

The inspector bowed as he said : 'I have had the pleasure of seeing Miss Vecchi act many times.'

'You are an old friend of mine, and therefore I come to you in this great trouble. This lady is engaged to be married to my friend Ross Gordon, who has not yet recovered from his accident at Rosehill. Last night she went by appointment to see Paolo Vecchi, who is supposed by everyone to be her father. He is not her father, and she went to him last night to learn the secret of her birth, and who she is. He was a dangerous man——'

The inspector nodded, and noted the word 'was.'

Danby then gave the inspector a clear and concise account of all Vera had learned from Paolo Vecchi. Then he said : 'I have placed the reason for her visiting him fully before you in order that you may thoroughly understand the situation. Miss Vecchi, as I will still call her, has the proofs of her birth with her, and will show them to you. She had better tell her own story of what happened in the house.'

Vera spoke slowly and clearly, which impressed Inspector Forrest in her favour.

'I put the money, two thousand pounds in notes, on the table,' she said. 'They are there now. He would not permit me to leave, and locked the door, putting the key in his pocket. He then vowed he would force me to marry him, and if I did not consent he would drug me again as he did in Melbourne, and as Mr. Widdrington has described to you.'

'It is most extraordinary,' said the inspector. 'I must obtain possession of the drug if possible.'

'I had a revolver with me. I knew the man I had to deal with, and took it to protect myself. We were alone in the house. I fired at the lock and shattered it, and then opened the door. He sprang forward to detain me, and I levelled the revolver at him, saying there were five shots left. He defied me, and said he was not afraid of a woman, or a toy like my revolver. I said if he came nearer I would fire upon him. He crouched down, and I saw he meant to spring under my guard and wrench the revolver from my hand. It was to save myself from him that I fired when he sprang upwards, and towards me. He fell forward on his face. I pulled him over, and he looked at me once with a terrible glance. Then he seemed to be convulsed for a few moments, and afterwards he did not move. I shot him, and he has paid the penalty of his crimes, for he died in two or three minutes after I fired. I covered the body with a cloth, and then drove to Mr. Widdrington's and told him what had happened. I locked the door of the house, and this is the key.'

Inspector Forrest looked at her admiringly, but said, with a grave face: 'This is a very serious business. I believe every word you have said, Miss Vecchi, and you are a courageous woman. I will do what I can to help you, but I am sorry to say you must consider yourself in custody. However, you may remain here, in my office, until I return. I must examine the body at once. Perhaps Mr. Widdrington will go with me?'

'I will,' said Danby. 'It is very kind of you to permit Miss Vecchi to remain here.'

Vera thanked the inspector for his thoughtfulness, and also for the belief he had expressed in the truth of her story.

'What a woman!' said Forrest to Danby as they went to Vecchi's house. 'Mr. Gordon ought to be proud of her.'

'He is,' said Danby. 'Will she be in any danger? Is there any chance of a verdict against her? Not for murder, of course; that is out of the question.'

'No,' said Forrest slowly; 'but she will be sent for trial. No jury will convict when they hear the facts as stated to me.'

'Cannot a trial be avoided?' asked Danby.

'To be plain with you, Mr. Widdrington, I think she ought, for her own sake, to stand her trial. You know how people talk. If she is not sent for trial, it will at once be said the affair has been hushed up, and that justice has not been done to the dead man.'

'You are right,' said Danby. 'As you say, the evidence will clear her entirely.'

'If I mistake not, she will be regarded as a heroine, and Vecchi's name will be held up to execration,' said Forrest.

'As it deserves to be,' said Danby.

Inspector Forrest unlocked the door and entered the house, followed by Danby.

They found the body of Paolo Vecchi lying in the position Vera had stated. The inspector removed the cloth, and Danby shuddered as he looked at the dead man's face. Even in death Paolo Vecchi wore a sneering, hard look upon his face, that was not pleasant to see. Inspector Forrest made a thorough examination of the body and the room. All he saw tended to confirm Vera's statement in every particular.

'Shot through the heart,' said the inspector, 'and the bottle shattered in his watch-pocket. See, the drug has stained his waistcoat and shirt. It has a peculiar scent.'

The money was on the table, and the inspector took possession of it.

That afternoon the news of the tragedy spread like wildfire. The evening papers made the most of the sensation. The headings they displayed were start-

ling, and the statements made exaggerated. Vera
Vecchi's fame as an actress caused every scrap
of information to be eagerly sought for. Paolo
Vecchi, too, was a well-known man. The sensation
caused by the manner of his death was eclipsed by
the extraordinary story told of Vera Vecchi's life,
and how the dead man had deceived her. All kinds
of romances were concocted by the ingenious press-
men. At the coroner's inquest the true facts came
out, but not fully. The jury brought in a verdict of
manslaughter, and Vera was committed. After the
inquiry before the magistrates, she was admitted to
bail in a heavy amount, Danby Widdrington and
Robert Heath being sureties for her.

It was Danby who first told Ross Gordon the news,
breaking it to him as gently as possible. He thought
it better for him to know, as the papers could not
very well be kept from him.

'Poor Vera!' said Ross. 'It will be a heavy trial
for her, but of course she is in no danger. That devil
Vecchi deserved his death.'

'Vera is very anxious as to how you will take it,'
said Danby.

'Tell her to come and see me at once,' said Ross.
'What she has done binds her still more closely to
me. I love her even better than I did before.'

Danby brought Vera to Ross and left them together,
and it was with a bright face she said to Danby
afterwards: 'I am very happy now. I fancied what
I had done might cause a difference between us.'

When Danby heard that Nora Heath had insisted upon Vera going to stay with them at Mount Royal, he came nearer to loving her than he had ever done before.

'What a good-hearted little woman she is!' said Danby.

'Has it taken you all these years to make that discovery?' said Ross.

'This caps the lot,' said Danby. 'It shows her pluck to stand by a woman in trouble.'

'Has it never occurred to you, Danby, that you are missing a great chance?' said Ross.

'What do you mean?' asked Danby.

'You imagine you are in love with Vera,' said Ross kindly. 'Now, you cannot have Vera, because I have a strong objection to it. But there are other women in the world. There is Nora Heath, as charming a woman as you need wish for, and she is hopelessly in love with you. If you were not such an unselfish, big-hearted slowcoach, you would have seen it long ago. You are not the man to make Vera happy, but you can make Nora Heath happy, and in time you cannot help loving her. She will win you in spite of yourself.'

Danby thought over what Ross said.

'If I thought it would make her happy, I'd ask her,' he said to himself, or rather to Nero, who, as usual, had his huge head on Danby's knees and was scanning his face and softly licking one of his hands. 'But would it be fair to her? I must tell her about

my love for Vera. It may pass away in time, but I
doubt it. When she is married to Ross I dare not
love her. Then they will go to Italy and search for
her father. They may be away for years, who knows ?
The temptation to love her will be removed. I think
I'll ask Nora if I can make her happy.'

Nora Heath's kindness to Vera touched her deeply.
She forgot she had ever been jealous of Nora, and
thought what a sweet, affectionate disposition she had.

'How she loves Danby!' thought Vera, as Nora
explained the points of Danby's namesake—the bull-
dog—to her.

'And he's so like Mr. Widdrington,' said Nora.
'Not in looks, of course, but in the many good
qualities he possesses. I could feel myself safe with
either of the Danbys near me anywhere,' she said
artlessly, and then blushed, thinking how she had
committed herself.

'I must give Danby a hint,' thought Vera, and
next time he called she did.

'You remember *he* said you were in love with me ?'
said Vera. 'I felt half inclined to believe it, but you
soon dispelled the vain idea.'

'It was not a vain idea,' said Danby.

Vera looked at him quickly.

'I mean it,' said Danby. 'I have always loved
you. There, it's out ; now I feel relieved. But you
are to be my friend's wife, therefore I do not love
you. You understand ?' he added sadly.

'I am very sorry,' said Vera softly. 'You are

dearer to me than any man except my Ross. You are the dearest, best friend I have ever had, and I want you to be happy. Ask Nora to be your wife. She has one Danby in her possession. Give her the other Danby.'

'Do you think I could make her happy ?' he asked.

'I am sure you can,' she replied.

'I must tell her the truth,' he said.

'Tell her you once loved me, that will be the truth. You do not love me now because I am to be your friend's wife,' said Vera.

CHAPTER XXIX.

A TRIUMPHAL ACQUITTAL.

VERA'S trial created a great sensation, and the court-house was crowded to excess. No one believed her guilty of murder, but opinion was divided as to whether she would be found guilty of manslaughter.

One of the cleverest barristers in Sydney had been engaged by Danby for the defence. This was Rowland Earlswood, a determined and wonderfully eloquent man. He knew he had an opportunity of distinguishing himself in this case, and he did not throw opportunities away. Moreover, he had a firm belief in his client's entire innocence, and he had learned to admire Vera's many good qualities.

Vera was accommodated with a seat next to her

18

defender, and Danby Widdrington and Ross Gordon were close at hand. Nora Heath accompanied Vera into the court and remained with her. There was a buzz of excitement when Vera was called upon to plead, and her 'Not guilty' sounded clearly throughout the crowded court.

Then came startling revelations as to her birth, and the manner in which Paolo Vecchi had stolen her from her parents and passed himself off as her father. The evidence for the prosecution merely gave the details of the tragedy, and, as there were no eye-witnesses, Vera could alone give the true facts. This she did without any hesitation, and her manner created a favourable impression.

'I will let her tell the story in her own way,' said Rowland Earlswood. 'It will be far more effective, and I can address the jury afterwards.'

Danby agreed to this, and Vera proceeded to relate all that Paolo Vecchi had told her.

'Until that night,' she said, 'I was unaware of the secret of my parentage. It had been well kept. Paolo Vecchi never gave me the slightest clue. Many times I have told him I did not believe him to be my father. I could not imagine such a man standing in that relationship to me, but I remained with him in order to try and obtain the secret from him. In Melbourne he confessed he was not my father. On one occasion he drugged me by force, and I was un-conscious of all I said to Mr. Widdrington. Under the influence of this drug Paolo Vecchi, in the presence of Mr. Widdrington, induced me to consent to marry him.' This statement caused a sensation in court. It seemed well-nigh incredible.

'When I recovered from the effects of the drug, Paolo Vecchi told me all that had happened. I wired to Mr. Widdrington, who had returned to Sydney, and he came back to Melbourne just in time to rescue me from a great danger.'

'Mr. Widdrington will tell the story himself,' said Earlswood.

'I will come to the night I shot Paolo Vecchi,' said Vera. 'That night I learned who I am. I have the proofs in my possession. I am the daughter of Count Enrico Francesci, and my mother before her marriage was the celebrated singer, Aidée Calve.'

In a dramatic manner Vera told the story of her abduction as related by the dead man. She thrilled her hearers as she had never done on the stage. This was a tragedy in real life, and the sensational story lost none of its effect by Vera's telling. Her clear, sweet voice resounded through the court, and every word was distinctly heard. Vera spoke as a woman who had nothing to fear, and was not afraid to disclose the whole truth. Her beautiful expressive face and tall, lithe figure attracted attention and created sympathy. As she told her story, there was a sudden revulsion of feeling in her favour. Her words bore the stamp of truth, and not a man on the jury doubted her.

' I placed a bundle of notes upon the table, amounting to two thousand pounds, and prepared to leave with my proofs. But Paolo Vecchi did not mean me to go. He wanted me, not the money ; he was playing for a much higher stake. His past misdeeds were such as to prevent his returning to Europe in safety. Married to me, he thought Count Enrico Francesci would protect the husband of his child. I fired and broke the lock, and then as he sprang upon me I fired at him. I had no intention of killing him, nor did I wish to do so. I am very sorry he died by my hand. But I had to protect myself, and what was dearer to me than life—my honour   I do not ask for mercy or pity, I demand justice, and I say I was justified in firing upon him in self-defence. The shot proved fatal, for that I am sorry ; but under similar circumstances I feel I should act again as I did then.'

There was some applause as Vera made this statement, and the judge threatened to have the court cleared.

' I have nothing more to say,' added Vera. ' I went armed, in case it became necessary for me to protect myself. The necessity arose, and I acted in self-defence.'

Danby Widdrington's evidence was also startling. He told the strange story of Vera's confession, and how she stated she would marry Paolo Vecchi as the only means of saving her reputation. He then described how he arrived in Melbourne in the nick of time, and rescued Vera from Paolo Vecchi's clutches.

'He was attempting to drug her again for some vile purpose of his own,' said Danby. 'I thank God I was in time to prevent him.'

Inspector Forrest gave evidence as to the finding of the body, and stated that Vera Vecchi's story, as told to him in his office, was corroborated in every way by what he saw at Vecchi's house. The medical evidence disclosed the fact that Paolo Vecchi's waist-coat was stained by an extraordinarily powerful drug. Dr. Ransom stated that a few drops of the drug had been extracted from the waistcoat. The drug was unknown to him, but he had tried its effect upon a dog, and it was marvellous. The animal appeared to lose all its instinct and sagacity, and did things it would have been impossible to make it do under ordinary conditions.

'For instance,' said Dr. Ransom, 'the dog would have actually put its paw into the fire at my com-mand, had I not prevented it. I watched it for several hours, and everything I told it to do it at once attempted. In twenty-four hours the dog was all right again, and quite another animal. I believe the drug has the effect described by Miss Vecchi, and I can quite believe all she has stated about it.'

Rowland Earlswood made an eloquent speech, in which he praised the courage of his client, and de-nounced Paolo Vecchi in no measured terms. 'He is dead,' said Earlswood, 'and gone to his account, with all his imperfections on his head. I have no wish to vilify a dead man's name, but, in the interest of my client, I have felt it my duty to point out to you the character Paolo Vecchi bore. He attempted to ruin the character of a pure and noble woman in the eyes of one of her best friends, and of the man she was engaged to marry. This man, who had passed himself off as Vera Francesci's father, wished the world to believe she had lived with him as his mistress, and that the supposed relationship was concocted to hide the infamy of their lives. Could anything be more vile or despicable? Such men are worse than murderers, and deserve more than an easy death. There cannot be a spark of pity felt for the dead man. Gentlemen, you know the facts. They have been placed before you in a manner seldom heard in this court. There can be no misunderstanding my client's statement. She does not ask you for mercy or pity, for she needs none. She demands—demands, remember, gentlemen—justice. Had Paolo Vecchi lived, she would still have demanded justice, and he would have been placed in the dock, and that justice would not have been denied her. Paolo Vecchi has met with a far easier death than would have been meted out to him in a court of justice. That my client acted in self-defence, no one can doubt, and I confidently appeal to you, gentlemen of the jury, for a triumphal acquittal.'

Rowland Earlswood's address lasted an hour, and was a brilliant success.

' My best, my warmest thanks,' said Vera as he sat down.

'You deserve far more than my humble effort on your behalf,' he replied ; but he was gratified at Vera's praise.

Counsel for the prosecution replied briefly, and the jury, without leaving the box, immediately returned a verdict of 'Not guilty.'

'You are discharged,' said the judge to Vera. 'The jury, by their verdict, have decided that you acted in self-defence. I am entirely of that opinion. I fail to see how they could have thought otherwise. May I add that I hope ere long you will be welcomed by your real father, whose fame as a statesman is well known to all who study the history of our own times.'

'Neatly put,' whispered Rowland Earlswood to Danby.

The trial was fully reported, and being of such a sensational character, the papers sold like wildfire. The news was flashed abroad, and the Continental and English papers told the extraordinary story.

Count Enrico Francesci, lying ill at the Villa Foggia, had the news gradually related to him, and then eagerly read the accounts in the Italian papers. The news, he felt, was almost too good to be true. It revived him, and he seemed a different man ; but his physician knew better, and did not give him a long lease of life. Cablegrams were despatched to Sydney to Vera Francesci, urging her to at once sail for Italy to see the Count. The Count's physician sent a message on his own account, in which he stated the condition his patient was in.

'To think,' said Vera, with tears in her eyes, 'I have only found a father to lose him again. It is very sad, Nora, after all these years.'

'There may be hope,' said Nora. 'Go to him as soon as possible. The sight of his child may bring him back to life.'

A consultation was held at Mount Royal, and it was arranged that Vera and Ross should be quietly married, and then leave for Italy. To this Vera agreed, although Ross said she had better wait for her father's consent.

'It is unnecessary,' said Vera. 'I cannot allow anything to come between us.'

The wedding took place at Randwick Church, and the week after Ross Gordon and his wife sailed by the *Austral* for Naples. Danby, Nora, and her father saw them off from Circular Quay, and were consoled by the thought that their departing friends had promised to return to Sydney before many months were over. Danby felt very lonely at Branxton that night. He sat in his den thinking over all that had passed since he stood in the sale-yard bidding against Paolo Vecchi for Killara. Vera was married, and he felt her loss, but also a sense of happiness and security.

'It's no use living in a big place like this by myself,' thought Danby. 'I shall never make such friends with any other man. I loved Ross, and all the more because of his faults. I promised to stick to him through thick and thin, and I have done so.

He is happy, and I can do no more for him. I think I'll try and turn selfish, and look after myself.'

Then he fell to thinking of Nora Heath, and fancied how pleasant it would be to have her bright, cheerful presence at Branxton.

'I'll chance my luck, Nero,' he said. 'I'll make a bold bid for a wife. I believe I can make Nora happy. I'll have a desperate try if she'll have me.'

Danby had a habit of talking to his dogs, and they usually seemed to understand and sympathize with him. On this occasion, however, Nero failed to grasp Danby's meaning. Contemplated matrimony was beyond Nero, and he looked foolish. Danby recognised the dog's difficulty and proceeded to demonstrate. He had a boudoir portrait of Nora, and he showed it to Nero. The dog looked at it solemnly, and then raised his great eyes to Danby's face.

'That's the lady,' said Danby. 'She is very fond of dogs, Nero.'

The mention of his name caused Nero to wag his tail, which Danby accepted as a favourable sign.

'I'll take you with me to-morrow,' said Danby, patting his head, 'if you will promise not to eat my namesake.'

CHAPTER XXX.

'ALL'S WELL THAT ENDS WELL.'

DANBY walked to Randwick accompanied by Nero. The exercise did him good, and braced up his spirits,

and Nero's frolics and demonstrations of delight
banished the sense of loneliness he had felt since the
departure of Ross Gordon and his wife.

Nora was reading, when she heard the gate bang
and the sound of steps on the walk. She hastily put
down the book, went to the window, and was not
surprised to see Danby.

'So you have brought Nero,' she said. 'I am glad
of that. He's such a dear old dog. Come and be
petted, Nero.'

Nero rubbed his head against her dress, and she
patted him, and he shook hands with her sedately.

'You may come inside if you promise to behave,'
she said to Nero, 'and do not knock valuable articles
off the table with flourishes of your tail.'

Nero went in at the open window, and Danby
followed.

'I brought him on one condition,' he said: 'that
he promised not to eat my namesake.'

Nora laughed as she said : 'I am afraid he would
have some difficulty in doing so, even if he felt
inclined. Danby has a habit of defending himself
pretty stoutly when attacked.'

'I feel awfully lonely now Ross has gone,' said
Danby, looking at her in a way that made her heart
beat fast.

'And I miss Vera so much,' said Nora. 'Fancy
Vera the daughter of a Count ! She looks a thoroughbred.'

'You are quite right,' said Danby, 'she is a

thoroughbred. There is no up-to-date vulgarity about Vera.' As he looked at Nora, he thought : ' I need not tell her I loved Vera. It is all past and done with. It would hardly be fair to her to tell her. I am sure I can make her happy.'

Nora thought Danby unusually silent. He generally had plenty to talk about.

' I must make a start,' thought Danby, ' or I shall never get to the winning-post.'

' Nora,' he commenced, and at his tone she looked up quickly, ' I have come this morning to ask you to be my wife. It's out now,' he added with a sigh of relief. ' I'm not a good hand at speech-making or love-making, but if you will have me, Nora, I believe I can make you happy. We have known each other for some years. I am considerably older than you, and have watched you grow up from a child to a beautiful woman. It is very lonely at Branxton. Will you take compassion upon me, and bring light and sunshine into the old place ?'

This was the moment Nora had been waiting for. She loved Danby, and thought him the manliest of men. She respected and honoured him, and knew her happiness would be safe in his keeping.

She put out her hands, and he took them, looking down into her eyes with his honest kindly smile.

' I will be your wife, Danby,' she said quietly, ' for I love you very dearly. I think I have always loved you. As a little girl I remember looking forward to seeing you more than anyone else. That feeling has

never left me. You have always been my best friend
and part of my life. The love I bore you as a girl
has strengthened now I am a woman. I will try to
make you happy.'

Danby kissed her fondly, and said: 'Now I have
someone to care for, and I will do all in my power to
deserve the prize I have won.'

Robert Heath and his wife were delighted at Nora's
choice of a husband.

'You have always been like a son to me,' he said
to Danby ; 'I can safely trust my girl's happiness to
you.'

'The sooner we are married the better,' said Danby.
'There is no necessity for a long engagement. We
have known each other so many years.'

Six months after Ross Gordon and his wife left
Sydney, Danby Widdrington and Nora Heath were
married at Randwick.

One of the handsomest presents they received was
from Horace Walsden, who had a great respect for
Danby. The news of their engagement had been
sent to the Gordons, and both Ross and Vera wrote
in reply. From their letters it appeared that they
arrived at Rome and went direct to Count Francesci's
villa.

'He is a glorious old man,' wrote Ross ; 'a grand
specimen of a patriot. The meeting between Vera
and her father was very affecting. There is a striking
likeness between them, as you will see from the
portrait I send you. The Count can never bear Vera

to be absent from him, and I am glad to say he has expressed his pleasure at her choice of a husband. That's one for me. I score there. We can easily see Count Enrico is not long for this world. He knows it himself, and has informed me that the bulk of his wealth is to be settled upon Vera and her children. He also wishes our eldest boy, if we have one, to take his name. We shall of course remain here until his death. It seems sad for Vera to lose him so soon. To all outward appearances he is a fine healthy man, but his physician tells us that he cannot live many months. How are the horses going on? You ought to keep up the stable, as you have a real good lot in training. Killara ought to win you another big race. Tell Newton to give him plenty of work, as I know he can stand it, and if you want to win races your horses must not be short of gallops. When we return, I hope to find you comfortably fixed at Branxton, and I am sure you will be happy.'

Vera's letter to Nora was full of good wishes, and she gave a glowing description of her father's home, and of the surroundings of the Villa Foggia.

'It is very sad to think I shall lose him so soon,' said Vera, 'but a consolation to me that we have been united before it was too late. I gave him a full account of my life in Australia, and also of Paolo Vecchi's end. The mere mention of that man's name puts him into a violent rage. He applauded my act, and says the villain deserved a far worse end. Personally I do not feel the slightest remorse for having been the cause of his death. I feel I have nothing to reproach myself with. It is, no doubt, a dreadful thing in the minds of some people for a woman to have killed a man. I know you have no such sentimental feelings about it; you would probably have acted as I did under the circumstances. I wish you every happiness in your married life. Mr. Widdrington is a man I have always been proud to call friend, and he has been a true friend indeed to me, and also to Ross. I look forward to meeting you in your new home with very great pleasure. Ross seems determined to return to Sydney after my father's death, and I am content to do as he wishes. Sometimes I feel a strong longing to return to the stage, but the feeling may wear off in time. After an active, struggling life, such as mine, it is difficult to settle down quietly.'

*   *   *   *   *

Ten years have quickly passed since the marriages of Ross Gordon and Danby Widdrington. At Branxton great preparations were being made to spend Christmas in true Australian style. The sound of merry young voices could be heard as the decorations were being completed. Danby's eldest son, a fine lad of eight years, was superintending everything with the assurance of being obeyed, two younger lads and a bright-eyed little dot of a girl looking on, evidently well pleased. The preparations were completed in excellent time, and on Christmas Eve Branxton resounded with shouts and laughter as the children—

Danby's and Ross's—played and romped to their hearts' content. It was a charming scene. The windows were thrown open wide, to allow a cool breeze to blow in from Rose Bay. The moon glistened on the waters of the harbour, tipping the faint ripples with light, and shedding a lustre all around. Lanterns were suspended from the trees in the garden, and a flood of light poured from the open windows on to the lawn. The hum of insects was in the air, and the perfume of flowers wafted on the breeze. Peace on earth and good-will towards men ruled supreme in the happy household. It was late when the children went to bed, and then preparations were made by Vera and Nora to keep up the visitation of Santa Claus, so dear to the hearts of the youngsters.

'Where are our wives?' said Danby, as he sat smoking on the veranda with Ross.

'Hovering round the children's beds like good fairies,' said Ross. 'By Jove, Danby! we have developed into family men with remarkable rapidity.'

'We're a lucky pair,' said Danby.

'Agreed,' said Ross ; 'and if it hadn't been for your kindness, old fellow, in days gone by I should never have been so happy.'

'Nonsense!' said Danby. 'I only helped you. Any man would have done as much for a friend.'

'That's your way of putting it,' said Ross. 'There are not many friends like you in the world.'

'Come and look at our work,' said Nora, coming

into the room ; ' but you must promise to be very quiet.'

They followed her and joined Vera in the children's bedroom. Santa Claus had paid his visit, and the beds were covered with a variety of presents from the venerable father of Christmas gifts.

It was a pretty sight to see them looking at the sleeping children, all unconscious of the joyful surprise their mothers had prepared for them.

That Christmas Day was well spent, and a merry time it was for everyone within the hospitable walls of Branxton. During the day Hector St. Albans, who was in Sydney, came in and amused the children by his excellent recitations and impersonations of a variety of characters well known to juvenile minds. He, too, had successfully combated his love for Vera, but he was still unmarried, and there was every prospect of his remaining so.

In a paddock at the rear of the house Killara was quietly standing under the shade of a large fig-tree, and Nero, now an ancient dog, slumbered quietly on the lawn.

There was nothing to mar the happiness of the two families, and Danby Widdrington felt grateful for the many blessings that had been showered upon him.

THE END.

www.ingramcontent.com/pod-product-compliance
Lightning Source LLC
Chambersburg PA
CBHW030623030726
47497CB00006B/1611